Karen ~
The Dream live or
or die with each
of us.
Lee Mun Wah

LET'S GET REAL

WHAT PEOPLE OF COLOR CAN'T SAY
& WHITES WON'T ASK ABOUT RACISM

BY LEE MUN WAH

Edited and Proofread by Barbara Imhoff
Proofread by Paul Psoinos
Cover Design by Allison Rolls
Cover Photograph by Stephen Weiss
Production by Allison Rolls
Production Assistance by Keri Northcott

Copyright ©2011 StirFry Seminars & Consulting

ISBN 978-1-4507-6367-7

Dedicated to Naraya, my friend in life, crime, and love

ACKNOWLEDGEMENTS

In Chinese culture there is a belief that it is at the source that we each must give thanks. That is no less true for the many who have supported me along the way in not only creating the essence of this book, but in helping to bring it to its actual fruition. I wish to acknowledge and to give homage to each of them. For, like all good artistic collaborations, each played an important part in birthing and completing this book.

First of all, I owe my deepest gratitude to Barbara Imhoff, our staff editor, conference coordinator, and renowned harpist, who painstakingly read through the morass of entries, and who helped me to choose the final entries, to edit them, then to categorize and finally to help name the appropriate chapter headings. Without her patience and persistence I would have still been wading through hundreds of pages, overwhelmed by the enormity of the task. So thanks, Barbara, for being such a great editor and friend. Your enthusiasm for the topic and commitment to social justice issues only added to the beauty and depth of this important work.

I also wish to thank Allison Rolls, who helped format and design the cover. And thanks to Melissa Sweeney, our Director, whose heart, talents and energy went into support of this book project and into all the diversity work being done at StirFry Seminars.

And of course, my heartfelt thanks and admiration to Stephen Weiss, whose beautiful photograph graces the front cover of this book. Thank you so much for volunteering your time, patience, and artistic eye to the final rendering that was literally chosen from hundreds of pictures that were taken. You captured the fear, pain and anguish I was hoping to portray.

I would also like to thank John Lenssen, Henry Bourgeois, and Jim Langemo for continuing to be such good friends over these many years. Each of you has inspired me by your humility, wisdom, and friendship.

To Bill Howe, a good friend, inspiring mentor, educator and author, your contributions to the field of diversity and education are admired by hundreds and are models for all of us. You are a true warrior and co-conspirator on the road of life and social justice. Thank you so much for writing the Foreword to this book. It was your early efforts that have allowed many of us a voice and a place to stand proudly and with dignity as persons of color.

But, most importantly, I would like to thank all those who took the time to share their truths with us. It was their willingness to share a part of themselves —both the wounds and the hopes—that I believe will help begin a conversation that has long been ignored and feared. No words can ever fully describe my gratitude and honor of being a witness and a bridge for each of you to be heard and believed.

And lastly, I would like to thank the thousands around this country who stand up every day in the face of racism by not only telling the truth, but modeling what it will take for us to heal, to understand, and to change. Your words and your courage do not go unseen and unheard. You have taught us that by breaking our silence, we can change the world and the future of our children. The secret to ending racism is only one person, one question away.

TABLE OF CONTENTS

SECTION ONE: FOR PEOPLE OF COLOR

Chapter One Telling the Truth about Racism to Whites

   What's hard about telling whites the truth about racism?
   What's the price of telling the truth about race relations in the U.S.?
   Why do you think it's so hard for whites to hear the truth about racism?
   What "blind spots" do you notice about white allies?
   In what ways do whites keep people of color from telling the truth
   about race/racism?
   What are your honest thoughts about white folks?
   What would you say to whites if you could tell them the truth
   about racism?

Chapter 2 A Question of Safety

   How have you learned to "play the game" to appease white folks?
   What does assimilation mean to you? Why?
   When you have told the truth about racism, what have been some
   of your experiences? How have those outcomes affected you?

Chapter 3 Personal Journeys

Chapter 4 Unlearning Racism—What It Will Take

How can white people help raise issues of racism when many whites like to believe that we have "transcended" race divisions and inequity is a thing of the past?
What makes a white person "safe and reliable"?
What can a white person do to alleviate racism?
How do you think whites can be effective allies to people of color?

What do reparations look like for you?
What signposts do you keep an eye out for that signal the overcoming of racism in our society?

SECTION TWO: FOR WHITES

Chapter 5 Telling the Truth

What's good and what's hard about talking about racism?
What percentage of your life is impacted by racism? Why or why not?
In what ways have you been able to avoid talking about or dealing with racism?
How does guilt keep you from dealing with racism?
How do you think you benefit from racism?
What are some of the things that you are afraid to say to people of color?
What do you think keeps people of color and whites apart?
Where did most of your stereotypes about people of color come from?
How did those stereotypes affect your perceptions and attitudes toward them?
What part do you think you play in perpetuating racism?
Do you believe that racism is a learned behavior and attitude? If yes, why? If not, why not?

Are there two Americas? Why or why not?
What does assimilation mean to you?
What does diversity or multiculturalism mean to you?

Chapter 6 Working with Other Whites

*What are some of your fears in bringing up the
issue of racism with other white folks?
What do you need from other whites to feel safe to talk about racism?
Why do you think many white folks don't identify as a group?*

Chapter 7 Working with People of Color

*What are some of your fears to bring up the issue of racism with
people of color?
If you could say three things to people of color about racism,
what would you say?
What would be some questions you would like to ask people of color?*

Chapter 8 Personal Stories

When did you first experience racism? What happened and how

Chapter 9 What Is Needed to Unlearn Racism

*What opens you up and what closes you down to talk about racism?
Why?*
How do you think whites can be effective allies to people of color? Why?

Chapter 10 What It Will Take

*What do you think it will take for people of color and whites to trust
each other?*
*What do you think it will take for the United States to heal from
racism?*

What do you think it will take for white folks to unlearn racism?

Afterword: Letter to Mun Wah

FOREWORD

by Dr. William A. Howe

Everything now, we must assume, is in our hands; we have no right to assume otherwise. If we do not falter in our duty now, we may be able, handful that we are, to end the racial nightmare, and achieve our country, and change the history of the world.

James Baldwin
The Fire Next Time (Vintage, 1963)

James Baldwin has always inspired me with this quote. Baldwin's message sends a shiver through me each time I read these simple, yet powerful words. This latest work by Lee Mun Wah has the same effect. No human being could possibly read the words that seem to spring alive from these pages without feeling hurt, anger, sadness, outrage, and despair. Yet, by listening to these stories, re-told by people like you and me, there is a powerful urge to reach out and talk about our differences, to seek healing beginning with honest conversation. Each and every person who reads these pages should find words that resonate with them, as the following did with me:

Shawn Patrick writes:

> *… talking about racism to people who are white is hard because I often find myself having to soothe their feelings. So in order to promote the possibility of having a useful conversation, I must put aside my own personal feelings of injustice and hurt in order to provide empathy to the other, who frequently does happen to be someone who engaged in racist acts. This is a duality of experience that becomes, quite frankly, maddening.*

So often I have these same experiences as Shawn, so reading his articulate words was validation for me of my life experiences. It is exhausting to have to constantly comfort others, while at the same time, holding back your own feelings of frustration. I don't know Shawn, have never met him that I can recall, but I know that if I ever do I can look him in the eye, shake his hand and say, "I understand."

Toni Adams writes:

> I've heard more than one person say, 'Slavery happened a long time ago and I wasn't a part of it, so give up on that excuse.' So many blacks reared by elders were taught to be 'careful' around white folks and NOT to say certain things around white folks. These are all lessons from the plantation that live on today.

Toni's words ring true to me. As a parent my heart aches when I hear African American mothers and fathers talk about having to teach their young children painful lessons about racism early on, especially the boys—"Never run in public, especially if you are carrying a parcel." "If you get stopped by the police, no matter how rude they may be or what racist things they may say to you, always call them sir and be polite."

Some stories about institutional racism will have you nodding your head in agreement while feeling that awful pain in your gut at the same time. Erin writes (regarding her challenging the constant use of JAP as an acronym at her work):

> This work experience cost me a part of my soul and a little piece of me died from it. To have an entire line of managers, one African American, not get involved, for an HR professional to turn the table and 'tattle on' me, and for my manager to chastise me made me lose faith in humanity and the corporate system. Each time I tell this story, it costs me a little bit more because I know that I can never get back that part of my soul that died that day.

I am not one of those people who think all white people are racist. There have been many wonderful white men and women, famous and otherwise, who have overcome the plague of racism and come to a higher enlightenment. So I am encouraged by the words of Janet Carter, a white female, who writes:

> White people can't be trusted until we understand that we are white and that that means something beyond checking a box on a form...We need to understand that our good intentions can sometimes result in hurtful situations and that we can take responsibility for that in ways other than falling back on our intentions, feeling paralyzing guilt and/or expecting the other person to take care of us.

I first learned about Lee Mun Wah in 1995 when a colleague gave me a video to watch about a Chinese American film producer on the *Oprah Winfrey Show* talking about a film he had made about racism called *The Color of Fear*. I didn't know any other Chinese American working in the diversity field, especially with the same last Chinese name of Lee (my family name). The Oprah episode is perhaps one of the best ever done on daytime television about racism. Mun Wah's appearance on the *Oprah Winfrey Show* was a significant event in the history of race relations in this country. For the first time, an Asian American entered into the national discussion on race through mainstream media. *The Color of Fear* is a riveting film and I have used it constantly for fifteen years in my work. No other medium has had that much impact on me personally or been that effective in getting people to truly understand racism.

In 2000, when I finally met Mun Wah in person, I was in awe. Growing up in Canada there were no Asian media role models for me. The television show *Bonanza* had that horribly racist character Hop Sing, a jabbering Chinese cook. David Carradine, a white male, was given the role of Kwai Chang Caine, a wandering Chinese monk on the television series *Kung Fu*. Carradine was given that role over Bruce Lee, who was an actual Chinese martial artist and actor. Greeting me was a gentle soul, someone who obviously took the time to actually connect with people. Perhaps it was his years of teaching high school or his training as a psychotherapist, but it was apparent that he could get his message across, but more importantly, he knew how to listen. It was this approach to diversity work that told me he was someone I should study.

My first opportunity came on 9/11. The annual conference of the National Association for Multicultural Education is held each fall. Many thought that so soon after such a tragic event might not be the right time to hold a national meeting. But the immediate backlash against our Muslim brothers and sisters and others convinced us we needed to be together. We set aside Friday evening of the conference to hold some type of "healing event." In thinking of who best could lead this, I thought of Lee Mun Wah. One short phone call and he immediately agreed to come to speak. The evening began with a well-attended Shabbat service. For the main event, instead of coming alone, Mun Wah brought with him many of his colleagues and members of the cast of his films. Not only was he appearing without a fee, but he brought others with him to join in the ceremony. Through laughter and tears, he got us all talking. In a packed hotel conference room, Lee Mun Wah managed to start the healing, to help set the universe straight again, to ground us in the fact that racism can be overcome. But it must start by walking across the room to have a conversation.

This book is an embodiment of his philosophy of learning to communicate and listening to understand. The stories you will read in these many pages will surely jump start a conversation that will lead to another conversation and further. Students, activists, teachers and others will find it a valuable tool. *Let's Get Real: What People of Color Can't Say & Whites Won't Ask About Racism* will leave you with hope—hope that someday we may all finally come together as one "to end this racial nightmare."

Dr. William A. Howe, Past-President of the National Association for Multicultural Education, is the education consultant for culturally responsive education, multicultural education, gender equity and civil rights at the Connecticut State Department of Education. He is also an adjunct professor of education at the University of Connecticut and Albertus Magnus College.

Introduction

This book has taken me over 64 years to finally express into words. For as long as I can remember, I've been acculturated on a daily basis in how to edit, censor, hold back, withdraw, protect, defend, and swallow my anger—in almost all of my relationships with whites. Regardless of whether or not the consequences were big or small—I have always suffered some kind of loss in the process of trying to express what it is like to be a person of color in this country. And though the wounds were not always seen or believed, they have exacted their toll on me. It is only now that I wish to give light to what happened to me and millions like me on a daily basis, one generation after another—in families, communities, and workplaces all over this country.

I'm not sure whether growing older has given me more courage, but it has certainly instilled me with a certain kind of reckless bravado—I really don't care any more what will happen to me if I speak out. What I am more concerned with is what will happen to me if I don't. A good friend of mine once said that it isn't the pain that hurts, but rather our resistance to it. I can unequivocally say that it is the resistance to my pain that hurts, more than the truth of what happened to me.

When I first thought of this book, I assumed that it would simply be a community conversation about asking each other hard questions regarding issues we didn't know about and listening to the answers. But, as the months passed and more and more submissions began pouring in, I was astonished by the honesty and directness of each entry. It was as if each person was not only baring their souls, but relieving themselves of the heavy burden of holding back what they had kept silent all these many years. They described what they felt in public, but couldn't put into words. They placed before this country a mirror that painfully reflected both our hypocrisy and our illusions of equality and justice. But they also shared their desire for a more authentic conversation and relationship—one based on risking and self-reflection, honesty and responsibility.

Perhaps that is really what this book is all about—not only what has happened, but what has not, even after years of civil rights marches, countless diversity classes and never-ending yearly celebrations all over this country in the form of ethnic foods and costumes, holidays and dance performances. We cannot keep moving on or building a better world without facing the root causes of the issues we face today. And that requires talking about and taking responsibility for our past actions and how what we have done and not acted on affects us all on a daily basis in this country.

There are thousands of unfinished conversations and experiences between EuroAmericans and people of color. This book is about breaking the silence of our fears and hatred and replacing them with compassion and authenticity—understanding that we are all a part of the problem and the solution. It is not a journey free of anguish, fear or denial. It will stretch us all and it will hurt and it will make us feel like leaving the room when it gets too hot or too close to the truth.

So the real challenge of this book is about what it will take for us to not only begin this conversation, but to stay in the room, to speak our truths and to hear the truth, even if it differs from our own. And to that discourse, be willing to reflect, be curious, take responsibility, and to change personally and institutionally.

Respect and understanding of diversity issues are simply words until they are practiced and integrated into the very fabric of our workplaces and communities, relationships, attitudes and behaviors. They are what inextricably bind us to our destiny as a nation and as a community. Will we be separate, unequal and divided or will we work together by honoring and making use of the beauty of our differences and the contributions of everyone? The choice to act is not for tomorrow or waiting for some charismatic leader to save us all, but for today—with those we love and with those we have been taught to fear.

INSTRUCTIONAL GUIDE

LET'S GET REAL
INSTRUCTIONAL GUIDE

When using this book for group discussions, classroom study or trainings, it is best to be prepared for the possibility that many intense emotions and conflicts may arise when discussing it. The questions in this book are extremely intimate as well as the responses they evoked. An excellent in-depth facilitation guide to prepare you for these types of diversity discussions is "The Art of Mindful Facilitation", which encompasses my twenty years as a diversity trainer and facilitator working with universities, government agencies, corporations, therapists and educators all over the country. This training manual will show you how you can prepare a group for these types of discussions. In detailed steps you will learn how to create a safe container, ways to de-escalate a conflict within seconds, listening and responsive techniques that will deepen and enhance authenticity and intimacy, as well as a variety of diversity exercises that are enjoyable and educational, and inspire more authentic relationships and insightful conversations. I would like to encourage all of you truly interested in this field to take some of our workshops to better facilitate unlearning racism and to learn to de-escalate the conflicts that might occur in the future.

One of the first steps in beginning working with this book is to carefully read the Introduction and Table of Contents, both of which give an overview of why the book was written and the particular topics inherent in each group of questions. Furthermore, when perusing the book, choose which sets of questions best meet the needs and issues of your participants. For example, if your group is predominantly white, it might be more useful to begin with the questions for whites instead of people of color.

In preparation for reading the book, have the group read and discuss the "9 Healthy Ways to Communicate" and the "The Art of Mindful Inquiry." "9 Healthy Ways to Communicate" is a communications guide to help the group relate to each other in a healthier and more nurturing way when someone is sharing a traumatic story or has an emotional response. "The Art of Mindful Inquiry" is a set of questions that will help the group when a conflict arises or someone is feeling emotionally vulnerable or misunderstood. Have the group memorize these sets of inquiries. It will be invaluable when the discussion gets emotionally charged. Included is also a variety of other helpful diversity tools that will help support the level of dialogue you are hoping to stimulate.

The goal of this book is not to determine who is wrong or who is right, but rather to explore the myriad of ways to connect and reconnect when our feelings and our experiences distance and separate us from each other. The key is our willingness to be open to hearing another's journey and truth, as well as our willingness to remain curious and self-reflective. What I am asking is not going to be easy to accomplish when nothing in our past experiences has modeled for us a truly healthy and honest dialogue on diversity issues—particularly race. Maybe what we are about to venture into is a new paradigm. One that requires equal risk from each of us. We must begin with ourselves and those around us, with those we love and with those we have been taught to fear and to hate. It is my belief that we must first begin with the issues at hand that separate us, before we can come together as friends and as a community. As Martin Luther King, Jr. once said, "We hate each other because we fear each other. And we fear each other because we do not know each other. And we do not know each other because we are separated from each other."

THE ART OF MINDFUL INQUIRY

The following reflections and questions are helpful when there is a conflict or when someone shares with you a traumatic story. These reflections are most difficult to put into practice when someone is yelling or angry with you, especially when you disagree with someone who holds political, religious, gender, class, racial, or personal viewpoints that you're opposed to. And yet, it is precisely at those moments that perhaps these reflections and questions can help keep the conversation open and flowing, instead of defensive and adversarial, because they come from a perspective of curiosity. As Buddhist philosophy tells us, "Curiosity is the gateway to empathy."

1. What I heard you say....
2. Tell me more what you meant by....
3. What angered you about what happened?
4. What hurt you about what happened?
5. What's familiar about what happened?
   How did it affect you? How does it affect you today?
6. What do you need / want?

1. What I heard you say...

One of the quickest ways to connect with someone is to use their own words. This is especially important when there is a conflict or a traumatic story has just been shared. (Also, reflecting back is a good intervention when you don't have any idea what to ask or do). When reflecting back, try to be succinct. Listing too many things about what they said will only overwhelm them. Begin by using their name and then, "What I heard you say was..." Choose a key phrase that they shared that best represents what is important to them, not to you. If they truly connect with you because they feel heard by you, they will add to their story and drop to a new level—trust.

Keep good eye contact and pause after using their name. In that way, you can "sense" whether or not a connection has been made by looking at their reaction to you. Also, be aware that, for some, eye contact is a cultural taboo. When that is the case, you can ask if that is an issue. For example, "I noticed you looked away when I started talking. I was wondering what that might be about or if it is a cultural issue for you."

2. Tell me more what you meant by...

This one statement is always a conversation-maker. It signals to the speaker that you are interested and also open to hearing more. When using this technique, remember to finish the sentence with something you heard them say. For example, "Tell me more what you meant by 'not feeling safe.'"

3. What angered you about what happened?

Often anger is one of the emotions that is most feared in conflicts, conversations and relationships. However, avoiding or trivializing its importance often creates an escalation of the problem. Someone once said that to tame a wild bull is to give it a wider field. That is contrary to conventional thinking, which is to contain anger or send someone down the hall to a counselor or a human resource specialist. Thus, we seldom get to witness anger being dealt with or mediated out in the open, which might explain why we lack the skill sets needed to work through our disagreements and anger. For anger to be successfully transformative, it requires not only freedom of expression, but belief and understanding on the part of the listeners. That is why when someone expresses their feelings of anger, it is good for folks to repeat what they've heard and to share what they understood about what the anguish was all about.

4. What hurt you about what happened?

Many times, underneath one's anger is a hurt that has not been acknowledged or validated. Validate the hurt and you are halfway there. Also, along with validation must come the willingness to see our part in the conflict or misunderstanding and to take responsibility for our actions and inactions.

Expressing one's hurt is very emotionally vulnerable. It can only be helpful if there is trust and safety created by authentic sharing and compassionate listening. Take your time by first allowing the story and anguish to fully express itself. Be patient and look for an opening so you can ask what hurt about what happened. Allow for the relationship to develop and grow.

5. *What's familiar about what happened? How did it affect you? How does that affect you today?*

This is the past tense question and one of the most significant reasons why most conflicts become heated. When someone is being triggered by a past experience or what another person said/did, we mistakenly take it personally and the conflict escalates. That is why this question is so important—it unveils the source of the anguish.

One of the tricks of moving from working with an individual to a larger group is asking, "Does this situation sound familiar to you in your own life?" In this way, the individual doesn't feel like they are the only one who has this problem, and you, as the facilitator, get to find a way to involve the entire group so it doesn't become an individual therapy session.

6. *What do you need or want?*

We often go quickly to this question so we can skip all of the above questions. Unfortunately, if we do, it is only a temporary stay from the real issues that need to be discussed and will only return later—unresolved and maybe even more heated. When I use this question, I often follow it up with, "Do you believe that this other person will follow through with their agreements? If not, what would it take for you to believe him/her?"

9 HEALTHY WAYS TO COMMUNICATE

1. Reflect back what is being said. Use their words, not yours.

When in doubt, the fastest way to de-escalate a conflict is to reflect back what is said. Though it may sound simplistic, it is often the most over-looked need in most conflicts—to be validated and acknowledged. It is also imperative to use their words, not yours. That is because there may be class and cultural differences when words are substituted. You have thirty seconds to make a connection. How they feel, what they need and what they don't need is right in front of you. The work is to be present and to listen carefully and with an open ear. Be a dedicated tape recorder and reporter. Reflect back only what is heard and seen.

2. Begin where they are, not where you want them to be.

Anaïs Nin once said that we don't see the world as it is, but rather as we are. That is why is it so critical to learn where another person is coming from, so that we can begin from where they are, not where we are, which often comes from our own needs and ways of doing things. In other words, love thy neighbor as they would like to be loved.

3. Be curious and open to what they are trying to say.

So often we make statements rather than asking a question. The Buddhists say that we do not learn from experience, but rather by our willingness to experience. Thus, curiosity is the gateway to empathy and understanding.

4. Notice what they are saying and what they are not.

From the Western perspective, we have been trained to listen carefully to what someone is saying or doing. However, from an Eastern perspective, it is equally useful to notice what they are not saying and what they are not doing. In other words, looking at the subtext. So that, as one is talking about their experiences with their father, notice that they haven't mentioned their mother. Or if they talk a great deal about their high school years, notice that they haven't mentioned anything about their lives in the present tense.

5. *Emotionally relate to how they are feeling. Nurture the relationship.*

Many times, it takes a lot of courage to emotionally share one's story in front of our peers or strangers. That is why it is equally important to reciprocate with some kind of reaction that shows that we are empathetic to what they have gone through and/or are experiencing even today. It is what I call "nurturing the relationship." A way of earning their trust by truly being present, authentic and emotionally supportive. In many cultures, this is often a "rite of passage" between two strangers. In group process this is about "emotionally aligning" ourselves with the client.

6. *Notice how you are feeling. Be honest and authentic.*

For someone to truly trust us, we must be willing to be honest about how we are feeling. If we are afraid, not sure, or don't know what to do, it is important not to pretend and to be truthful. Honesty and sincerity are what make others feel safe in a scary or uncertain situation. Not saying something or pretending everything is all right only makes it more unsafe.

7. *Take responsibility for your part in the conflict or misunderstanding.*

We all have been acculturated to be defensive, adversarial, and blaming of others when criticized or questioned. We have few, if any, models from any of our institutions about taking responsibility for their actions and behaviors. When was the last time you remember any politician, CEO, or president taking responsibility for doing something wrong before they got caught? How many companies have you known that have paid millions in lawsuits and admitted no wrongdoing? President Obama was told at a town hall meeting that he really erred in his first two cabinet choices, and he responded by saying that, yes, he had screwed up.

During his campaign he said that that because he had very little knowledge in those areas, he would appoint experts to help him and the person who disagreed with him would be the person he wanted to hear more from. No wonder he has more mail from folks offering ideas than any other president in the history of this country, because people feel they will be heard and that he is open to new ideas and solutions.

8. *Try to understand how their past affects who they are and how those experiences affect their relationship with you.*

Learning about one's past is essential in understanding why they react or don't react to you in a certain way. The key to learning about another person's journey comes from truly listening and being curious and not taking their reactions personally.

9. *Stay with the process and the relationship, not just the solution.*

Too often we rush to solve something rather than just listening and being supportive. I think that we rush to solve something because we need to be in control and to have all the answers. Staying in relationship with someone also means letting go of control and allowing a wide range of emotions to be expressed.

THE ART OF LISTENING

"To die, but not to perish, is to be eternally present."
-Buddhist Proverb

1.   Listen to what is being said and what is not.

2.   Observe the language of the body.

3.   Notice how something is being expressed and what words are used.

4.   Know that what you feel is as important as what you hear and see.

5.   Be willing to adapt and to adjust to the moment.

6.   Notice how your body and words express your projections.

7.   Notice when you are asleep and why.

8.   Keep breathing. Allow space for humor, warmth, and grief.

9.   Know that compassion is one of the highest forms of being present.

10.   Acknowledge and utilize the wisdom that is in each person.

11.   Accept and validate the truthfulness of each person's perception.

12.   Notice where someone begins and ends.

13.   Notice what is in the middle of the room.

14.   Model the acceptance and openness to conflict, anger, and pain.

15.   Acknowledge the courage and intimacy of being vulnerable.

16.   Be kind to yourself and others.

FACILITATING A CONFLICT

1. Breathe. Notice how you are feeling.

2. When you are not sure what to say or do—be still.

3. Allow for silence after the speaker has shared.

4. Mirror back the concerns and feelings of the speaker.

5. Non-verbally acknowledge the feelings of the speaker. Connect with the speaker using your eyes and body and voice.

6. Use your ethnicity, gender, etc., to make a connection with the speaker. Notice when any of these is a threat or an obstacle.

7. Stay with the anger until it has been fully expressed. Then gently move towards the hurt.

8. Stay connected to your co-facilitator. During breaks, discuss what is coming up for you and what you are observing about the group.

9. When one facilitator is listening, the other facilitator is observing the reactions of the group.

10. Ask about the life context of one's statements. Get to any past experiences. Discover how this affects the person today.

11. Watch for signs and clues that the group might be emotionally withdrawing. Notice and acknowledge their departures and determine why that might be occurring.

12. Trust the wisdom of the group. Use their stories.

13. Conflict is an opportunity for intimacy. View anger as an intimate opportunity and a catalyst for change and illumination.

14. Let the participants tell you where to go next. Allow the group to emerge at its own pace and in its own direction. It is their workshop.

15. Observe the listener as well as the speaker. Be aware of intent and impact.

CONVERSATION STARTERS

1   What's hard and what's good about talking about racism? Why?

2.   What was it like when you first noticed you were different? How did it affect you then and how does it affect you now?

3.   What opens you up when talking about racism and what closes you down? Why?

4.   How consciously aware of race are you? What areas don't you know about? Why or why not?

5.   What does "white privilege" mean to you as a (your ethnicity)?

6.   What kinds of experiences/memories have you had about race that have impacted your attitudes and behaviors?

7.   What has it taken for you to get to this room as a (your ethnicity)?

8.   Are there two Americas in terms of race? Describe what that looks like. How are you affected by this division? Why or why not?

9.   What would it take for you to heal from racism? What do you need and what don't you need? Why?

10.   What's the fear of talking about racism? What's at stake?

11.   Describe an experience in your life in which you were racist.

12.   How do you benefit or not benefit from racism? Why or why not?

9 WAYS TO BEGIN A DIVERSITY CONVERSATION

1. Have everyone share their ethnicity, when they first discovered they were different and how it affected them then and now.

2. Have each member share their ethnicity and one thing that is special about their culture and why. If they don't know what it means to them, why not?

3. Have everyone share their definition of multiculturalism and how they actualize that in their lives, work settings, and relationships.

4. Have each member share what is good and what is hard talking about diversity issues.

5. Have each member share how race/racism plays itself out in this group. (Additional options: class, gender, sexual orientation, age.)

6. Have each member share how racism has affected their lives and what it has taken for them to get to this room. (Additional options: class, gender, sexual orientation, age.)

7. Have each member share how discrimination affects their attitude, self-esteem, behavior, and sense of safety in their family, workplace, and in the world. If they don't have this experience, why not?

8. Have each member share what opens them up to talk about diversity issues and what closes them down.

9. Have each member bring quotes/pictures from their culture(s) and discuss what it was like doing this and what it meant to them to bring these to this group.

10 POINTS OF ENTRANCE

In all communications, there are entrances and departures, moments when we are either connecting or feeling disconnected. Here are some guidelines for developing healthy ways to relate and stay connected. Staying in the moment with someone requires that we notice the intent and impact of all our communications and those of others.

1. Ask questions based on what's important to them.

So often, we ask questions that are important to us, but not to the speaker. I think this happens because of our need to be in control. So we conveniently steer the conversation towards what is familiar and comfortable to ourselves. A good gauge of our connectedness is to observe the reaction of the speaker when we ask our questions. Are they more engaged or disengaged? When did they disengage and why?

2. Let them know how you feel about what they've said.

One of the main reasons why folks stop sharing is that often no one responds to what they are saying. The silence is deafening. That is why it's imperative to share how you feel about what they've said. It's a sign to the speaker that someone is listening and feels what they've shared is important.

3. Believe what they've shared.

This is one of the hardest ones to practice—believing what they've said, even if it is outside our experiences and beliefs—because it is their experience and truth. So many times there's a competition of who has the real truth, which means that someone is either the winner or the loser. The hard work is hearing each other and learning the roots of our separate truths and experiences, asking questions, being curious and staying open.

4. Equally risk in the exchange. Be willing to be emotionally vulnerable and available.

This isn't easy, but so needed when someone shares something about themselves that is personal. They often feel vulnerable and worried about what others are thinking about what they've shared. That's why I often go around the room asking folks to share what's familiar about they've just heard in their own lives. In that way, the one who has shared doesn't feel so isolated or unique in their feelings or reactions. It is also another important step in creating community and more authentic relationships.

5. Be willing to take action on their requests.

In all the trainings and workshops I've facilitated, I've learned that one of the main reasons participants don't want to share what they need and want from their workplaces is that they don't believe that anything will be done about their requests. That is why it's essential to understand the importance of following through on requests for changes. Trust is the key to all relationships—accounting for their success or failure.

6. Let them know that you've heard them by reiterating their major concerns.

The secret to de-escalating a conflict in seconds is to reflect back their major concerns instead of being defensive, adversarial, or in denial. The same is critical in almost all communications—listening and responding to another's needs. This may appear simple as a concept, but it's extremely difficult when faced with someone with whom you socially, politically, morally, spiritually, or religiously disagree. That's why it's important to practice reflecting in your daily relationships and communications, so that it becomes more natural and a part of your everyday life.

7. Tell the truth, even when you are scared.

To paraphrase Tom Booker, from the the movie *The Horse Whisperer*, "The truth is always there. To say it out loud, now that's the hard part." We are often surprised that others know when we are not telling the truth. It is something you can feel sometimes—the insincerity, the half-truths that linger in the air like the smell of an old apple filling a room. There is a saying, "If you accept and acknowledge your mistakes, what I see is your goodness. If you cover up your mistakes with excuses, claiming your goodness, all I see are your faults."

8. *Stay in the room even when it gets confrontational or uncomfortable.*

Participants can often feel when someone is getting scared or wanting to find an easy exit or distraction when things are getting heated or confrontational. Breathe and be real. Everyone feels fear or is scared when they are feeling out of control or past their comfort level. I often share with participants that I'm scared, too, but am willing to keep finding a way to support the process and those who are in conflict. The hard work is our willingness to stay in the room and to work things out.

9. *Curiosity is the gateway to empathy.*

To truly understand where someone is coming from, we need to be curious about who they are, what they have gone through, and how their past experiences have affected who they are today. In that way we can better relate to them with compassion and understanding.

10. *Be open to hearing new experiences/ideas outside of your own world.*

Albert Einstein once said that a fish doesn't know it is in water. The same can be said of our personal experiences. Just because we don't believe something doesn't mean it doesn't exist. Sometimes we need to expand beyond our world to see what is outside of our vision and experiences to truly understand another's life story and beliefs.

SECTION ONE
FOR PEOPLE OF COLOR

CHAPTER ONE

*TELLING THE TRUTH
ABOUT RACISM
TO WHITES*

——·— WHAT'S HARD ——·—

What's hard about telling whites the truth about racism?

SHAWN PATRICK

I find what can be most hard exists on two levels. One is the place where I must constantly defend the truth of the experience. There will always be someone who insists that what happened to me or another person of color was not actually racism but just a "misunderstanding," or an "innocent mistake," or my being "oversensitive." Not only does this become tiring, but after a while it starts to erode my own sense of what has happened—I begin to doubt my own judgment, my own feelings, my ability to interpret what happens around me. I usually leave this type of discussion with a tremendous headache.

On another level, though, talking about racism to people who are white is hard because I often find myself having to soothe their feelings. There is often an immediate defensive reaction on the part of the person who is white, so that I find the only way the conversation can proceed is to validate how they feel judged, misunderstood, discounted, which ironically is exactly what I think people of color need from those who are white! So in order to promote the possibility of having a useful conversation, I must put aside my own personal feelings of injustice and hurt in order to provide empathy to the other, who frequently does happen to be someone who engaged in racist acts. This is a duality of experience that becomes, quite frankly, maddening.

INDIGO VIOLET

It is hard in this post–Civil Rights era to tell whites that racism is more insidious and persistent than obvious, hateful, deliberate acts and attitudes. It is hard to explain that racism and white supremacy are embedded in the mainstream white culture of America, in the everyday ways that white privilege and white power work—through oblivion, through not seeing, not knowing. It is hard to tell whites that regardless of their intentions they are probably still racist, that they would have to unlearn and remake a tremendous amount in order to overcome racism. It is hard for whites—especially liberal whites

and those who see themselves as color-blind, inclusive, or even anti-racist—
to understand that a profound spiritual/emotional liberation process, a deep
unlearning of ingrained dominating behaviors, an unlearning of the subtleties
of white supremacy is the work that they really need to do. Being somewhat
aware doesn't cut it; racism is deeper and the process of undoing it is harder
and more rigorous than mere awareness. It seems hard for them to hear that
this work might take more than one lifetime and that in the meantime we
might not be able to be the best of friends.

INEZ TORRES

What is hardest about telling white people about racism is that they retain
the privilege of disbelief and the mythology of this country's formation and
history that supports that disbelief. The fact that race informed this country's
origins and its foreign policy is completely missed in our educational system.
This alienates people of color and disabuses white people. One result was that
when the highly-contested civil rights bill was finally signed—after the lon-
gest filibuster in the entire history of the U.S. Senate—white people, who were
kept ignorant of their own history, still saw racism as only a personal issue.
Therefore, if they treat the few people of color that do come into their sphere
the same way they like to be treated, racism cannot be a factor. They use this
framework for processing the life experiences of others and when that framework gets challenged (usually by a person of color) they resort to the privilege
of discounting or redefining the life experiences of people of color—that is,
disbelief.

WAYNE DOWNEY

Generally, whites do not have to operate from a race-based perspective on
a daily basis. As a consequence of this, the experience of racism is arbitrary,
unknown, and foreign. When I am placed in positions where I have to explain
that people are treated differently on the basis of skin color, I have to provide
evidence. If I don't, I am perceived as being angry, having an agenda, or being
anti-white. It is equally difficult to comprehend that the lack of knowledge
that whites have pertaining to racism will eventually hurt them. Inequality is
not some altruistic venture to save people of color or to "do the right thing." It
is really about a system that is designed to provide economic advantages that
favor one group over the others.

Genny Lim

The difficulty in telling the truth is running the risk of friendship and misunderstanding. Whites tend to reject criticisms about white racism as untrue because they perceive them as personal attacks and often find it difficult to accept your feelings without attempting to temper, critique or censor them. Instead of just listening and trying to understand your point of view, they feel a need to argue, discredit or correct your thinking. This internalizes the oppression that ethnic minorities experience on a daily basis. Blaming the victim lays blame on the one who is being oppressed rather than the one who is doing the oppressing. Additionally, racial deflection abdicates responsibility for addressing, much less resolving, the source of the problem. It makes excuses for racism, which is a subtle way to reproduce or perpetuate racism.

Razia Kosi

I'm thinking back on several experiences of telling whites the truth about racism and many thoughts and feelings come up for me. One is the voice of Jack Nicholson from the film *A Few Good Men* and the scene in which he responds to repetitive questioning about the "truth" to shouting, "You can't handle the truth!" So my immediate response to telling whites the truth about racism is "Can you handle the truth?" Are whites able to hear my truth about racism without jumping in to defend the whites in the situation, without challenging me on the reality of my experience, without telling me that similar things have happened to them and it wasn't because of race, and without a condescending look of pity?

Carol Walsh

For me the difficulty is their perceived indifference, disbelief, defensiveness, and projection. Living in a predominantly white community in the Pacific Northwest, I often hear that racism no longer exists and that my discussions about it are based upon my personal agenda to either make them feel guilty/cause trouble where none is present, or because I'm just an angry black woman. They also tell me they were equally discriminated against based upon being a red-head, fat, tall, etc., and that racism isn't any more painful or important than their pain or experience. I don't discount that discrimination, ridicule, and alienation of any sort is painful; however, why do we have to play this game? The historical legacy of racism and its continued burden, coupled with white privilege, is never acknowledged, and therefore, I don't feel acknowledged or validated.

Ralph Ellison, who penned *The Invisible Man*, noted in his prologue, "I am an invisible man. No, I am not a spook like those who haunted Edgar Allan Poe; nor am I one of your Hollywood-movie ectoplasms. I am a man of substance, of flesh and bone, fiber and liquids—and I might even be said to possess a mind. I am invisible, understand, simply because people refuse to see me." (1952, p. 3).

Racism keeps me invisible. Invisibility is the refusal to see, discuss, or even acknowledge the existence of racism and oppression and the deleterious impact it has on people of color.

Carolyn Bernard

They don't want to hear it. It's very difficult for white people to be told that they have invisible privileges that make their lives easier just because of the color of their skin. Even those whites who will acknowledge that life is harder for people of color do not want to also admit the obvious—that life is EASIER for them. They want to focus on individual experiences and have a hard time understanding the scope of institutional oppression. It is easier for whites to believe that racism only comes in the forms of the KKK, neo-Nazis, etc.—these are sources of racism they find easy to accept because they don't see themselves in these extremes. But what they resist seeing is the casual, institutional racism that surrounds us all, every day. They do not like to see that they are part of a problem.

Helen Ye

Whites do not feel they have received any entitlement or special privileges; rather they "deserve" to receive whatever they receive in their lifetimes because of their hard work and connections. I wonder if whites truly know how much more hard work, barriers and hardships people of color need go through to get even some of the simplest benefits whites take for granted. If whites had more meaningful relationships with people of color, they might learn more of our stories. If whites own up to being in more positions of power and authority as a result of racism, we could have more of an open dialogue.

DAVID LEE

My primal response to this question is that whites won't want to be my friend any more if I tell them the truth. The truth is an insult to their character; after all, "I'm not a racist." In my experience, white people claim to be hard on themselves until you tell them the truth. Then suddenly they're better than or above the characterizations you make of white racism. And shame on me for making this mischaracterization. They'll accuse me of being too sensitive, generalizing too much; after all, they're the exception, as every other white person claims. Well if every white person is the exception, then why do we still feel slapped in the face everywhere we are? What's hard about telling white people the truth is that white people continue to lie.

——•— THE PRICE —•——

What's the price of telling the truth about race relations in the U.S.?

INDIGO VIOLET

Whites get guilty, they get fearful, they are confused, they start to backlash, backpedal, condemn, hide out, protest, freeze up, resist. If they have access to power and media, they start spinning distorted discourses like "reverse racism," pointing the finger at the victims of racism, blaming the truth-tellers. It's a neurotic dance and if one has the spiritual resources to stay calm and shielded, it is interesting and fascinating to watch. Yet the price of truth-telling can be high if one is a deeply-aware person of color, or a particular community of color, who has to bear the psychic brunt of this kind of misguided energy, defensive avoidance, [unintentional] white supremacist posturing.

YUKARI TAKIMOTO AMOS

I have been called "racially hyper-sensitive" for talking about white privilege to white colleagues and friends. I have been called racist for talking about white racism because, to them, just to talk about the reality of race relations in the U.S. is enough to make a person a racist. To them, if we stop talking about race issues, the problems will disappear. I totally disagree. So, most of my friends are minorities, as a result, or those whites who are married to minorities. I have been called a "racist professor" just because I always talk about white racism in my multicultural education class. By honestly talking about the truth, I have been labeled and watched by whites, which makes me very uncomfortable and sometimes physically unsafe. But this behavior of labeling and watching just because they don't want to hear in itself is white power.

TONI ADAMS

The price is being tagged a "radical" or a person who feels race is an excuse for every issue in life. I've heard more than one person say, "Slavery happened a long time ago and I wasn't a part of it, so give up on that excuse." There is a real lack of understanding of the residual effects of an interlude in our history like racism. So many blacks reared by elders were taught to be "careful" around white folks and NOT to say certain things around white folks. These are all lessons from the plantation that live on today.

TRAVIS SMITH

Part of the difficulty lies in being too often redirected and possibly relegated to "one of those angry blacks who think everything is about race." When I say redirected I mean being told, "That's not what was meant," or, "You're overreacting."

We live in a system designed to create a labor class in service to white society, in particular a white elite. When it appears that 98% of the whites have bought into the illusion of "whiteness," the mythology concocted by their ancestors, it's very difficult to conjure up the nerve to trust those who identify as such.

People of color are totally dependent upon whites to prepare children of color to compete with white children for a place in a white-dominated society. Schools have always been mirrors that reflect the values, goals, needs, and priorities of the society/communities they serve. So if white hegemony is the order of the day, and it is, then students of color are brainwashed and trained to be passive participants in the process.

Despite their legacy of violence and injustice I still have to deal with whites in order to navigate their society. Only 3% of doctors and lawyers are black. So when I'm ill or my children are ill I have to place a level of trust in one who, if they've been through five years of the United States school system, could very well see me as inferior. If I'm wronged in some way or an injustice befalls a loved one, I must place my hopes in the hands of—in all probability—whites.

Therefore a great part of the difficulty lies in telling them the truth on how it feels to walk in a world of those who slaughtered the Native Americans, enslaved/tortured/murdered millions of Africans, dropped "Little Boy" via the *Enola Gay* on Japan, placed guns and drugs in your own communities, designed unjust laws to protect the grand theft of an entire landmass—we may be forced to pay the price of being fired, blackballed, set up, imprisoned and even murdered.

Erin Yoshimura

In my mid-30's, I worked for a very hip and progressive international software company. During my seven years there, I would often have to educate people that using the abbreviation "JAP" for our Japanese-language product was not only inappropriate, but highly offensive to people of Japanese descent. I did this with much diplomacy and understood that most people just didn't know that "Jap" was very derogatory term.

Imagine walking into various departments at work and seeing JAP written on white boards, file folders, notebooks and shelving labels. Each time, it was a punch in the stomach and took me back to those school days when white kids would yell, "You dirty Jap, go home!" and throw rocks at me just because of my race.

There was one department in particular that I had to constantly remind to stop using it. Although the manager complied (reluctantly, with rolling eyes), it seemed to continually pop up.

The final blow that made me decide to leave the company came when I received a group e-mail with a document attached labeled "JAP." With less diplomacy, I asked the sender to rename the file and said that I had repeatedly told her department and her department manager to stop using that abbreviation. I received a scathing e-mail response from the department manager, who also took it upon herself to send it up the food chain to my manager, his manager and her manager. To quote the e-mail word for word (I saved a copy of it):

> Erin, you did NOT tell me several times, you told me ONCE and I never wrote it that way again. Mary* was not aware of it and now that she is, she will NOT write it again. If I had noticed, I would have told her, but I did not, and I apologize for that. However, please be also aware, as I already explained to you, that the word JAP is meaningless to us, as foreigners. We are not Americans; we were not involved in making up the term or using that term in a derogatory way. And again, please do not say that you have told me this several times. I find this offensive and untrue. I am very sensitive to cultural issues, and I don't need to be told several times to respect them. Joan*   (*Names have been changed.)

What came after was much worse.

A short time after this e-mail exchange, I had other Japanese Americans come to me to complain that they went down to the department and saw JAP written on the whiteboard. I went down to verify this was true and went straight to HR to complain, only to be met with silence and a strange look from the HR person that I took as disdain.

Within moments of leaving the HR office, my manager stomped into my cubicle and said, "Erin, is this the way you want to handle this?"

He thought I was out of line to go to HR about this. Suddenly, I was scared that I could lose my job.

The only way this issue got some resolution was when one of my white colleagues stomped into HR and said the word JAP written on the whiteboard was offensive to her. My colleague was transgender, so the company was enlightened about some diversity issues.

This experience cost me a part of my soul and a little piece of me died from it. To have an entire line of managers, one African American, not get involved, for an HR professional to turn the table and "tattle on" me, and for my manager to chastise me made me lose faith in humanity and the corporate system.

Each time I tell this story, it costs me a little bit more because I know that I can never get back that part of my soul that died that day.

CAMISHA L. JONES

When I tell the truth about racism (even when I speak peacefully without an angry tone or body language), I risk being seen as militant, an opposing force, un-American, divisive. The term gets turned back to me, "Isn't it racist to stereotype all white people?" This I find funny since the word "racism" is usually so charged and offensive to whites. Rather than have a real conversation, when I tell the truth about racism, I risk ending up in a tangential game of "I'm not racist. You are." Whites seem to want to use the word "racist" as a shield and a weapon when I want to use it to heal by taking off the crippling blinders they wear.

CAROL WALSH

There is a great risk to speaking the truth. It first makes you vulnerable to attacks and ridicule. These attacks have taken their toll upon me. It makes me hesitant, nervous, anxious, and prone to second-guessing myself. I also find

I have to give up a part of myself, meaning my time, my personal safety and peace of mind, to move out of my comfort zone to hopefully inform, raise awareness, or change the conscious and unconscious mind of those holding hate, ignorance, or intolerance around race relations in the U.S. Ostracism and isolation are the tools used to punish and silence those who dare speak the truth about racism in this country. Not only do our white brothers and sisters do this, but unfortunately I have felt the sting of internalized racism from my own racial group. When those of your own racial group tell you to "stop making waves," or "It's not as bad as it appears," or worse, "Racism no longer exists," where do you find community? Whom do you go to for support, solace, or encouragement? So, I find myself in constant debate with myself, asking, "Do I risk it or just let it go?"

Recently I attended an operations meeting in my organization and at the suggestion of the facilitator a brainstorming session ensued over the pressing issues for the upcoming fiscal year. Debating with myself, in my head, on whether or not I should broach a relatively volatile subject in the organization, I decided, "What the hell," braced myself, and commented, "Diversity is an issue of importance." Continuing, I noted that students, faculty, and staff have expressed multiple concerns over discriminatory and racist comments and treatment. I took a breath to form my next sentence and before a word could be spoken, the attack began. As I sat back and heard either a myriad of reasons why this topic was inappropriate for this group or feigned naiveté over how could we possibly operationalize and thereby "do" diversity, I was reminded of the debate which transpired in my head only moments before and my subconscious promptly teased, "I told you so." Weary of the battle, which had now been waged for several years, I said, "Forget it. I withdraw the comment; move on," to the obvious discomfort of those in the room and on the phone. The facilitator promptly did as I suggested and moved on.

For days after the meeting, whenever I bumped into the participants, I was met with how uncomfortable and/or horrified they were at the comments and treatment I received (despite the fact they remained silent at the meeting) for such a worthy cause, which they fully supported. I thanked them for their concern, briefly noted their silence, and remarked I will no longer attend the meeting as it was clear that I had no place there since diversity was the scope of my job and it was clear that diversity was not a relevant factor in the group. Disheartened and apparently saddened by my comments, I heard nothing more than, "I understand." However, one comment in particular that came immediately after the meeting was more striking to me. A meeting participant noted that whenever I speak about diversity it is perceived as a criticism or accusation of wrongdoing, failure, or even racism to those with whom I'm speaking. The profundity of the statement prompted me to question our ability to really have a conversation about race or racism, particularly when we can't even really discuss "diversity."

INEZ TORRES

I have paid a hefty price for answering the call to teach a largely white organization how racism works. I have been slandered, verbally attacked, misinterpreted, misrepresented (and not allowed to correct that misinterpretation or misrepresentation), ostracized, and despised by people of color and whites.

On the other hand, I live my life with my eyes and heart open because the very things that could have stopped me cold and turned me away from this work have contributed to my growing quite large-hearted as a person. My capacity for self-healing and regeneration of spirit has been multiplied several hundredfold. Others have had their lives touched and some have experienced healing. As a result, I cannot imagine ever wishing a return to the not-knowing of the first twenty-five years of my life.

Why do you think it's so hard for whites to hear the truth about racism?

YUKARI TAKIMOTO AMOS

While I was living in Japan, I never questioned my own racial and ethnic privilege. It was not because I was not aware of the privilege (I was keenly aware of it). I simply did not care about other racial and ethnic groups and took it for granted. This non-caring attitude itself is a privilege. When my Korean friend discussed institutional racism in Japan against her, all I said to her was, "That's the way it is in Japan."

Racism is always related to privilege. Those who live a daily life based on the birth-given privilege due to their race and ethnicity find it difficult to listen to others exploring the truth about racism.

SHAWN PATRICK

I think the real difficulty is that people who are white in this country also have suffered because of racism. They experience the hurt of being associated with, related to, or perhaps as being themselves perpetrators of harm and injustice upon others. But facing that reality forces people to ask very hard questions about themselves and take ownership of their role in this process. In short, it's hard because no one wants to admit they could be or are "one of those people." Add to this the value in white culture of independence and self-determination —accepting racism means also accepting that your success has come at the price of millions of people losing their rights, privileges, even lives, and not just because of "hard work." I think this is a very painful thing for a person who is white to come to terms with.

INDIGO VIOLET

Hearing the truth exposes so many of the lies of U.S. history, that the nation is good, that the process of making it was righteous, that the blood and brutality were not all that bad, that for the most part America is good. As part of white supremacy, whites have internalized a powerful idea that they are good people, nice people, generous people, well-intentioned people. While there are definitely good-hearted white folks out there, the attachment to the idea of goodness is profound. It is profound partly because it is linked to the historical ideas (both overt and covert) that Africans, American Indians, Asians, Mexicans, etc., were/are bad, problematic, inferior. Goodness—in the present-day implicit/embedded racist system—is not simply a neutral idea; it is attached to the long-standing ideas of white supremacy. The idea of white goodness was constructed in contrast to the Other.

So, to tell a modern-day, liberal-minded, do-good white person that a lot of people of color don't think white people are very good people, that white people have not always been good, that in fact they've been really horrible, that even when they are nice and well-intentioned the impact of their power, privilege, and oblivion is not good—this upsets a very deep construct and psychological anchor for whites.

INEZ TORRES

Most of the activist whites I have encountered in the twenty years I have been doing this work more often appear to prefer chastising and castigating members of their own group more than they are willing to find their own healing and clarify or provide a road map for themselves so that they can become part of a healing historical movement of counter-cultural resistance.

BILL HOWE

It makes them feel uncomfortable. It is much safer to stay in one's comfort zone and pretend that racism does not exist, that other people are not suffering, that white people are not the beneficiaries of their skin color. People can talk themselves into anything, rationalize anything, blame others for the problem. It is much easier to deny there is a problem if by acknowledging it there would be a cost to you. White people aren't fools—why give up a good thing?

TRAVIS SMITH

Sociologists spent a century calling blacks intellectually inferior, evil, and lazy. Never mind that for over a century it was illegal for us to learn and the free labor we provided generated the wealth that made America what it was. It's hard for whites to hear the truth about racism because they're paper tigers! Also, one cannot escape the reality of how the modern world was created: through the murder, deception, and robbery of people of color. Not only have they deceived the world, but they've fooled themselves into thinking that humanity revolves around them, and it never has! Wherever they are in their development we've been! Civilization did not begin in Europe and everywhere Europeans have gone they've done their best to put out the lights of the people, the likes of which the world has never seen!

True racism exists only when one group holds a disproportionate share of wealth and power over another, then uses those resources to marginalize, exploit, exclude and subordinate the under-privileged group. In the Americas, it is "whites" who use wealth, i.e. resources/power, to marginalize, exploit, manipulate and divide humanity.

According to *The Color of Wealth: The Story Behind the U.S. Racial Wealth Divide*, for every dollar owned by the average white family in the U.S., THE AVERAGE FAMILY OF COLOR HAS LESS THAN A DIME. Whites typically have assets more than 10 times greater than do persons of color. This difference was created not only by government policies that impeded wealth building for people of color, but also policies that actually boosted white wealth policies, like land grant and homestead programs, low cost mortgages, farm loans, and social security checks, all at times available only or mostly to whites. So, typically, it's hard for people to hear that the gains they think they've made have actually been afforded to them via an unjust, biased, and racist system.

DAVID LEE

Centuries of privilege have given whites a real ego trip.

DENNARD CLENDENIN

It is difficult for whites to hear the truth regarding racism because in my opinion they have difficulty getting past their own complicity as it relates to racism. In other words their own "white guilt" is difficult for them to own up to. They realize that they've benefited from a white racist society. For the most part, they feel that they haven't engaged in overt racist activities. More specifically they have never been members of the Ku Klux Klan. They've never protested the presence of women, gays, of people of color. They may have even voted for Barack Obama. That somehow exonerates them from being racist.

More than likely buried in their subconscious are the painful memories of their parents' attitudes towards people of color. Perhaps they've gotten entrance to an educational institution, acquired a job or promotion, as a result of racism. Perhaps they were privy to, or in the presence of, racist comments by other whites regarding fellow students or co-workers of color and were silent. It is difficult for them to admit that even though they do not engage in those comments, they were silent.

Last, and I think most important, is their own self-image. That is, when hearing about the painful experiences of people of color, most whites are unable or unwilling to think about the offended person. They simply don't want people of color to think that they are racist. That is what I call the "self-centeredness of white guilt."

GENNY LIM

You risk being written off, blackballed or dismissed as angry, paranoid or racist. You're only allowed to discuss racism in a sterile framework removed from living reality. The objectification of racism as a formal, academic discourse can have the dangerous side-effect of treating racism as some sort of antiquated phenomenon or as a relic of post-colonialism, rather than as an ongoing, operational system of complex social, economic, and political relationships embedded in the national fabric. The dominant discourse of racism, moreover, allows the dominant institutional structures to frame and define racism as well as to determine how it is to be discussed and understood. The underclass and ordinary folk continue to be excluded from the dialogue, to the point where they are relegated to field subjects or research specimens for the fulfillment of academic theory. The folks most oppressed by racism are questionable beneficiaries to the privileged discourse on race and are the least likely population to speak for themselves. This is problematic and results in the phenomenon of double racism, whereby the oppressed class is not only being discriminated against, but their oppression is exploited by outside experts, politicians or business interests that presumably represent their view or desires.

ERIN YOSHIMURA

The hardest part about telling some white people about my experience with racism is they don't believe me. They don't have to say anything because "the look" says it all. I told a white woman about my project, visualizAsian.com, and said the reason I'm doing it is because Asian American Pacific Islanders are still invisible in the mainstream and when we are visible, it's often an inaccurate portrayal based off of centuries-old stereotypes. As soon as I said this, the smile dropped off her face, she lowered her head, tightened her jaw and her eyes became very steely and cold as if to say, "Oh, c'mon now, that's not the truth."

The look is so familiar to me and most often comes from white people. A surprising number of them are highly educated, in positions of high rank and power and are considered progressive thinkers. The frightening part is how quickly and harshly they react to my stories and experience even though I don't use the words "racist" or "racism."

CAMISHA L. JONES

I can understand why white people tend to get defensive when racism is discussed, because if they really opened themselves up to hearing the truth about racism, their opinion of themselves would change drastically. It would be extremely uncomfortable to realize that even if they have done nothing intentionally harmful, they are complicit nonetheless in the oppression of people of color. It would be painful to realize that not seeing color doesn't equal being a "good" person. Actually, in my opinion, a person who claims to be color-blind is more likely to be an oppressive person. It is not an easy thing to learn that you are not the fair, open and inclusive person you believe yourself to be and that your silence and blindness has reinforced a status quo that discriminates in your favor and denies the humanity of those who are unlike you. It is hard for whites to hear the truth about racism because of what racism says about the influence, actions and the impact of white people.

CAROL WALSH

Fear is something we don't talk about enough when we have conversations around racism. "What will this mean for me, my kids, my family, my lifestyle, if I even entertain the conversation of racism?" is the question that comes to mind for whites when they even hear the word racism. The privilege they refuse to openly acknowledge they possess is the very privilege they're deathly afraid to lose! Can the colonizer understand the perspective or the language of the colonized? Generations of hegemony have resulted in the most profound disability among whites. They have become deaf, dumb, and blind to the truths of racism; and although they feign or show genuine disgust for the current conditions of race relations, they still maintain their helplessness over being able to do anything to change it. This "helplessness," however, has been fueled by the rhetoric and lies passed down through generations about the inferiority, danger, and limited usefulness of people of color. When these stories are believed and held as truth, it becomes difficult to unravel and deconstruct the lies taught by those closest to you and society as a whole.

CHIMI

They don't want to accept what they are doing or have done wrong.

ERIC LACKIE

A number of years ago I interned with a local mentoring agency. One day I accompanied the director (at the time) and another intern to interview "at-risk" middle school youth to see if they were eligible for our program. The director and the intern (both white and female) began to joke about how we should dress up like rappers with big gold chains, tilted hats, sagging pants, and big clock necklaces, and introduce ourselves to the youth by saying, "Yo!" I felt uncomfortable about their jokes for a couple of reasons. First, I don't want to dress up like a stereotypical rap artist just to recruit kids for mentoring. Second, I was uncomfortable because most of their humor sounded sarcastic and mocking and was directed at a form of expression of black culture (which has been adopted by other ethnic groups). Still laughing, the director finally turned to ask me what I thought about the idea. I told her, "Honestly, I feel offended." They both proceeded to tell me why I shouldn't feel offended because they weren't being racist, that they were just joking, and a whole lot of other justifications which only caused me to feel more unheard and shut down.

I later went to meet with the director one on one, but in defense she explained how she is not racist because she dated a black guy who used to play in a well-known jazz or blues band, and that she had been active in the civil rights movement. All I could think to myself was, "Even though you dated a black man, and even after your involvement in civil rights, you are still unwilling to hear and validate the pain that I experience." I wish white people would not use their positive experiences with other people of color as an excuse to ignore or dismiss the ways that I feel hurt by their behavior.

What "blind spots" do you notice about white allies?

SHAWN PATRICK

Blind spots I notice have more to do with some white allies believing they no longer have any hang-ups or biases because they have decided to fight against racism. I am very excited and encouraged when I meet someone who is white who takes on racism honestly, but I become wary if that same person uses this to insist that he or she knows everything about the experience of the person of color. It means more to me if that ally is able to fight against racism while admitting their own biases, prejudice, or expressions of racism, instead of insisting he or she never took part in it.

CAROLYN BERNARD

The biggest blind spot I see in white allies is that they want to believe they are incapable of racism themselves. I have seen white allies blithely say racist things or blindly exercise their white privilege or happily appropriate the cultures of people of color. When called on this behavior, these people are rarely ready to hear that they are not being a good ally; they often react defensively, wanting to believe that having declared themselves an ally, they are no longer culpable. It is an ugly situation, and I have seen fledgling "allies" decide that anti-racism is just "too hard" when they realize that they will always be held accountable for their words and actions. What they fail to understand is that racism is not something a person of color gets to walk away from—whether we like it or not, this fight is at our doorstep and we are forced, every day, to participate.

TONI ADAMS

It took me a long time to understand, my reality is not anyone else's reality.

TRAVIS SMITH

They see the world through a different lens sans the experience of being considered the other, even my white-sister-friend who recently wanted to argue that a "neighborhood" she took me to shop in that we'd never been to was safe without consciously realizing that the reason she thought this was because the people we encountered were all white. I took the position that no neighborhood was safe enough to leave her vehicle unlocked with our purchases in full view in the backseat, and that I was waiting for the day someone white would say that about an all-black neighborhood.

The biggest blind spot I find with white allies is that they're comfortable around people of color and they congregate with other whites who "get it," but seldom do I find them amongst the other whites who seem to be out of sync and even archaic in thought. I think that would do a great service to us (people of color): for more white allies to fight those battles amongst those who feel they can say some old racist shit to you, about people of color, because you're "white like me." And if they're not saying it, I think whites "who get it" should have a technique to check and see if their family members or old friends from high school are harboring racist feelings and thoughts. And not be afraid to check that friend or relative.

CAROL WALSH

On some levels, because whites have befriended a person of color, they can easily make the mistake of believing that person of color has somehow "transcended" race by virtue of their friendship. As if the friendship with the white ally has elevated the person of color's status. For example, I was looking a picture of a white ally and their friend on a yacht. The picture was taken at a time before the ally became truly aware of racism. My comment was that the picture was a representation of privilege, of unearned wealth that was taken for granted. In the picture were probably two individuals that benefited greatly from their privilege to the point of a slap on the hand for criminal offenses, job offers without interviews, and admissions to prestigious colleges without adequate credentials. My white ally friend commented that I was being judgmental and unfair; however, my comments and observations were 100% correct (as they admitted to), and, in fact, both individuals received one if not all of the benefits of their privilege I named. These benefits could not be bestowed upon me nor would the assumptions be made about me. When asked, if you saw me on a yacht, would you think privilege or would you think, "What white person was kind enough to allow me on their yacht?" My friend responded yes to the latter question.

CAMISHA L. JONES

Some people I know who believe themselves to be allies think they have "arrived." I think this is a huge blind spot. I believe unlearning bias to be a lifelong process and to be an ally is to know that you never "arrive." You might become better at detecting stereotypes and discrimination but you don't ever "arrive." To me, being an ally means you have come to the realization that you have a predisposition to act biased (not from any fault of your own but simply because biased messages in society are targeted for your consumption). Being an ally means you are actively working against digesting those messages so they will not inform your decisions or influence your actions. When a white ally declares themselves not to have a "racist bone in their body" they are declaring that they have stopped actively defending their minds and hearts from the onslaught of racist messages being sent for their consumption.

YUKARI TAKIMOTO AMOS

I have a white colleague who is married to a woman from Latin America. He claims he is a multiculturalist. One day he said to me, "These days it is difficult to get a job at an institution of higher education because I am white." Are you kidding me? If that's the case, why am I surrounded by white professors at my university? A self-claiming white multiculturalist like him still doesn't understand white hegemony. In other words, my colleague still defends his whiteness unconsciously.

INDIGO VIOLET

I recognize that white people who are involved in anti-racist work are at different stages in their own understanding of the historical, cultural, and social issues pertaining to racism as well as in their own anti-racist white identity development. I try to be patient and offer compassion, recognizing that stages shift and deeper understanding can be had—that we are all works in progress. Some specific blinders I see are as follows (and this is based on my definition of a white ally as someone who is able to be critical of whiteness, white culture, white ideologies, and white privilege):

- Slipping into "I'm a good white person," aligning themselves primarily with people of color, and separating themselves from other white people that they see as somehow beneath them in their understanding.
- Not recognizing that, even though they are white allies, people of color may still be suspicious of them, that people of color still do not have to be intimate on a personal and spiritual level with white people, even those who desire to be allies.

- Still holding on to a sense of entitlement to people of color's friendship and knowledge, rather than having a humility and clarity that their work as a white ally does not depend on whether people of color like them or not.
- Falling into old white supremacist patterns—not listening to people of color, capitalizing from their white ally status, taking over conversations, seeing themselves as people who know and can take the upper hand.

RAZIA KOSI

The "blind spots" that I notice about white allies are that they may become such advocates in addressing racism and biases in others that they may have become less adept at examining their own biases with others. If the allies aren't willing to examine themselves and be a part of the journey in ending racism in this country, then they have become a part of perpetuating the issues that caused racism. This is also true of people of color who do not examine and address biases and internalized racism in themselves, their own communities, and with other racial, ethnic and cultural groups. In order for all of us to get past our "blind spots" we have to be willing to see the things in ourselves we'd prefer to be blind about.

ERIN YOSHIMURA

I often notice that being white means you have the "right of way." Whether it's walking around at a crowded airport or grocery store, I often get cut off or am forced to move out of the way so as not to knock into white people. There's unconsciousness about physicality that communicates entitlement and I imagine that if you have the right of way all your life, it's as natural as breathing. This also applies to conversation.

I know some white people who are pretty culturally fluent who don't realize they cut people off while conversing or take over a conversation before the other person is done. While they may do this to all people, it's monumental to people of color because often we're not fully heard or are easily dismissed because we're not white.

White allies also need to be cognizant of using a "universal cultural template" when interacting with people of color. We're not all the same nor do we have similar experiences. For instance, the term "Asian American Pacific Islander" is an umbrella for more than 28 different ethnic groups. Just as white people are afforded the privilege of being seen as individuals, extend the same consideration to people of color.

As a fourth-generation Japanese American female, I will always be a student of diversity and racism. My hope is that white allies also become lifelong learners because there is no end to what we can learn about others and, most important, about ourselves.

——·—— OBSTACLES ——·——

In what ways do whites keep people of color from telling the truth about race/racism?

STACEY GIBSON

Even and especially in the race discourse, there remains a requirement for people of color to "take care of whites" in the time of new-found white crisis. Because the white person MAY, for the first time, feel a small percentage of the unrest, dis-ease, outright hatred and trepidation that oppressed people of color live and die in every day, it is still an expectation that the white person (the person most taken care of and valued since Columbus' arrival) becomes the most taken care of and valued in the race discourse.

INDIGO VIOLET

We don't understand racism in our culture, we don't talk about white supremacy nearly enough, so the charge of racism is treated more gravely than we treat the brutality of racism.

SHAWN PATRICK

I don't think whites just prevent people of color from telling the truth, I think they also prevent other white people. I think this is done through establishing norms that say we can't talk about these things. I think it is also done by challenging every story of racism that comes out, to fight strongly against the notion that racism exists. I also believe there are still intimidations, threats, and other real harms that are used to keep people quiet.

INEZ TORRES

Duh, it's the power. Power. The one thing whites have that controls people of color like me from sharing what I know about racism is power. Their institutional and systemic power decides who will be heard and how broadly that *who* gets heard. Power determines what will be allowed to have impact. Power decides what is made public or widely known and what does not. That power is demonstrated along a continuum that ranges from rejection or failure to believe to the benign neglect of those things that are known to be true (the most damaging) to the actual persecution and desire to harm those who speak this truth.

JEAN MOULE

Blame the victim.

DENNARD CLENDENIN

Whites keep people of color from telling the truth about racism by changing the subject, exhibiting frustration aimed at the person speaking about racist experiences, or, lastly, especially in a business environment, making it clear that the subject is not appropriate for the workplace. It is their way of controlling the environment and thus insulating themselves from the issue.

Whites also keep people of color from speaking to issues of race by not allowing any visible signs of diversity. In an office or home settings, there are no items expressing cultural diversity. The allowable items include paintings, statues, pictures, etc., that are steeped in white culture or otherwise neutral. The absence of these items for people of color sends a silent message that diversity is not part of the dialogue.

GENNY LIM

White people's friendship always seems conditional on not rocking the boat. As long as we never bring up anything disturbing or difficult, we can be the best of friends. We can talk about anything from relationships and children, to love, sex and death, but when it comes to confronting the truth about racism, it is not up for grabs. It is neither proper nor appropriate to mention why it is so important that their kids go to expensive private schools but not yours, or why it is out of the question for them to clean their own houses and chauffeur their kids to soccer, ballet and sports camp.

COZ

The reason why they don't tell the truth is because they don't want to feel bad about having done wrong, so they keep it from everyone.

J.C. Eaglesmith

Obviously the strategy of "divide and conquer" has been achieved: non-white tokenism, that is, "allowing" a small percentage of non-whites to enjoy a more visible and comfortable life, i.e., to enjoy more "white-like" privileges. This strategy sends a message of appropriate and acceptable modeling. The only non-white in a group of whites is often privy to hear negative racial remarks and consequently be offered the old, "Oh, we don't mean you, Chief! You're okay!"

Again, we talk about people getting defensive about the role they play in perpetuating racism. I continually hear, "Those things happened hundreds of years ago, we can't take the blame for that." But they will gladly accept the unearned benefits. Or, "But look at Oprah or Bill Cosby," which are usually the only two "successful" people of color they can name. And if you asked them to name an Asian person, or an Aboriginal person, or a South Asian person who had a fraction of the success, they would be at a loss for words.

Or, "Why should we feel guilty for what our ancestors did?", which again brings me back to privilege. Or, "If you don't like it you should leave," which leads to a greater discussion about the fact that people of color have been contributing to the Canadian landscape for over a hundred years, African Canadians have been around for about 400 years, and First Nations' people didn't come from anywhere else.

Denise Hampden

We must constantly be explaining ourselves and justifying our right to be in North America and we're tired of it.

Carol Walsh

One of the most powerful ways whites keep people of color from telling the truth is to make them feel as if they are finding problems where none exists. Racism happens very subtly. It happens when the cashier places your change on the counter and not in your hands; it happens when you raise your hand and no one calls on you; it happens when someone asks you to get the garbage out of their office mistaking you for a cleaning woman; it happens when you walk with a white friend and people will walk between you assuming you couldn't possibly be together; it happens in each of these instances. Yet when you try to explain them to whites you are told, "You're exaggerating," or, "You're trying to cause trouble," or the classic, "You're just being overly sensitive." Because the slights can be so small and almost unnoticeable, as a person of color you at times begin to believe you are exaggerating and wonder, "Is it me?" These are the most damaging and productive ways whites silence people of color.

More recently, with the election of President Obama and the belief that racism no longer exists, it becomes more difficult to discuss the continual impact of institutional and personalized racism. Our white allies can also become defensive and unable to hear the pain of black folks. Instead of just listening when we need to unleash and unload the fury, the confusion, or just the pain, they immediately say, "But that's not how I see you," or "That's not what I do," or they provide a litany of advocacy and social justice work they have done. Yes, I can hear of your pain, and have been raised with the stories of the difficulties of the ruling, dominant and privileged class/race; but when is it my turn? Let down your guard, sit in the discomfort of my story and let's see what we can learn together to continue righting the wrongs of racism in this world.

CHIMI

Not teaching their kids the truth about history in school. They don't listen.

YUKARI TAKIMOTO AMOS

The price of telling the truth about race relations is high. Whites do everything to prevent people of color from telling the truth because it reveals their privilege. One effective tactic for whites is being argumentative or even combative. In my multicultural education class, I, as a minority instructor, ask questions related to institutional racism. White students usually get frustrated and defensive and as a result become argumentative and combative. To everything I say about white racism, they have something to counterattack. They do so in a group and in yelling voices. When they think they have lost the argument, they use silence as a weapon and show explicit defiance. White students' combative attitude and silence cause fear and anxiety for minority students in class. As a result, minority students are usually quiet throughout the class discussion. Finally, I lose allies. What is the price of this confrontational class discussion? In contrast to my other classes, I frequently receive low student evaluations for this class, which is detrimental to my tenure and promotion.

Another tactic is showing pseudo-empathy. When I honestly expressed my feeling of my voice not being seriously taken in our department to my supervisor (a white male), he said to me, "I understand how you feel. I was a minority in Uruguay. I am also from a low SES status. Class and race are the same." This simple statement really upset me and prevented me from further discussion. How can a white, European American male be a minority in Latin America? How can a class issue be equivalent to a race issue? Why doesn't he understand the power issue? By trying to be empathetic, whites actually discourage further discussion on race and racism because people of color realize that the level of their understanding is too shallow to even discuss face-to-face.

CAROLYN BERNARD

Whites keep people of color from telling the truth about racism by DENYING racism. By pretending that racism is "a thing of the past" or that it only comes in the form of white hoods and lynchings, white people effectively define racism. And they define it in ways that benefit themselves.

SONYA LITTLEDEER-EVANS

By not hearing the stories of people of color. I often choose to not go deep and tell the truth about racism with whites because I'm not sure how to help whites understand my experiences with racism outside of their white contexts—it's always hard for whites to see how their white experiences are directly related to my non-white experiences. Often, when this happens, the mentality from whites is that if they can't understand it (my experience) then it must not be true. Whites keep people of color from telling the truth about racism by not being vulnerable about their own experiences with racism. Just as I am willing to share about how racism has disadvantaged me, I would like whites to share about how racism has given them advantage, to be honest about this, to own it.

—·— SAYING IT OUT LOUD —·—

What are your honest thoughts about white folks?

CAROLYN BERNARD

I honestly think that white folks rule the world and they like it that way. I honestly think that white folks hold tightly to their privilege, even those who claim to be anti-racist. I honestly think we have a long, long way to go before white folks in this country allow people of color to truly stand beside them as equals.

MARY WEEMS

Many, when made aware of the spirit-killing impact of racism in America, are at least open to considering the history of its origin though most are unwilling to act to do anything to stop it. If this were not the case, there would be no need for questionnaires/projects like this.

TRAVIS SMITH

In my rage, I think you're a bunch of land-grabbing, people-enslaving, pathological liars and homicidal maniacs who rule the world through lies, terror, murder and exploitation. Any time you flood territories in order to build hydroelectric dams, destroy rain forests in order to mine the lands beneath, poison the land, air and water all in the name of leisure, pleasure, and capitalism —you're crazy! I think you're childish and really unworthy to be spoken of.

In truth, I'm in awe of your climb to the apex of human activity. When I look at your history I find a sick people living in ignorance and suffering from various plagues, a people constantly at war with one another, all the while braving the elements of this little peninsula called Europe. You fought several crusades, battled the Mongols in the east and the Moors in the south. Then you took what knowledge you learned from us, pooled your resources, fashioned weapons, built ships and set out to convince the world that your shit don't stink. Now there's nothing you can't have and no place you can't go and live like it's yours!

Yukari Takimoto Amos

Privileged, arrogant, and overconfident. Unfortunately, white folks are privileged even outside the United States. White privilege is an international phenomenon.

Carol Walsh

In many ways I feel sorry for them. It's much like a spoiled child who can never be happy because there's never enough, they didn't have to work for it, and their entitlement prevents true gratitude and appreciation. Also, because of their entitlement, they have an inability to deal with pain, loss, and denial which has caused them to oppress so many cultures and nations of people, as well as destroy others who thrive, survive, and achieve despite pain, loss, and denial. The envy and fear is overwhelming for them at times.

Camisha L. Jones

Honestly, I think white people are injured by racism just as much as people of color. I think they live in denial. I think our country has equated being American with having no cultural ties or consciousness. I think most white people are unconsciously racist. I think I have to be careful about what I share with white folks and what I do around them because they have had so little interaction with people of color they can easily misinterpret my actions in ways that will be harmful to me. I think white folks believe color-blindness is the remedy to racism and I completely disagree. I have heard so many white folks tell me, "I wasn't raised to be racist. I was raised to treat everyone equally." I think they believe this because their parents simply told them to treat everyone fairly, not because they were equipped to think critically about the ways that people of color (and other marginalized groups) are not treated fairly. I believe most white folks have never had significant close relationships with people of color or exposure to cultures different from their own. I believe most white people are unaware of the ways people of color have positively contributed to the development of our nation, businesses and the development of knowledge. I believe most white people were raised without much if any exposure to counter the negative stereotypes and imagery regarding people of color and because of this they were raised to be racist. I believe most white people would prefer not to talk about race and to believe everyone has the same opportunities to succeed in America. I believe white people see people of color as antagonistic and delusional when we talk about race and racism.

MICHAEL LESLIE

I think they are cunning, self-centered, greedy, selfish, backstabbing, racist, hypocritical and murderous. There are some exceptions to the rule, but that only proves the rule.

INDIGO VIOLET

Honestly, I think whites are at a disadvantage culturally, spiritually, and psychologically, since so much of their identity in the U.S. has been built on the idea that they are better and somehow more deserving than people of color, rather than positioned as equal with the rest of the world based on the virtues of some of their cultural outlooks, their interconnections with non-whites, and the human spirit that all people reflect. At this stage in my life, I often feel sorry for the overwhelming ignorance of many whites, while simultaneously resenting their power, ignorance, and control of so many institutions.

ERIC LACKIE

I think white folks are often unaware and insensitive to the value systems and rules of respect that exist within the cultures of people of color. The establishment of slavery and racism gave whites an ability to thrive and succeed with hardly any need to adapt to other cultures. Today's white ignorance about the cultures of people of color comes from generations of not having to care. Here are a couple of examples of hurtful and insensitive comments I have received about people of color from "decent" and "upstanding" white people.

CHURCH EXPERIENCE

An elderly male fellow church member told me, "My wife and I recently visited a black church. The congregation was nice but we didn't really care for their music." His comment frustrated me in two ways. First, churches whose members are predominantly people of color are typically identified by a cultural prefix, like "black church," "Chinese church," or "Mexican church." However, churches with predominately white members are not referred to as "white church" but rather "church" because white is considered normal. While subtle, our language can reveal a lot about white attitudes of superiority in this society. Second, in stating his displeasure at "their music," I wondered if he realized that he was making a criticism of black music while speaking to a black person. I presented my concerns to my fellow church member and he apologized, although I'm not sure how much he really understood. Another white male church member who overheard our exchange approached me afterwards and thanked me for speaking up. Did he feel the same discomfort I did about my elderly member's comments? If so, why didn't he speak up himself? At this point I was too emotionally exhausted to ask.

MY GRADUATE SCHOOL EXPERIENCE

In graduate school I attended a weekend training on a specific model of family therapy that was held in the home of a local family therapist. I arrived with four female Taiwanese peers/friends from my cohort. For lunch the group of participants agreed to order Chinese takeout. I overheard the host's wife mention to three other white women, "I love Chinese takeout but let's just hope they didn't cook dog." She and the other women laughed. I thought the comment was distasteful and culturally offensive, yet I heard no one express disapproval. Also, my Taiwanese peers had just stepped outside to get snacks and drinks when the hostess made her comment. I remember thinking to myself, "If you can make this kind of insensitive comment in the absence of my fellow Taiwanese students, I wonder what you'd say about African Americans behind my back."

I decided to confront the hostess, yet felt afraid that she might take offense and kick me out of her house. I asked her to step aside for a moment and nervously expressed my concern. I remember feeling rushed and not articulating my thoughts as clearly as I wanted. For some reason I don't remember exactly how she responded. I think she heard me but may have felt embarrassed and wasn't sure what to do or say. I wish that another white person would have taken the initiative to confront her. It would have shown me that someone else cares.

SHAWN PATRICK

I don't believe all white folks are evil, or openly desiring white supremacy, or hating people of color. I think that most typical white Americans would desire an equal society. I don't think most typical Americans recognize how systems of racism and oppression hurt them as much as they hurt non-dominant groups. Because of the history of pitting groups against each other, I think whites have been fed the same lies about how non-dominant groups will take rights away from white folks, or steal jobs, or other such nonsense typically used to breed xenophobia and promote the status quo. So I think many who are white are afraid and uncertain, and want to provide a decent life for their kids, but have also inadvertently bought into the same oppressive system that hurts non-dominant groups. I believe whites in America are lost and have little idea about what it means to be white. I believe that when white folk in America can realize these lies and myths for what they are, they will want to cast them off and recognize how the embracing of diversity will only strengthen everyone rather than diminish.

What would you say to whites if you could tell them the truth about racism?

CAROL WALSH

Stop feeling sorry for yourself and your white guilt and shame and do something about it! I'm tired of having to walk on eggshells to protect the delicate nature and sensibilities of whites. They will allow people of color to crawl over broken shards of glass to prove the existence of racism, but will not subject themselves to "feeling sad" or to sit in the pain to accept the existence of racism. Your denial and indifference is killing me; slowly and surely I die a little each day when I'm stared at because they haven't seen someone black before or in their circle. I die a little each day when I'm followed in the store and asked repetitively, "Can I help you?" I die a little each day when you feel comfortable telling me a black joke or make derogatory comments about blacks because, "I'm different and not like 'other' blacks." Stop feeling sorry for yourself and complaining about the discomfort you are experiencing from me as I adjust to get your foot off my neck.

CAROLYN BERNARD

I would tell them that sometimes just being around them is painful in ways that have no words. I would tell them that there are layers of meaning in the world around them that they do not see or experience because they are white. I would tell them that the world caters to them in ways they don't see, that there are hurtful nuances that they do not hear. I would tell them that their skin color is a sort of armor that the rest of us do not have.

C. Spencer

Racism is fear-based illusion that whites utilize to further separate themselves from any other human that doesn't look, feel, or act like them.

Many whites will contend that they've had to work hard for what they've achieved in life. I would submit that people of color have had to work twice as hard to get to the same level. So, I think white people need to closely look at how they got there. If you are expected to go to college based on your family history, then do you really have to work that hard? Did George W. Bush work really hard or earn his way into Yale? Methinks not.

Dennard Clendenin

Several years ago, I went to a California Highway Patrol graduation ceremony. The top graduate was a white male, whose father was a CHP officer, and his grandfather was a retired CHP officer. Did that officer work hard? He probably did. But, one must ask themselves, "How do people of color and women build up those legacies that ease their transitions into opportunities?" The three generations of white CHP officers resulted from some kind of Affirmative Action. Did it not? Could we refer to this phenomenon as "Legacy Action?" The question becomes: How do people of color build up those legacies?

Wayne Downey

I would tell whites that black and Latino youth are not born with guns, knives, and bombs. The killing of black and Latino youth has become a blood sport for the six o'clock news. When you return to your gated communities, are you locking yourself in or are you locking "them" out? Black and Latino children are dying and being murdered because of the luxury you perceive you have to not become involved. The first racial epitaph that your children will learn will often be heard in your home. The first race-based hostility your child will learn will come from your home.

David Lee

Stop giving so much credit to themselves.

Denise Hampden

There is a long list of things that I would say; unfortunately many of the things I do say fall on deaf ears and whites become defensive about their roles in eliminating the problem. In less formal settings I don't have any patience for racism. I am very blunt, frank and sometimes ugly. In my workplace I challenge it head-on every single time. Within my union I use what means I have available to also challenge it. I am fortunate that I can surround myself with people to whom I don't have to explain everything all the time. They know the truth.

In a classroom setting, however, my role is to plant seeds that grow into a strong anti-racism sentiment. Telling the truth means saying how racism affects us in real ways. Not simply saying, "That hurts," but explaining the ways it hurts. The sleeplessness, the anger, the frustration, the sickness, the bitterness. The fact that racism or sexism or homophobia for that matter is about things we cannot change about ourselves is even more frustrating.
I would explain to them that in many cases overt racism leads people of color to wish they were white. Even if it is only for a fleeting second.

Helen Ye

It hurts. It hurts you, it hurts me. It is a man-made barrier that creates division and tension, rather than connectedness, intimacy, humanity and peace. It's hard for me to even write this because anger, hurt, frustration, and impatience come up. I see so much injustice and disregard for people of color, I cannot help but feel the whites are just truly blind to what is going on.

Indigo Violet

I am so done, in my personal life, with telling white folks the truth about racism. I mostly say nowadays, "Do your work with other white people, figure out this stuff about whiteness, find some anti-racist therapy, deal with your own emotional liberation so that you are actually equipped to do this work, and maybe I'll see you again sometime in the future."

If I believed white folks would get it, would really understand the emotional/psychic implications of the statement, I would say, "Hey, we are hurt, we are devastated, we have been robbed and violated by this history and ever since you/we got here, we have been busy trying to put ourselves back together, to make ourselves anew while dodging the persistent blows."

While there was a time in my life where my personal, emotional, and political work was tied up with white people that I believed to be progressive or even radical, now I am untying all of that. I would rather put my energy into healing paths and knowledge for my own people and put a priority on the struggle for understanding and solidarity between people of color.

SONYA LITTLEDEER-EVANS

I would tell whites that racism is not just about putting some at an unearned disadvantage—but about putting others (whites) at an unearned advantage. And that this unearned advantage is a form of oppression that silently kills the hopes, dreams and futures of our children. I would tell them my story of how, as a little girl, I didn't know words like racism, unearned disadvantage or prejudice—but I did know that what I wanted to be when I grew up was "white." Even as a child I could see the advantage of being white and how it could get me further, get me more. Innocent and at the same time naïve, I thought "white" was something I could earn or be given. Once I realized that my color was something I had no control over, and that it would never change, I fully grasped what my experiences of being treated and looked at differently than my white friends were all about: racism in its most subtle and disguised form. Although it wasn't said out loud, it was every day implied that because I was brown and looked different than all the other children—I was less. And even when I worked harder in school and out-performed my white classmates, it didn't matter. I was still not trusted, still called "dirty Indian" and still treated as less. This is the truth about racism that I would tell whites.

GENNY LIM

I'd tell them that racism hurts everyone. Whether you're on the receiving end of racism's benefit or abuses, the tension between the two poles is explosive and violent when the situation bursts. It's inevitable because discontent simmers like a pot of boiling oil. When it spills over, containment is always a problem. Inner cities are pots of boiling oil; the violence and crime can't be confined only to that area. If the sources of social injustice rooted in race and class aren't addressed sooner or later, the chickens come home to roost every time. Look at Watts. Look at Oakland and Richmond. Gated communities and upscale neighborhoods have not been immune to widespread crime. In fact, many middle class white kids exhibit the same dysfunctional behaviors with drugs and violence that used to characterize their poorer ethnic-minority counterparts. We live in an interdependent society and isolation is no longer a viable escape from the growing tensions of race in America.

The proliferation of guns is a manifestation of growing fear in a fortress mentality that can only resolve social conflicts with aggression and violence. This attitude only escalates the problem and ups the ante so that the ultimate consequences become that much more violent and explosive. Our cities are war zones and even the suburbs have become repositories of antisocial, criminal activities.

The extremism, fundamentalism and nationalism of the extreme right are a direct response to protecting white racism at all cost. White supremacy, however, can't thrive if everyone on all sides unifies and cooperates to transform and neutralize the effects of racism. To white liberals, I would say this requires a full engagement with the contradictions that privileges raise, both within us and outside. Approaching racism as an external problem always evades the issue. In the end, you will be part of the problem rather than the solution.

Razia Kosi

If I could say my heartfelt and emotional truth about racism to a white person, I would say, "Wake up! What kind of world do you want for yourself and your children? Do you want your children to continue to live in guilt, anger and fear? What will it take for you to sit in the pain of racism and not become defensive or try to minimize the experience of racism as people of color try to share their stories with you? I want you to know I don't want racism to continue and I and those who have similar skin tones can't do it by ourselves. We need you to be a part of this journey to ensure each person is treated with human dignity, with the same opportunities and hope for the future. We need to work together to end racism!"

CHAPTER TWO

A QUESTION OF SAFETY

FITTING IN

How have you learned to "play the game" to appease white folks?

BILL HOWE

I play the game every time...I walk into a room full of white people and I sense they are uncomfortable with a person of color in the room ... and then I take a deep breath, put on a big smile and "work the room" so they become comfortable again. I ease them of their anxiety.

I play the game every time...someone tells me how well-behaved, polite and smart Asian kids are (implication—not like those other colored kids)...and I thank them politely.

I play the game every time...I hear someone say, "You speak English really well and you were born here, so you are not really Chinese," thinking that is a compliment. And I have to tell them I am okay with being Chinese, but thank you anyway.

I play the game every time...one of the bosses calls me Jack (the name of the other Asian guy) and asks me how my wife Nancy is (the name of his wife) and I tell him she's fine and our son Peter is doing well too. (My son's name is Christopher).

I play the game every time...new people I meet ask me if I know the people who own the Chinese restaurant in Fargo, ND, and I tell them "no" politely.

I play the game every time...people act surprised when they find out that an Asian, like me, loves Elvis, Meatloaf and Joe Cocker and I don't smack them upside the head.

I play the game every time...

WAYNE DOWNEY

Watching other people being taken out for not playing the game, I have learned to play the game because I desire to sleep indoors and drive an automobile that is mechanically sound. I prefer to have running water and electricity. I prefer to have access to healthy food and medical attention. Having had the experience of being homeless and only being to afford 40-cent loaves of bread is a reminder that learning the game or keeping your game-playing skills up to par is a requirement.

DENNARD CLENDENIN

Having been exposed to the whims of white people for 60 years, for my own survival and sanity I've learned to appease them. This was more critical in my younger years. Now that I am of an advanced age, I no longer wish to accommodate or appease white people.

I remember making a conscious effort to make white people feel comfortable. If I found myself walking behind a white woman on a dark street or in an underground garage, I would instinctively rattle my keys or whistle loudly to alert her that I was in the area. Why was I doing that? It was annoying that I had to make her feel comfortable. That wasn't my responsibility.

I also learned to maintain my silence, especially when I was the only person of color among the group. If racism was an issue in a seemingly non-racial conversation, I would not bring up the possibility that race was a factor. I would argue that my ability to "appease" white people has cost me my self-esteem.

SONYA LITTLEDEER-EVANS

I have learned to "play the game" to appease white people in many different ways: sharing my individuality (education, occupation) first before sharing who I am in the context of my ethnicity, remaining quiet until I know it's "safe" to speak about topics regarding race, having to demonstrate that I'm intelligent and able to speak English without an accent before whites give me credibility, not bringing up race/racism unless asked and then knowing how "deep" to go and when to stop, and, even though I notice, I never share or point out when I'm the only person of color in a meeting, on a board, or at a gathering.

GENNY LIM

There is a way to ignore racism without denying it. To survive institutional racism, for example, you have to play the game by the rules without being self-righteous or belligerent about your perceived rights. You have to pick your battles and strategies to resist or counter racism. If you know it is a no-win cause, it is best to wait for the right opportunity or moment to make your case or act. People of color often take the path of least resistance or act passive-aggressively, because they know directness isn't an option. This breeds internalized racism, so playing the game too well can be a double-edged sword. We've seen how people get ahead in the system by acting white to the point where they've lost a sense of who they are. There is a point at which you have to stop playing and stand firm on your ground. Where the line lies is different for every individual. Once you stop acknowledging the limits of your endurance to withstand racism, you've been, as they say in the jargon, "sold out." You've become blind to racism like the frog in the well who doesn't believe in daylight.

MICHAEL LESLIE

I keep quiet about race and discrimination at work unless I am forced not to. I also try to appear as contented as possible. I keep a low profile and just do my work and go home. I stay away from whites as much as I can.

RAZIA KOSI

The website "Things White People Like" is a humorous and sad example of how many things I have internalized, so that at this point I'm not even sure if I really like the things that white people like. When did this happen? Was it the first time I picked up a fork at dinner and chose to eat my Indian food with my parents with a fork and knife instead of with my hands as I was taught to do? Was it when I asked my mom for silver "American" jewelry so the kids in elementary school would stop making fun of my "gaudy" Indian gold jewelry? Was it when a boy on the school bus questioned all the students who looked Iranian? The boy would literally say whether he thought we were "okay" or "not-okay" based on our answer, by saying, "Yeah, you're not I-raynian, you're okay," and the kids on the bus would cheer. I realize now, that I learned at an early age how to "play the game."

DENISE HAMPDEN

I always remember three things:
1. Nod and smile while really listening.
2. Decide if it is a battlefield upon which I am prepared to die.
3. Remember that they have been a part of a dominant culture for a very long time and it might take some time to un-learn that dominance.

CHANCE WHITE EYES

When it comes to the American workplace in general (with a few exceptions), I believe that the culture is inherently capitalistic, which can be quite contradictory to many American Indian traditions. (Teamwork as opposed to the cut-throat "me first, I am the best and I will take what is mine" mentality.) There is also a level of assumed respect for people you do not know, as opposed to everyone earning their own respect among their co-workers and superiors. My current position means that I must appease both my superiors (who may or may not be white, but must follow the same guidelines) and still maintain a strong sense of cultural identity.

That being the case, I am not out to "appease the white folks," I am out to try to help my people (specifically young American Indian students), while maintaining a "professional" (white?) appearance. This in and of itself is a very difficult thing. There are elders in Indian country that still remember boarding schools. Those elders more than likely remember their elders as well, who lived through an even more horrific form of ethnic cleansing with westward expansion. These elders heavily influence the decisions of the American Indian youth (as well they should). How does one convince American Indians that higher education is important, given the white American history of education and ethnic cleansing?

Currently, I am beginning to notice there is a big difference between being Indian and simply claiming it because of family history. Being Indian involves a great level of traditional retention, as well as cultural knowledge. American Indians from reservations can see this a little more clearly, and when an outsider claiming to be Indian comes and tells them the "benefits" of higher education, I think there is a population of American Indians that immediately question their sincerity. This is also something I struggle with personally. Am I in fact taking part in ethnic cleansing by taking children from Reservations and placing them in institutions that will shape them to be more "white"?

J.C. EAGLESMITH

The old saying Don't Burn Your Bridges! has been institutionalized to the point that many folks won't speak justly before atrocities. We would be well served to adopt Burn All Bridges to Infested Islands!

IJEOMA NWAOGU

I straighten my hair and put extensions in it to reach the length and volume of white people's hair, I stay away from the sun to prevent my skin from getting darker, I wear clothing from stores white people shop at, I make my face expressions "soft" to avoid squirming my nose and looking angry, I use lotions from Bath and Body works to smell like white females and refrain from using lotions many black Americans may use, such as cocoa butter, as this may leave a specific scent. I abstain from using certain hair products that have a certain scent so that my hair won't leave the smell of oils or fragrances found in black hair products, I articulate my words and expressions in a way that mimics white folks, I am hesitant to cook certain ethnic foods because I am afraid that the aroma will annoy my white neighbors. Sometimes, I refrain from using slang around white people.

CAROL WALSH

I have a dear colleague who recently cut off his locks so as to appear less "scary" and "militant" in order to gain employment as an educator. An educator! Educational institutions supposedly provide the platform to help students move beyond the limitations of their mind, or so I thought. I appease white folks by remaining silent on issues of race and racism when they arise. I also tend to use humor and make jokes about things to not appear angry or aggressive so that I'm not intimidating.

I also downplay my educational achievements (I have a Doctorate in Jurisprudence, a Doctorate in Philosophy, two Master's degrees, and have done post-graduate work at Harvard University and the University of North Carolina–Chapel Hill) so they don't feel threatened or intimidated. I have learned when whites are intimidated they will try to destroy you in the most passive and seductive ways. My parents understood the significance of "playing the game" and so they provided and afforded me a traditional education as well as an education in racism, or, more appropriately, how to be as "white" as possible. Our music, our readings, our travels, our living environment, and our entertainment were all for the purpose of teaching us the "tools of the master's house." However, as Audre Lorde noted, "The master's tools will never dismantle the master's house." These tools only served to reify internalized racism. This is why playing the game to appease white folks can be deadly. If we are not careful, we will internalize these patriarchal oppressive practices and indeed become lost in translation.

Carolyn Bernard

We are raised from infancy to fit in, to assimilate, and above all, to not complain too loudly. I have excused the ignorance of white people and I have put their feelings above my own, even when they are the ones who have insulted me. We are taught to play the game by teachers, by parents, by the media—we are taught to be quiet and polite and to be happy with whatever bones we are thrown. We're taught not to make a fuss. I'm beginning to think that I have always played the game and am just learning now NOT to.

Helen Ye

Not being combative, angry, keeping quiet, not speaking up for yourself or others, not tooting your own horn and accomplishments are different ways I have learned to "play the game."

But I no longer am the passive, quiet Chinese girl. I speak on the behalf of others who are in the process of finding their voices, or are uncomfortable bringing sensitive concerns forward. I've found my voice, grown a strong backbone and speak up in ways that allow for dialogue, respect and feelings, and observations and personal experiences.

What does assimilation mean to you? Why?

Carol Walsh

Assimilation means don't be you. It means don't be the "you" that makes me uncomfortable, confused, scared, bewildered, or forced to tolerate you or to deal with you. It means don't wear locks, don't be passionate, don't get angry, don't defend or speak out against injustices, and, for a black woman, it also means don't be smarter than me, more successful than me, more talented than me, more financially stable than me, date, love, marry someone like me, or, God forbid, be better looking than me! It means deny yourself, your spirit, your uniqueness, your individuality, your wonderfulness. It means deny your race or ethnicity and any relationship to it. Although we won't fully accept you into our race, you must reject your own in order to even be tolerated by ours. It ultimately means to die spiritually, emotionally, and, eventually, physically. Assimilation means don't be you.

GIA OVERTON

I absolutely detest the idea of assimilation. Assimilation means giving up who you are and where you came from in order to be like everyone else. This is death! I believe in acculturation, not assimilation. If you acculturate, you expand who you are by adding on pieces of your new culture. You don't subtract parts of yourself in order to survive.

PATRICIA CORTEZ

Assimilation is the assassination of who I am, is the stripping of my spirit, traditions, customs, language, world views. It represents the selling of my soul for a cheap price. It is not feeling welcomed, valued, appreciated. It is to leave behind all that I love, all that is important to me, to my family, to my childhood. It is nothing once I show my face and the beautiful color of my skin. It is speaking English with no accent and accepting a life full of material garbage and a heart full of emptiness. It is to hide under a pile of false pride and endless nonsense. It is what divides me from those who look like me, but think like them.

Assimilation is the pervasive instrument used in this country to build up stairs to heaven, so those who assimilate can easily step on others without regard. It is the melting pot which some preach about and are so proud of without stopping to think what that way of thinking really means. Why assimilation? I don't know; my mind can't find the proper answer, but my body experiences it as the tool for oppression, as the obsession for the confused, the weak, the fake to adopt supremacist views and the doctrine to prepare those who assimilate to join the malignant power to forget who they really are.

TRAVIS SMITH

I'm saddened when I see my people celebrating Halloween, Christmas, Thanksgiving, or wearing green on St. Patrick's Day, chanting in Latin during Mass, and looking down on their own people who do otherwise as pagans. When my own people are saying, "That's bad English," or are speaking Spanish and French with such pride, begrudging African music and dance while straining their toes in ballet, and upholding the notion that going to see European symphonies is a "sophisticated" thing to do, I'm deeply saddened!

I know many of us feel "American" and that "those are American traditions and thus ours too". The sad truth is that these are European traditions that we've grown to accept and share with our children as though they were our own. The reason is that we've completely been stripped of our own traditions!

When an educator of African descent is an expert on Freud but is ignorant of Franz Fanon; has read and recalls the words of John Dewey but nothing of W.E.B. Du Bois, Paul Robeson or Marcus Garvey; when I see a black educator preferring to teach Chaucer and knowing nothing of Chinweizu; or who loves the works of Hemingway but has never read a word of Zora Neale Hurston, I'm saddened! Assimilation means the death of my personhood and the covering of the footprints laid by my ancestors to guide me into and through the future! Without them I am lost and at a loss for words to contextualize the world in my own unique way.

According to the modern notion of "brilliance," or excellence, you can have 1200 on the SAT, 18 on the ACT, and know absolutely nothing of African, Asian, or Indigenous literature. We would applaud such a person. You can earn a Ph.D. from an Ivy League university and be completely ignorant of the fact that people of color have contributed tremendously to the development of human thought and actually contextualize the world in a different light. It is this type of ignorance that fosters white supremacy and black/brown/yellow inferiority.

Jean Moule

Ugh, what a loss to have everyone be "white like me."

Francine Shakir

Assimilation means always questioning myself about whether or not I've "got it right." Am I using a vocabulary that demonstrates a "suitable education"? Are my mannerisms on target? I'm really not so different, see? I'm drivin' the cool hybrid car—I'm not like those other blacks. So, let me in your club, won't you? Look at how I'm working to lose myself! Certainly I'm worthy now. Don't you think?

And in the process, I have to psych myself up to feel comfortable in your presence. But I'm really not—comfortable, that is. Where are the others who think like me, feel like me, love like me? I look around for something in the room that says "safety" because I know that centuries of hatred are hard to wash away—like a bleach stain on a dark shirt.

Assimilation has caused my people to hate the color of their skin, their hair, their lack of "good" English. They choose to turn their backs on the rest of us—too black, too ghetto, too poor. It means I have to hate myself and love something that doesn't fit—like size 8 feet in size 6 shoes. Can't wait to take these tight things off—so I can breathe...so I can be free to be authentically Me.

DENNARD CLENDENIN

Assimilation is a loss of the essence of who you are. The irony here is that, as white people continue to preach assimilation, no matter how hard people of color try, they will never be viewed as "everyone else." Assimilation has been thrust on every immigrant group that has arrived on the shores of America. Assimilation was also the doctrine for Native Americans, and look how that worked out for them. I am not a proponent of assimilation and will resist with every fiber of my being.

WAYNE DOWNEY

Assimilation means that you give away unique qualities about yourself because they are perceived as threats by people who have more than you do. Assimilation means that you do not act in your own best interest so that others will feel comfortable being around you. Assimilation means that you cry yourself to sleep at night because people cannot accept the uniqueness about yourself that you cannot change.

JESSIE EWING

Assimilation to me means to hide. But it's a matter of survival and creating opportunities for success. In this country you're not supposed to bring up race. When you want to be taken seriously you don't use Ebonics. You try to lose your accent. The problem is that people of color will never be what's wanted; we can't make ourselves white, therefore we're tainted. So since you have that "fault" you have to try and lose/hide everything else you can. I call it hiding because I like to believe that one day people can come out and not have to conform to find success and live a long life.

HELEN YE

Assimilation means that I have to be a certain way to fit into mainstream society. The reason? So, I can succeed—get a good education, win scholarships, make a good impression on the right kind of people, to get the job, make enough money to pay my bills and help my family out.

Assimilation means my hair and clothes need to look a certain way to fit in. I certainly shouldn't wear any topical Chinese herbal ointment if I have some kind of pain, and I need to be sure my teeth are pearly white, and really should consider having my eyes surgically enhanced to make my small eyes more round. And, I should learn how to speak properly so I can be seen as professional and of "good substance, good material"—job-worthy. I really shouldn't fall into my Chin-glish language or mixed family language of English, Ilongo (a Filipino dialect), Cantonese, and a number of other Chinese dialects that no one except my family members can understand.

The richness of my unique background and experiences goes unseen because of the lack of inquiry, interest or personal stories shared in the workplace. If mine are overlooked, I know many other people's unique background and experiences are overlooked too—not considered valuable in a typical American organization.

When I felt Chinese medicine was my calling and quit my full-time job, I got an earful. "That's witchcraft!" "Why are you studying something old? Why not Western medicine?" "Can you earn a living doing that?" "Why are you wasting your time and money?" "What are you doing with your Berkeley education? What a waste!" My whole family, immediate AND extended, again did not support my decision—in fact, belittled it over the next several years.

Even my non-Asian colleagues in the field of Chinese medicine believed that my decision to go into Chinese medicine was easier than theirs because I was Asian and Chinese. When I tell them my story, they are quite surprised to hear the opposite. Yes, being one of the Model Minority doesn't always mean you get to choose to follow your own dream, but the American and Chinese dream that is defined as a well-educated, well-respected, high-achieving, high-earning individual.

GENNY LIM

There is a positive as well as a negative connotation to the word "assimilation." At its positive, it means taking on qualities and attributes of a dominant culture and society in order to better function and get ahead. Every immigrant wants to assimilate as soon as possible for economic reasons, though not every immigrant wants to lose his or her distinct cultural identity, language and culture. The two aren't always compatible or easy to negotiate and some might say that assimilation is a tool for erasing ethnic identity and creating a homogenous population whose values can be easily shaped and manipulated by the governing power structure. I see its definite benefits but I also see its downside in terms of whitewashing Americans into believing that if we're all the same then there will be no more racism. We've all seen many people of color who deny that racism exists even more vehemently than whites do. I don't see any merit ultimately in eliminating cultural diversity or racial pride, so long as it doesn't end in the old identity politics of the 1970's. We need to acknowledge our differences, yet embrace our commonalities, because by only focusing on difference, we forget to connect with our common humanity. So it is a constant interactive process of give and take. I believe assimilation works this way too. I pride myself in being American, but I can also pride myself in being uniquely individual, which happens to be Chinese and Chukchak.

When you have told the truth about racism, what have been some of your experiences? How have those outcomes affected you?

INEZ TORRES

There have been three camps, if you will:

- There have been those who embrace the truths I share, often finding relief simply in hearing their experiences mirrored and their pain understood.

- There have been those unable (purposefully or not, I do not judge) to hear the truths—they decide I am sharing personal experiences and insights that have nothing to do with them and do not inform their own lives in any way.

- And then there is the group that sort of enjoys hearing the facts and figures—totally left-brain.

Over time, I have decided one camp is no worse than another because unless those in the first camp do their own work, they can be as draining as the other two.

WAYNE DOWNEY

I was questioned, cross-examined, asked to provide evidence, accused of having an agenda, accused of being racist towards whites, accused of being bitter, angry, and petty. As a consequence, I became unemployed.

RAZIA KOSI

When I have told the truth about racism to white women, I feel my experience has often been minimized and I am immediately told the situation was similar to something they have faced because of sexism. I then hear their story without an acknowledgement or even silent empathy to sit with me in the pain of the truth I shared. When this has happened, I have felt that my truth to them was not a truth and that they needed to share their truth or invalidate my experience. I have left those situations with quiet anger, a distance between me and the people I have shared with, and a sense of frustration as to whether I can truly open up and trust them. As I think about intent and impact in those situations, I truly do not believe the white women's intent was to minimize my experience; however, the impact on me was that of marginalization. I believe their intent was to actually "bond" with me to create a sense of sisterhood in our experiences. While they may be clearly able to identify experiences of sexism, I cannot as easily make those distinctions, nor do I want to. I am a woman of color. My ethnicity does not stay at the door when I walk in a room, nor does my gender. I am impacted by people's perceptions and stereotypes of both and my experiences reflect both, so minimizing race over gender minimizes my experience.

MONIQUE RIEKE

I have been labeled as "crazy, politically correct, fanatic," and also a "pimple on an elephant's ass," and have felt that this criticism has harmed my professional reputation. I am unable to apply for certain jobs because my views have been published in newspapers and other forms of media in my communities. I have been commenting on race and diversity for several years and sometimes these outspoken moments come up in interviews and many other instances, which serve to belittle my intelligence and professionalism.

GENNY LIM

It has always been a painful experience to speak my truth about racism. I've lost longtime colleagues in some instances and on some occasions deepened friendships. It is especially difficult because people see my feelings as an act of betrayal. They ask why I've never told them before that I've deceived them into thinking otherwise. How can I convey to them that racism is complex? My appearance often belies my sensitivities. I give whites the impression that I'm very sweet, easy-going and cheerful. They misread these qualities sometimes as being somewhat of a "pushover" and oftentimes make the mistake of taking advantage of my good nature. When I react in the negative, it comes off as over-reactive or shocking to them, because their stereotype of me doesn't fit the message. I frankly think they're angrier at their misreading of me than they are at my reaction. That is why they feel so betrayed.

I don't want to change the way I am because I like to be open and friendly. These days I try not to internalize resentment and hurt the way I used to and try to approach the problem at the outset to nip it in the bud. If it doesn't work out—and often it doesn't—I have to understand that it probably wouldn't have worked out in the end anyway and it is better to know this sooner than later. If it does open the door for better understanding and communication, however, then both parties will have benefited. It takes two, however, to come to this awareness. You have to accept that you can't win every battle.

DE ANDRE DRAKE

Whenever I have spoken up about racism I am either the angry black man, or the hypersensitive black man. I am never just a man with a serious issue I am asking to be openly addressed. But, in the long run, that conditioning from those responses now has made my reactions lean towards "the angry black man." It's my way of keeping power in the situation.

SHAWN PATRICK

I have been challenged, laughed at, questioned, told to shut up. Those outcomes make it hard for me to continue talking, and sometimes I quit. I go back home, cry, yell, and then try to find some inner resource to get back up and do it all again.

I've also seen people affected by my experience or the experience of others; I've watched people choose to tackle their strongest prejudice and face their role in oppressing others. I've had people (typically people of color) come up to me and say "thank you" for bringing it out in the open. These outcomes give me hope, and help me recommit to the work of ending racism.

I conduct research in the area of diversity, specifically ways to help increase cultural competence and awareness of privilege for students in the helping professions. I had the experience of presenting some of this work at a conference in Australia. This work has been very dear to me, and it is also work that some of my colleagues find unimportant. When I presented my work, one of the conference leaders commented about how deeply touched she was by what had been done, and also that it had been done by a woman of color who also has to overcome these difficulties. This reaction has honestly been one of the most profound for me, because I didn't realize until I heard this recognition, not just of the work, but of my status as a person of color engaged in this work, just how desperately I needed to know that this work, this sharing of "the truth," mattered. I have had so many invalidating experiences that I think I had become used to it, and it wasn't until this one moment that I felt like the hard work of telling the truth had finally made a difference.

——•— ILLUSION/REALITY —•——

What is the illusion about race relations in the United States?

CAROLYN BERNARD

I think the primary illusion about race relations in the United States is that "things have gotten better." I think the truth is that things have just gotten more subtle, and in some ways that is more dangerous. We fool ourselves into thinking that race relations are somehow improving all by themselves, and that somehow frees us of any obligation to truly improve them.

TRAVIS SMITH

The illusion about race relations in the U.S. is that we've come a long way. I say this is an illusion because for every gain that people of color have made, from politics to astrophysics to popular culture, we still serve the best interest of white folks! And if any of our luminaries voice their true feelings about the road they've traveled and the hoops they've had to jump through, they're labeled as "reverse racist" or "sensitive," even "extreme" and sadly made to feel "wrong." I say, as El Hajj Malik El Shabazz said, "If you stick a knife nine inches into my back and pull it out three inches, that's not progress. Even if you pull it all the way out, that's still not progress. Progress is healing the wound, and America hasn't even begun to pull out the knife." I would only add that the knife has moved three inches since he spoke those words.

GIA OVERTON

This is a very leading question! If one were to believe that there is an illusion about race relations in the U.S. (as I do), the illusion would be that race relations are improving! This is not so. I think we're just getting better at being polite about it. Race relations aren't as ugly right now as the battle between homophobes and those seeking equal rights for homosexuals, but they are bad. In my town, for instance, in 2009 we have four elementary schools that are basically racially segregated. Two have majority white students, two have majority Latino students. How on earth could this have happened and how could it still be happening? And no one wants to talk about it. I have brought it up at least three times in the past six years and no one seems to give a darn about it. Not the whites, not the Latinos. As a biracial person, I wonder sometimes if I am the only one who cares.

RAZIA KOSI

While great strides have been made to increase positive race relations in this country, the undercurrents of distrust, anger and fear have resided side by side with the illusion that race relations in this country are in a post-racial state. The illusion is immediately broken when a situation such as the arrest of Professor Gates, or anger over the myth of "illegal immigrants" accessing health care, become polarizing issues in this nation.

CAMISHA L. JONES

The illusion about race relations in the U.S. is that we've "arrived." Because we see black faces winning athletic games, creating popular music and sitting in the White House, we think we no longer have a problem with racism in this country. We as a country believe we are the land of the free, where anyone who works hard enough can become a success. But that's not what the statistics tell us. The statistics tell us that people of color are drastically poorer, sicker, incarcerated more often for longer periods of time for lesser crimes, falling through the huge gaping cracks of our education system more than white people.

Our media and entertainment paint a picture that reinforces this idea that we've "arrived." It's as if people of color (black folks especially) are still dancing and singing in blackface for whites—as long as we're entertaining them we're deemed successful. What we really are is successful at keeping white people comfortable and helping them to continue to believe they have created a grand country on their own with grand principles that benefit all people. Well, it's not true. While it is no longer politically correct to use derogatory language, create laws that discriminate or act in violence against people of color simply because of the color of their skin, racism is still alive and well. Hate crime is real and rarely discussed. Hate groups exist throughout our great nation along with the more subtle and persistent forms of racism.

HELEN YE

The United States has been traditionally known as the "melting pot" of all cultures and immigrants from around the world—perceived as a positive experience of societal blending of all cultures working alongside each other and raising children alongside families from different backgrounds.

Yet the truth is quite the opposite. Many groups stick within their own communities and only the predominant English-speaking communities from different backgrounds may share the same neighborhoods, but still do not mix and mingle socially. Native Americans of this country are rarely included in this conversation of history.

MICHAEL LESLIE

That things are getting better and that given more time, the animosities and social inequities between the races will disappear. This is the great white fiction and it appears to be increasingly shared by blacks.

DENNARD CLENDENIN

The grand illusion, especially in the wake of President Barack Obama, is that race relations are somehow not an issue. No doubt, race relations are getting better; however, one only needs to listen to the language and tactics that are being used to attack our new president, as well as see the continuing police brutality that is being perpetrated on people of color. White people feel that they are now off the hook, and finally don't have to deal with the "R" word.

Recently, a white mother fled her home with her daughter. She left a cell phone message alleging that two black men had abducted them and they were locked in the trunk of the car. This turned out to be false. I would remind you that several years ago a woman let her vehicle slip into a lake while her young children were strapped in their child seats. She then claimed that two black men had abducted them. Several years earlier in the city of Boston, a white man by the name of Charles Stuart shot and killed his pregnant wife then shot himself and proceeded to make a frantic 911 call claiming that a black man had shot them both. This turned out to be false. However, in the examples I just cited, the public and police were quick to respond to a purported crime of black on white. I would argue that that formula still has value today.

TONI ADAMS

That we don't have a race problem—and that only white people are mass murderers, child molesters and pedophiles, while black people are dopers, Latinos are gang bangers and Asians are still model minorities. BS to all of it. I believe as long as we are stereotyped by our ethnic heritage there will be strained race relations in the U.S.

INEZ TORRES

That they have always been not so bad! This country was slave for centuries more than it has been non-slave. The Indian Wars? Like they never happened. Every generation has had its illusion about race relations in the United States. Before this nation was constituted, Indians and Africans were catching the heat—but we aren't taught about that. The first half of the last century taught how slavery was really one of the best things that could have happened to African Americans—for their labor, these people were sheltered, fed, received medical attention, and they were relatively happy, right?

The sixties had the illusion of erasing our differences with the civil rights and the free love movements. We all sang, "This is the age of Aquarius." In the seventies we had affirmative action. In the eighties we had the illusion of opportunity for all, and the only ones that didn't have anything were those who didn't want to work for anything. Right now we are in the supposed post-racial era simply because Barack Obama was elected president. Now, we are pretending that we all have privilege—sort of the 1980's turned inside out but this time with an African American president to silence any nay-saying.

DAVID LEE

That as long as we treat ourselves equally and don't look at color, we're being fair. The illusion is that one can accurately gauge what equality is to the other.

Are race relations getting worse or better in the U.S.? Why or why not?

DENNARD CLENDENIN

The election of the first black president and the election of the first black mayor of the city of Philadelphia are testaments to America's progress as it relates to race relations. However, I would submit that instead of "genuine" progress, the notion of racial tolerance is greater now than ever. Look at the language used to describe then candidate Barack Obama. His rivals for the nomination used code words like clean, attractive, well spoken, credit to his race, etc.,—all code words for reminding us that he is black. Even the liberal "I got an office in Harlem" Bill Clinton engaged in code language in describing Obama's victories in the south. He dismissed them by equating them to Jessie Jackson's victories. Let's face it; there is no comparison between Jackson and Obama.

Going back to Obama, I see parallels in the careers of Obama and Colin Powell. They are both light-skinned and therefore more acceptable to the white population. While making them acceptable to whites, this lightness causes problems in the black community. Both Rev. Al Sharpton and Jackson claimed that Obama wasn't "black enough" to become president. Colin Powell, growing up poor and black in the Bronx, and getting out of that environment, was taunted with the same charges from the black community.

Their lightness aside, both Obama and Powell are conservative in race matters. Both don't overtly come out and blame racism for the plight of black America. They implore blacks to take advantage of opportunities and take the initiative themselves. This indeed worked for them; however, not every black is afforded the same opportunities. These arguments essentially let white America off the hook. They can sit back and say, "See, even Obama and Powell think you need to pull yourself up by your bootstraps."

I would argue that if someone who looked like Isaac Hayes or Mr. T decided to run for office, he wouldn't stand a chance because he is frightening and dark. I know lots of white folks would rather forget slavery feeling that the institution is behind us, but frankly speaking, these dynamics are a result of slavery and perpetuate the "plantation mentality." That is, house slaves who are acceptable are generally lighter in skin color, and allowed to work in the home with certain privileges, while the darker field slaves are less valued and relegated to hard labor. It's no wonder that Obama resides in the "White" House.

KYE LOCKHART

An optimistic person will say yes, race relations are better because we have a black president. On the other hand, I've never heard "kill him" (Obama) screamed out in a political campaign until recently.

SHAWN PATRICK

In some ways, I think they are improving in that I do see more people, including white people, talking and trying to take a stand against racism. I think there is more of an effort at providing real education about what has happened in this country to non-whites and Indigenous populations. But I also think in many ways it hasn't changed much; I think people have become savvier about sounding as though they accept others when in reality they hold just as many stereotypes and biases as before. I also believe we are not so far removed from things like Jim Crow to think we would be free of that influence.

INDIGO VIOLET

Some of the daily assaults have improved, largely for middle class people of color who have various passing abilities and cultural capital. But the psychological landscape of race relations is getting worse because the original problems were never addressed; there has been no move towards a national dialogue or healing. So, new pathologies are emerging.

Yet, there's always the usual stuff: racial profiling and police targeting, everyday stereotypes and bad energy in public and on the street, and the profound, institutional quagmire that keeps so many people of color in poverty. Race relations are really not much better if you look at structural and economic realities.

TONI ADAMS

While racial mixing has eased some race relations in certain parts of the country, there is still a divide in the U.S. along geographical lines. In Atlanta, for instance, I once told my friend who was the Chief of Staff to the Mayor that I was "too black" to work there. Southern communities like Atlanta and New Orleans are still defined by how much white blood (and color) can be found in a black person. The kind of job you are able to secure, how you are treated when you walk down the street, where you live and much more is still defined by color.

GENNY LIM

There is hope, but there is also an insidious undercurrent of racism, which we've seen evidence of in recent tragic mass murder rampages. One horrific case of reverse racism at Virginia Tech was perpetuated by a Korean American loner, who found his own perverted brand of justice and revenge in the mass slayings of innocent students and faculty. These incidents are not isolated. They are obvious clues about the state of crisis the country is facing in regards to the polarization and hatred fanned by extremist groups and right-wing media, who radicalize social problems as a direct consequence of immigration and illegal aliens. Fear of displacement, joblessness and integration loom in the last bastions of racist America. The equal rights espoused in the Constitution were never intended for all peoples, only for whites.

INEZ TORRES

Look at the incarceration rates of college-age Latino and African American males; that ratio did not exist in the middle of the last century. The proof is in the pudding.

CAROLYN BERNARD

Worse or better than what? Than the days of slavery and the Chinese Exclusion Act? Yes, in a sense, things are getting better. But we still have justices refusing to marry interracial couples. We still have colorface on *America's Next Top Model*. We still see white kids cast in the leads of *DragonBall Z* and *The Last Airbender* in Hollywood. We still see too many white faces on TV while people of color rot in stereotyped roles. Racial humor is still accepted as great comedy. Things are not better ENOUGH.

RAZIA KOSI

I truly believe race relations are getting better in the U.S. and I also believe we still have a long road ahead to form meaningful relationships with each other beyond our external features and internal beliefs. I believe there is still a long road ahead because each of us has to come to terms with our own biases and assumptions about people. Unearthing those biases and wanting to truly form a relationship with someone who has either hurt me or people who look like me takes a great deal of belief in humanity. Some people argue the nature of humanity is inherently the "survival of the fittest," and those who have been oppressed become oppressors once they are in a position of power.

I believe in order to for us to move beyond ourselves we need to have a higher belief in the good of humanity and take ownership of our actions and inactions. As a person of color I am benefiting from both people of color and whites before me who have given their lives for equity. I need to work harder to improve relations among people in the U.S. and also around the world because the work is not done. I believe race relations are getting better because I am able to live a comfortable life and surround myself with those who value positive relationship between the races. Unless I am working towards ensuring that everywhere in the world each person is valued in the same way, the work is not done.

Can you ever envision a world without racism? Why or why not?

DENISE HAMPDEN

I cannot. To do so would mean I have to envision a world where keeping people oppressed is not valuable to others. I would have to envision a world where war wasn't profitable. I would have to envision a world where capitalism was not deeply intertwined with racism. I would have to envision a world where the word "socialism" was not a dirty word and socialist ideas were not viewed as fringe or lunatic ones.

INEZ TORRES

My ability to envision a world without racism is part of my own stubbornness to live. I refuse to surrender to the low energy of inevitability that vibrates beneath the surface of this question. I will continue to sow the seeds of peace and healing that I believe can feed the energy of a vision of healing and wholeness. I will continue to open myself to the possibilities of living racially reconciled. Not believing it is possible hurts just too damned much.

TONI ADAMS

We will always find something to divide us—whether by nations, hair color, body size, etc., and I think there will always be a religious divide that may or may not be racially motivated.

JEAN MOULE

Sometimes I try, sometimes I cry.

DENNARD CLENDENIN

I do not see a world sans racism. Being who we are defines and shapes us. There will always be mistrust and greed in us as human beings. This mistrust and greed manifests itself in the taking advantage of others. The poor economy increases the continuation of racism. As capitalism continues to take advantage of the world economy, the divide between the haves and have-nots will increase. Why should anyone believe that racism will somehow disappear from the world?

WAYNE DOWNEY

A world without racism is an experience that has not occurred before. I suppose that if they can invent flying cars, they could figure out how to create a social system in which racial discrimination is not a part.

GENNY LIM

We have to envision a better world before we can manifest it. Racism is an ugly disease and I can't see any parent in their right mind who would want their children exposed to it. It is an unenlightened way to function in the world. We must get beyond our baser instincts and evolve our thinking and actions around this barbaric mindset for all our sakes.

KYE LOCKHART

I can absolutely envision a world without racism. That's what makes the human mind so great. We come up with cures for diseases, we can build spaceships, we can teach children right from wrong. So, YES, WE CAN and should envision a world without racism and work toward that. After all, racism didn't always exist.

DE ANDRE DRAKE

No, I can't. There's always evil and hate in society and these hatemongers will always find something that makes us different in order to keep us separated.

HELEN YE

I do envision a world without racism, but not in my lifetime. Each of us from all ethnic backgrounds, representing all colors, must be able to speak our truths, share our stories, become connected with each other in more intimate life experiences in order for racism to be etched away into history. So little of this happens today without intention that I cannot envision a world without racism for many generations.

Perhaps in the future, when our children are so mixed across all cultures, ethnicities and colors that all of us will no longer be boxed into one racial or ethnic category. When all of us may be seen as unique individuals rather than a group fitting certain stereotypes.

Razia Kosi

I must envision a world without racism because I am a part of shaping the world for my children and my children's children. In the world that I envision, my children's background of having a South Asian mother and white father will not be viewed as "exotic" or unusual because their parents do not share the same external features. In this world the strengths of my daughters will be valued equally with those of my friends' sons and the shading of their skin tone will not play a part in deciding whether they deserve a particular job. In this world, my daughters will also engage with and value people who look different from them and learn to value traditions and cultures that are not the same as the one they have experienced. I have a clear vision of a world without racism and I have a belief that the inhabitants in this world will create this world.

What can't you say about racism? Why or why not?

Inez Torres

In all my writing and in all my training experience, I still do not have the words to say what racism has cost me.

Camisha L. Jones

Each time I talk about racism, I must package my message in words, tone and body language that will not scare the white folks. I have to be mindful to balance how boldly I speak about racism (or any "ism" for that matter) and make sure the white folks still feel secure having me at the table when decisions are being made. I wish I could just say what's on my mind without being afraid that I'll lose my job, or be labeled, silenced and shut out of opportunities I need to sustain my life. When we're brainstorming speakers and committee members, I wish I could just say, "Could we add some people of color to the list?" When we're hiring people, I wish I could say, "Were there really no qualified people of color to consider for this job?" I wish I could talk openly about the ways I have felt dehumanized. But if I did, I'd be deemed the enemy and a troublemaker.

CAROLYN BERNARD

I can't say almost anything about racism to a white person who is not already involved in anti-racism. Your average white person has no idea how to think about racism, and they certainly don't know how to talk about it. To use academic terms, I can talk about racism at a 101-level, and I can listen to other people talk about racism at a graduate level, but most white people only understand racism at an elementary level, and that makes it almost impossible to discuss. I feel like white people need a basic primer before they can even understand what anti-racists are saying.

Do you ever say what you are thinking to a white person? Why or why not?

SONYA LITTLEDEER-EVANS

Sometimes I do and sometimes I don't. I will say what I am thinking to a white person if I feel it is safe. By "safe" I mean for both me and the other person, that the setting is appropriate, that the environment is such that I am not jeopardizing my or their job or status. To feel safe, I need to know that saying what I am thinking is not just for my gain, but will benefit the other person as well. Now, I can't always know if someone is ready or not to hear my truth, but I can try to gauge if they are seeking truth or not. Sometimes I will say what I'm thinking, but put it in a more "white-friendly" manner. This might mean toning down the emotion I feel about something, or articulating appropriately for my intended audience. These are ways I might say what I'm thinking but doing so in a way that brings some safety for me. To be safe for the other person, the white person, I might notice who else is present; if there are other whites, I might not take such opportunity to say what I'm thinking because I don't want anyone to lose face—especially with other whites. I would take into account their role in discussing whatever subject I am having thoughts of. If it is something they sought out, despite who else is around—I might speak up.

But then, other times, I don't think about any of the above and will say what I'm thinking regardless of the setting. This is usually when I feel very strongly or emotionally about the subject and I feel that to not say anything would be oppression of myself. So I will speak up regardless of the consequences—and at the same time, be ready to accept the consequences.

MARY WEEMS

Absolutely. As a social foundations professor I teach courses which always deal with America's real history as it pertains to race, and other social "isms." I consider it my responsibility to share my thoughts with my students, colleagues, and others in this setting as part of my commitment to work against racism and toward an inclusive, just, democratic society. In my personal life, which is inextricably linked to my professional life, I speak my mind because after years of not doing this, I realized that the person I was hurting the most—was me. Holding in feelings is damaging to the mind, body, and spirit and I can't encourage my students to speak their minds if I'm not modeling this behavior.

SHAWN PATRICK

I certainly have, but not always when it comes to issues of race. If I find myself talking to someone who clearly displays a lack of interest in hearing my point of view, then I am less likely to offer all of my thoughts. I don't think this totally justifies my silence, though, as I believe silence in the end will only perpetuate racism. So I am working on more ways to introduce at least pieces of my thoughts, even with someone who seems uninterested.

Other times I have kept silent when I fear that my thoughts could lead to some form of harm to myself. Because of my appearance (light-skinned), I often run into a person who is white who presumes I am white and will share very negative thoughts about someone who is not white. Or this person discloses the acts of aggression he or she has taken against someone who is non-white. In these instances, I will not share my thoughts because of the potential retaliation.

ERIC LACKIE

As a person of color, it can be risky to express my honest thoughts to white people and also damaging to hold these feelings inside. If I open up, I risk being invalidated, ignored or criticized, which can cause me to feel even more hurt. When I don't speak up, it can build into resentment with no proper channel for resolution. I personally prefer to be vulnerable and honest in healing conversations about race with white people. However, these conversations quickly bring up strong emotions that white people are often unprepared to handle effectively. Therefore, while I do speak my truths to white people, I am also gathering the courage to do it more. Here is one example:

Recently, a person of color from the community presented several concerns about culturally hurtful comments and behaviors made by employees within my place of employment. A meeting was scheduled for members of the communities of color to present their concerns to leaders of my agency. Although the complaints were not against me personally, I am one of the leaders, and I chose to attend the meeting to help build a bridge between whites in my agency and people of color in the community. I attended a pre-meeting with administrators of my organization to prepare for hearing the identified concerns in a constructive manner. Towards the end of this pre-meeting, a white female coworker asked the group if it would be okay to bring some Christmas cookies to the meeting. I shared my opposition to bringing Christmas cookies and articulated two reasons, "First, Christmas holiday has religious and cultural connotations that are offensive to some groups and individuals of color. Even when your intention is to extend a hand of friendship, this offering of Christmas cookies is another example of the cultural unawareness in our agency which feels insensitive to others. Second, if representatives of an organization who caused my grief were to offer me cookies, I would feel like they were trying to pacify my anger. This group can offer a better gift by listening to their stories, welcoming their expressions of pain, allowing ourselves to sit with the discomfort, and taking accountability when it's right to do so."

My white co-workers expressed appreciation for my honesty and the people of color in the room shared agreement with my words. Later that evening we had a difficult yet productive meeting with the participants from the communities of color. Afterwards, my coworker who offered to bring cookies invited me to her car to take some home. I gladly took several and we hugged. While she was outwardly gracious, I'm not sure how my comments impacted her. I hope she will take the initiative to tell me.

ERIN YOSHIMURA

No, but I strive to build up the courage and find the words to do so someday. If I had the courage and could come from a place of mindfulness I'd say, "Although you're well meaning, you are unconscious of your rank, power and privilege as a white person. Just because you may not feel like you have power and you've experienced adversity a few times in your life, it's not the same thing as being sized up, judged and labeled because of the color of your skin and the slant of your eyes."

"No matter how hard you try to immerse yourself into my community, there are times you're like a bull in a china shop because you lack the awareness of the damage you cause behind you. Learning about my cultural traditions isn't like learning how to ride a bike, where once you get the hang of it, it'll always be with you and is your badge of honor. Stop trying to prove you're more ethnic than me. There's a difference between coveting the external tangible elements of my culture and having deep insight on the internal intangible issues that I have to deal with every day."

"Telling me you're 'tired of political correctness and always hearing about racism' indicates that you don't have a clue about how much privilege you really have. And, this makes you very unsafe to be around, so don't be surprised or insulted that I don't trust you."

Would you be willing to teach me about your culture,
faith and traditions? If yes, what? If not, why not?

CAROLYN BERNARD

I would be willing to teach you whatever you asked, as long as you were respectful and attentive. I believe it is important to learn about one another's culture and traditions, and I believe that familiarity can help to breed respect and appreciation. What gives me pause is when white people seek to fetishize, commercialize, and appropriate the culture, faith, and traditions of people of color. Many whites simply accept the idea that other cultures are theirs to plunder as they see fit. It is a very colonial attitude, and can be devastating to observe in friends or acquaintances who hide behind a mask of "innocent curiosity." But when someone approaches me with respect and a desire to learn, I do not hesitate to share aspects of my culture that may be unfamiliar to them.

TONI ADAMS

I shouldn't have to teach you about our culture, faith or traditions in that they have been acculturated into mainstream society for decades. Almost everything we have has been adopted—our hairstyles (braids), dances, music, food. The Colonel made a fortune off some black woman's fried chicken recipe.

ERIN YOSHIMURA

My initial response is no because it's too tiring and usually involves debunking stereotypical thinking coupled with marginally racist remarks and snickers. It would depend on the situation, context and the person asking. If it were food-related, I have no problem with schooling someone because that's a pretty safe topic. It also depends on whether the person is willing to listen to learn rather than listen to discern. The latter can be a trap where I then find myself defending, convincing and ultimately walking away feeling bad about myself.

A few years ago, I was working with my chiropractor on releasing and clearing deep-seated fear and anxiety. The practice involved her asking me powerful questions along with muscle testing and adjustments depending on my answers. One of her questions resulted in an answer about an early racist incident from my childhood. She laughed at my story! Then she asked, "Is that what really happened? I can't believe it," and shook her head in disbelief. I brushed it off at first, but as I told her more stories, she continued to laugh and shake her head. She determined that the source of my fear and anxiety couldn't be because of these experiences and was resistant to go deeper.

Needless to say, the procedure didn't work, although I worked with her several times. The trust that we built over five years was gone and I no longer go to her. I realized that I made a poor assumption about her because she's gay and she could relate to me. This was a costly lesson—that I need to check my own assumptions about people.

Shawn Patrick

There is really so much I could say here. I would be willing to teach everything I could to someone who is interested. I say that because I do feel like much of my culture, faith, and traditions has been mystified by popular culture. As such, I run into many who think they know what my culture is, and when I attempt to offer a different picture, I am often told that my picture can't be correct. This is a baffling experience.

There is one specific thing related to being biracial that I would want everyone to know, and that is simply that we do exist. We do have a place. We are not "marginalized," we are out in the forefront; we are the largest growing ethnic group in the country; we will continue to grow, and we defy historical attempts to deny, ignore, and destroy us.

Mary Weems

Nothing. This is a painful question to even consider. My original culture, faith, traditions, language, country, ancestors, history have all been lost thanks to slavery. As a film I recently saw, *The Language We Cry In*, poignantly points out, I have no language to cry out in to my ancestors. I can't trace my family back beyond my maternal/paternal great-grandparents. I'm an Indigenous woman living in a country that hates me, with forced and unforced white blood coursing through my veins. The best way to learn would be to do your own formal research and to interact with us on a regular basis as much as possible.

SONYA LITTLEDEER-EVANS

I would be willing to teach anyone about my culture, my faith and my traditions—as long as they are genuinely interested. If this were the case, I would be willing to share my story of my mixed culture and heritage and how growing up was a bit confusing with the last name of Littledeer, though most of my family spoke Spanish; or being told I was Native American even though my family was making tamales and enchiladas at home. I would share with you my maternal grandparents' story of coming over from Ireland and where my mom's maiden name of McCully came from. I would share how some of my family is Catholic, some are Mormon and some are Christian. And how I grew up going to a Mormon church, but rebelled against this religion because it was forced on me. I would share about how my path later took me to finding God and accepting His Son as my Savior. I would share how sometimes it feels like there are walls between my ethnicity and my faith—and how depending on which crowd I am with, I am sometimes less of an Indian, less of a Mexican and less Irish because I am a Christian.

I would also share about my family traditions—traditions that exist around being of color, growing up poor, and being Mexican-Indian-Irish. Traditions from my childhood included making tamales at New Year's with my entire family, eating chadizo and eggs for weekend breakfasts, going to California in the summer to visit relatives and practicing my Spanish with those relatives. As a family of eight, with parents who had no higher education, we were often on welfare. My dad would send each of us six kids into the market with a $1 food stamp to buy a 5¢ candy and return the change to him—this was a Sunday tradition and we so looked forward to it because of the 5¢ candy! Christmas was always amazing because we usually had nothing and were down and out, so somehow our name always got put on the "needy" list, and firemen would always show up the day before Christmas with loads of gifts for us—gifts that we only dreamed of.

I would share with you about how my family traditions have changed with my own family. How I was able to earn an education, which created opportunity that would not have otherwise existed and therefore allowed me to create a tradition of education with my family. I would share about a tradition of always finding ways to give back to my community and how this tradition grew out of so many wonderful people along my journey who gave to me when I so needed it.

I would share these things because they are me. If you are really, truly interested—I would share all of these things.

MICHAEL LESLIE

No, that time has passed. Now whites must seek out that knowledge for themselves, by educating themselves. Enough has been written about people of color so that if whites are sincere, they can study us in a library. I am not available to serve as a guide dog for them.

RAZIA KOSI

I would be willing to teach you how I experience my culture, faith or traditions, but my experience does not speak for my South Asian/American culture, Islamic Faith or South Asian/American traditions. The fact that I have gone to far more rock concerts than classical Indian dance performance speaks more about my American pop culture interest than my identity as a South Asian. My experience is unique to me and I have traveled along this journey with full awareness that my culture, faith and traditions have been morphed into something that is new and unique to growing up in a place where I am not a part of the dominant culture.

My parents, who emigrated from South India in the late 1960's, tried to pass along traditions to my brother and me. They, themselves, were learning how to maintain an Indian household filled with traditions while living in a society that did not value difference. They had to quickly recognize and maintain all the components of their culture, faith and traditions that they valued and wanted to pass along to my brother and me. I imagine it was not easy for them. It became a battle between my parents, trying to maintain an image of India from the 1960's while living in the U.S. through the '70's and '80's. India had changed, my parents had changed, and my brother and I became individuals who, on the surface, looked like our parents, but didn't sound, act, think or express ourselves like our parents.

The aspect of my culture that I am willing to teach you about is our strong ties to family, high value on education, strong work ethics, celebrating religious events with family, eating our Indian foods and basing decisions on what's best for the family. One can watch the latest Bollywood film to soak in the colors, rhythm and drama of the pop culture that permeates the psyche of modern India, but this is not the culture that permeates my soul.

Travis Smith

Whatever it takes for you to get over your xenophobia! And whatever it would take for you to broaden your knowledge of reality! In the words of Frederick Douglass, "The American people have this lesson to be learned. That where justice is denied, where poverty is enforced, and ignorance prevails, where any class of people are made to feel that society is an organized conspiracy to rob, oppress, and degrade them, neither persons nor property will be safe. Hungry men will eat, desperate men will commit crimes, outraged men will seek revenge."

You have to understand my culture is one of survival! It is a culture created in the plantations and ghettos of the United States. What faith we have we learned from you, and the life we've given it, you could have never done! What foods we eat we've fashioned into a delicacy from the garbage you left over for us! And our music reeks with the sorrows and joys of being human in an inhumane society!

Though we're far from being monolithic, it is important for you to know that, "The common road of hope which we all traveled has brought us into a stronger kinship than any words, laws, or legal claims." (Richard Wright)

Carol Walsh

"Teach" is a strong word. My first question would be, Why do you want to learn? What will you do with this information? I would be willing to get to know you and have you do the same of me. I would like to engage in authentic dialogue and truth about your life and my own for the ultimate purpose of change. Will what I provide you help your self-actualization as a non-racist? Will you embrace not only my words, my cultures, my faith, my traditions, but me as well? Will you assume to know all about those of my culture, my faith, and my tradition simply because you shared a moment in time with me? I'm always willing to share in reflective exchanges, but when I am the "topic" I have to ask, Why, and What will you do with this information?

Camisha L. Jones

There is almost nothing I wouldn't be willing to share but I find it exhausting to do so when I am among people who believe their culture, traditions, and practices are the "norm" in comparison to other ways of doing things. If I sense that my experiences are deemed "abnormal" or "inferior," I will not likely continue to do much sharing. However, I love to be among people who are open to sharing the ways that our experiences differ and the ways they are the same without demeaning anyone's experience. Over the years, a conversation I have found to be meaningful is talking about race and faith with fellow Christians. In these conversations, we have discussed how our experiences and backgrounds differ and in doing so I feel we have learned more about what it really means to live our faith.

Yukari Takimoto Amos

If a person wants to understand other people's cultures, that person needs to live in that community or society for a long time. I know a lot of white students who say, "I know a lot about Japanese culture and traditions because I learned them in class." But I wonder how much they know about how we really think and behave and why we do so. Visible culture can be learned, but invisible culture cannot be learned unless a person is open to critically comparing others' cultures and their own.

Eric Lackie

I have two responses to this question. My first response will speak to distrust, and the second will be about education.

Distrust: One of the most uncomfortable requests that I have received from white folks is to teach them about my culture. I don't always know or trust the intentions of white people who ask me to tell them more about my culture. Here are some questions that may help you to take a closer look at your intentions and help you to better understand the hesitancy some people of color feel about educating whites on the subject of our cultures.

- How long have you been curious about my culture?
- What are your life experiences that have brought you to ask me about my culture?
- Prior to asking me, what efforts have you made to learn about my culture? What efforts have you made to learn about other cultures? What did you learn?
- Whose life are you hoping will be improved as a result of me teaching you?
- Do you believe that attaining knowledge about my culture, faith, and traditions will make you more culturally sensitive?

- Do you believe people can still be hurtful or hateful towards people of color even after learning about their culture?
- What do you suggest that I do with my pain if I feel hurt by your actions even after teaching you about my culture?
- What do you know about the history of whites using cultural information about people of color in ways that harm us?
- Can you assure yourself that what I tell you will be a benefit to me as well as to you?
- Do you know how to listen in ways that are validating and respectful?
- Are you aware of responses that feel invalidating and disrespectful?

Education: Your first assignment is to research your own cultural life history and your own history of cultural interactions with others. Then come to me with what you have learned and I will teach you about my culture, faith and traditions at an academic or grade level that seems most appropriate to your learning. If you like, you can use the sample questions outlined in the above paragraph titled "Distrust" to help you in your research.

Some white folks may have difficulty understanding the basis for my reticence to teach. It is mostly because I'm exhausted from a lifetime of investing energy into educating whites who often appear only minimally interested. Consequently, I'm working to learn new ways to help whites increase their cultural competency while avoiding burnout.

INDIGO VIOLET

I'm not too interested in teaching whites about cultural issues pertaining to my community unless they are politically and personally working to undo racism and I recognize them as strong allies who have done the work to be wary of cultural appropriation. There are so many dangers embedded in the complex intricacies of white supremacy, including the idea of embracing the "cultures" of people of color without working to understand the histories of oppression and struggle that have shaped people of color communities. If a white person was doing good anti-racist work, there may be some cultural logics and beliefs that I might share, if I knew they would use that information to hold the idea that people of color's cultural logics and practices can be liberating and in some cases, could help to heal the world generally.

Would you be willing to come to my home and have me to yours?
Why or why not?

Toni Adams

Been there, done that!

Carolyn Bernard

Yes, I would be willing. I want a dialogue between whites and people of color about racism, and I want it to be an intimate dialogue. I want us to be friends; I want us to feel safe in each other's homes.

Mary Weems

If invited—yes. I have been invited to the homes of white, African, Japanese, Mexican, Jewish, gay, and former Mormon folks, and any time I can—I go. I wish everyone in America were willing to have these kinds of experiences, because they highlight in the best possible way just how much we have in common as people born into this world dependent upon others to thrive. It's in these informal, intimate settings that we get to know each other in mundane and complex ways. It's how we come to know just how alike we really are, which is a good foundation for learning to respect and celebrate our differences.

Wayne Downey

Sure, and I often do. This is how the conversation becomes more relevant, when it's transpiring in living rooms and around kitchen tables. I think that as long as you are open and consistent, then I don't see why that wouldn't be a possibility. It requires me to acknowledge a shadow or dark side, in having to adhere to some self-preservation. I can't just go into any situation unmonitored or pre-inspected, because you never know what is going to transpire. What's key here is genuine, authentic, open, real relationships.

Eric Lackie

If visiting your home feels physically or emotionally unsafe, I may decline or ask that we meet in a more public place or with others. Also, it helps to know the reasoning behind why I am being invited. What do you want to happen during or as a result of this visit? Is this a party you are inviting me to? If so, what kind of party? Is there something you want to show me? Is there something you want me to know about you? Is there something you want to know about me? Visiting people in their homes is an experience that can be rewarding, traumatic, or just plain boring. This depends largely on how comfortable people feel during the visit. If I don't feel comfortable with you now, I probably won't feel too excited about going to your house or inviting you to mine unless I am in an extra compassionate or brave state of mind.

Carol Walsh

People often invite a person of color in an effort to change the mindsets of those in their home, or prove something to themselves. So, as long as I am truly welcomed—as you would be welcomed into my home.

Camisha L. Jones

I believe a person's home is sacred, a place of sanctuary, where they should be able to let their hair down and be their truest self. I do not invite everyone into my home. Mainly, I invite people I trust to my home, people whose company I enjoy or people I would like to get to know better. So, yes, I would invite you to my home and would want to visit yours if I felt I could trust you and enjoyed your company. However, if I felt you were not conscious about race and racism, I would not be very enthusiastic about inviting you into my home or visiting yours—unless perhaps we were visiting to discuss race and racism and I felt you were truly open to having an honest conversation.

Michael Leslie

I have already been to your home enough. In the past, I would have invited you to mine, but this no longer seems useful or even desirable to me. It is not a pleasant experience to be scrutinized in my own home—or by you in yours.

Razia Kosi

I would be willing to come to your home and to have you come to mine at least once. Whether we continue building a relationship would depend on how the first visit went. I say this with the intention and hope that we would continue a friendship, but I realize that the older I get the more my personal relationships are with people who have a similar background as me. I don't know if it's because of a surface level of comfort or a deeper feeling of trust or camaraderie, but I do have to recognize that I have been more willing to open my home and accept invitations to those of similar background when forming new friendships.

——•—— RACE/RACISM ——•——

What is the difference between talking about race and racism?

MONIQUE RIEKE

Race describes the ethnic choices people associate themselves with and racism is the act of rejecting a race of people.

JIM PEAL

Race is what makes us unique and adds to our contributions to life. Racism is what makes our differences separate us.

NORM

Race is a physical pigmentation, and often social and cultural differences. Racism is the usage of these differences of a dominant group to oppress a subordinate group.

RAZIA KOSI

Racism is perpetuated by the need of the dominant culture to feel superior to groups or individuals different from them. Talking about race is different than racism because it means having a dialogue about experiences that individuals and groups have gone through because of their external features. It also means looking at the construct of race and the illusion about the differences between people who look differently on the outside. A thorough examination of a person's mitochondrial DNA would reveal more variation among groups who appear physically similar and possible matches with people who have different ancestry and physical features. This discussion could be liberating, eye-opening and welcoming of more dialogue.

MICHAEL LESLIE

Talking about race most times is simply acknowledging the existence of difference in phenotype and ethnicity. Talking about racism calls the whole system of power relations based on race in our society into question, and points out the inequities and assigns responsibility for them.

CAROLYN BERNARD

I think most people, especially white people, are more comfortable talking about race than racism. Race is a sensitive subject, but racism is inherently uncomfortable and almost always painful to discuss. When talking about race, we can appreciate our differences and similarities and we can, as they say, "celebrate diversity." But racism is not a celebration. Discussing racism requires us to focus specifically on how race divides us and how it causes us to hurt one another.

INEZ TORRES

Anyone can talk about race and just about anyone will.

Few people talk about racism and fewer still understand and can explain the institutional and systemic dimensions of racism.

GENNY LIM

Whites like to talk about racism as long as they don't have to take personal responsibility for changing themselves or relinquishing certain privileges that come with the territory. It is human nature to accept and protect privilege and, because of this, the cycle of racism continues. Laws don't change racism. People do.

What's worse—overt racism or the buried-deep-down kind?

CAROLYN BERNARD

I'm not sure about worse, but I think the buried-deep-down kind of racism is more dangerous because it often sneaks into situations where overt racism would be dismissed or reviled. People allow themselves to be racist in "small" ways because they think it is somehow better or more justifiable than wearing a white hood or spouting off racial slurs. But both kinds of racism are harmful. The buried-deep-down kind is just sneakier, so it goes farther and influences more than the overt kind.

WAYNE DOWNEY

I'd have to opt for the very deep-down kind, especially from somebody you didn't expect, somebody you have a working relationship with, somebody you consider an ally, and then you discover that they've got some issues that you didn't catch so now your ally has become an adversary.

The overt kind is great because you know who is behaving that way and then you can choose whether or not to interact with them. It's the people that keep it hidden that make it scarier.

TONI ADAMS

THEY BOTH SUCK, but that's their issue, not mine.

ERIC LACKIE

They both hurt and I wouldn't want either. I challenge the asker of this question to meditate on times when you were hurt by others. Discover for yourself what was worse, when someone was overtly hurtful to you or when their hurtful behavior was buried-deep-down and not so obvious.

RAZIA KOSI

In asking whether overt racism is worse than the buried-deep-down kind, I feel like it's asking whether it's worse to die from a gunshot wound or a cancerous growth that overtakes your body. Racism in any form is an insidious construct that gives a privileged group power over other groups. The need to feel above others may either be fueled by fear, an ingrained sense of superiority or a hate propelled by a need to maintain barriers. I may have a stronger reaction of anger and fear to overt racism because it may cause a direct impact on me and my sense of safety but I am also fully aware that the buried-deep-down type of racism will have just as strong an impact on me and will cause just as much, if not more harm than overt racism.

TRAVIS SMITH

"I have more respect for a man who lets me know where he stands than the one who comes up like and angel and is nothing but a devil." – Malcolm X

Personally, the buried-deep-down kind! Because if I'm led to believe that my family and I are welcomed somewhere but in reality we're not, then our lives could be in jeopardy! That's how serious the sickness of "whiteness" is! Honesty is more commendable than deception. If we know we're not wanted somewhere then we don't go there!

Carol Walsh

The absolute worst is buried-deep-down racism. The overt racist is open about their feelings and proud to stand up for or behave in a manner congruent with their convictions. Overt racists, if they can be swayed to understand the existence, impact, and deleterious effects of racism, will be equally outspoken and proud to stand up for the eradication of racism as they were for its advancement. Those who bury their racism are untrustworthy and dangerous to me.

Yukari Takimoto Amos

Both. But I would argue that the buried-deep-down kind is more vicious since it is hard to detect. If it is overt, we can respond with clear evidence, but if it is buried, it is hard to convince others. But, in the current days, this buried-deep-down racism is prevalent. For example, when I announced to my white colleague that I was awarded the merit award, she said in surprise, "How could you?" When I said to my white boss that my paper was accepted at a prestigious educational conference, he said to me, "Oh, it's a round-table session, correct?" These put downs, in other words, microaggressions, are rampant in my university. Are these racist? I would say yes, because I am pretty sure that if I were white, they would have never said what they did. But how do we prove it?

Indigo Violet

Well, since I definitely do not deal much with white folks who exhibit overt racism, I tend to think the buried-deep-down kind is worse. It is worse mostly because of its lack of transparency, its rootedness in a good-hearted kind of ignorance, and the ways that white privilege and white power can continue to be perpetuated, even in liberal or progressive circles, on account of unexamined racism. However, overt racists pose a terrifying kind of danger—the threat of violence or death, particularly with the most vehement ones. So, I cannot say that one or the other is worse. The buried-deep-down kind can be more psychically damaging and painful; the overt kind is just plain scary.

SHAWN PATRICK

At one point in time, I would've said that the deep-down kind was worse because this type of racism often works "under the radar." Overt racism can at least be dealt with more easily because it can be identified directly. I think fewer people engage in overt racism; however, these acts tend to be highly aggressive with the intent to harm. Thus its impact can be catastrophic—such as ending in murder. But, as such, I think most people engage in covert or subtle racism, where they believe they have good intentions but inadvertently hurt non-dominant groups. For example, the company Christmas party that presumes everyone will bring their spouse also sends the message that non-Christians and same-sex relationships may not be accepted. These kinds of messages are encountered daily by non-dominant groups, and the end result is a continual process of self-doubt and building of defense that ultimately shapes who you are and how you think about yourself. Thus I think the damage can be done over a very long period of time and result in relational, psychological, or emotional difficulty. I think both result in terrible damage to many people and society—one is just "quicker" than the other. I think it may also be useful to begin to see "deep-down" racism as just as bad as overt racism, so people understand the true magnitude of the problem.

What makes you feel safe in a conversation about race?

CAROLYN BERNARD

Knowing that the person I'm talking to is willing to listen and reflect makes me feel safer in conversations about race. In group conversations, knowing that I am not the only one at the table with a basic understanding of institutional racism is also helpful.

MARY WEEMS

Nothing. The only time I feel truly safe in this country is when I'm at home or around people I know intimately and love. While I understand the need for and encourage the development of safe learning environments, where people believe they can share without being judged, open and honest conversations about something that causes as much misery, hatred and fear as race relations in this country cannot and should not be fully couched in notions of safety when there are millions of us who live each day knowing that our race is a constant negative factor in our way of being in America. Notions of safety make me think about political correctness and the nonsensical idea that being P.C. will help bring us together by making certain no one is ever offended by something another says or writes.

WAYNE DOWNEY

I feel the most safe when my race-based conversations are being acknowledged, aren't being scrutinized or subject to cross-examination. I feel safe when I'm believed. I feel safe when people are willing to step in and participate or to defend me in a conversation.

SHAWN PATRICK

I feel safer with a white person if that person is able to recognize that I am a person of color. I don't want my ethnicity to be ignored. I also don't want someone to constantly be remarking on how we are similar. I feel very safe with a white person who can acknowledge our difference and then say, "I'd like to learn more." I actually find a white person to be less reliable if they attempt to appear to have all the answers. I prefer the honesty of someone who can say they know nothing about someone like me and don't understand my experiences. At least then I know that person isn't presenting a false self to me. For reliability, that also includes seeing a white person back up their words with actions in public. For example, to see that white person question another person's bias, or not laugh at a racial joke—those small deeds build trust and show me that the person is at least taking these issues seriously.

TONI ADAMS

I'm old enough now to be comfortable in telling my truth and acknowledging it may not be your truth.

ERIC LACKIE

I feel most safe when talking with people who genuinely want to understand and see the validity in what I'm trying to say. Even if I don't use the best words, a good listener will not criticize my word choices. Instead, they will repeat what they think they hear me saying and allow me plenty of opportunity to clarify my thoughts and feelings. My feelings are honest, even though my word choices can be confusing at times and especially when I'm emotionally vulnerable. Try not to interrupt. If you do interrupt, do it with a tone of respect and love.

It's usually other people of color that I am able to get real validation from. I think white people are often too scared to hear what I think. On the other hand, many who do want to know what I think often start the dialogue by making provocative statements like, "I don't think Obama has what it takes to get our country on track. What do you think?" I don't remember ever being randomly asked by whites about my opinions on George Bush or Bill Clinton's effectiveness in office but I've frequently been invited into conversations about Barack Obama, Tiger Woods, and Michael Jackson. I typically engage more with whites who seem genuinely interested in listening and ignore whites who appear more inclined to mock, judge and be flippant with their ideas.

Michael Leslie

Having other people of color present who are not totally cowed by the white master race gives me the courage to speak and to act against racism.

Razia Kosi

The thing that would make me feel safe in a conversation about race is a true willingness from the other person in engaging in a dialogue, rather than debating their point of view about race. I would not feel safe if the person wants to express their perspective on how they do not feel they have any power because they are part of the dominant culture and how they have had it just as bad as people of color. I also would not feel safe with people who chose a stance of color-blindness, believing they are above any issues concerning race. Unlearning racism is an on-going process, and one in which all people have to be willing to engage with their eyes and minds wide open. It's not an easy process for both white folks and people of color to surface their biases, assumptions and beliefs about others to the world, but it is one which is necessary to truly have a conversation about race and racism.

Camisha L. Jones

When talking to white folks about race, I appreciate thoughtful questions, comments on the ways our experiences are the same and different, even a simple statement like "I never knew that." I hate it when conversations about race become a tug-of-war in which I am put in the position of convincing skeptical white people that racism exists and that my experiences are a valid expression of what it means to be a racial minority in this country.

Yukari Takimoto Amos

The presence of people of color makes me feel more comfortable. Since whites have their own distinctive discourse styles that put down people of color and elevate white people, in order for me to be safe I need minority allies. The other night I had dinner with my Japanese friend and her white husband. During the conversation, the issue of his cousin-in-law, who is Puerto Rican, came up. According to the white husband, the only reason why his cousin-in-law cheats on his white wife is because he is Hispanic. Face to face, both my friend and I argued against him saying his statement was a stereotype and prejudiced. My friend's presence made it easier for me to respond to her husband's prejudicial remarks.

Indigo Violet

Where defensiveness is absent and where an openness to listen and deal with the truth of history is present.

Erin Yoshimura

The only times I've felt safe to share my experiences of race and racism are in the 3-day workshops held by StirFry Seminars. Lee Mun Wah and other Stir-Fry-trained facilitators create a safe space to speak openly. They masterfully pick up on micro-expressions, slow down the conversation and guide participants to have real, in-depth and insightful communication that most diversity trainers overlook. Their workshops are very healing and cathartic experiences for me, as I've been able to unfold many years of pain and self-oppression that I wasn't consciously aware of.

The key to safety is to not hurry through difficult conversations, but to sit in the fire together knowing that it's okay to reach deep within and express feelings that you don't feel safe to share. Safety comes when there's a sense of equal responsibility on everyone to share and, most important, to listen to people who are different than yourself.

CHAPTER THREE
PERSONAL JOURNEYS

What was your most profound experience with racism?

How did it affect you and how does it affect you today?

DE ANDRE DRAKE

My most profound experience was very recent. It was in New York at a Jewish wedding where I was the only black person in attendance. I did notice a few blacks and Hispanics working as servers. I was approached by one of the guests in the wedding who asked, "Who do I talk to in order to get the air conditioning turned on?" My response was a shrug and a baffled, "Shoot, I don't know." The guest responded with attitude, "What do you mean you don't know?" It was as if he expected me to have the answer and I was wrong for not having the answer. He looked at me, I looked at him, and I could tell at that exact moment we both had the same realization of what and why he was asking me what he was asking. He simply walked away, no apology.

SHAWN PATRICK

For me it is more a collection of small experiences that all added up to the realization that I was not the "norm." When I was little, probably first grade, I remember other kids telling me jokes about Chinese people, or kids making Bruce Lee-type motions and noises at me. I actually remember laughing. Being a kid, this didn't feel like teasing, and I don't think they were trying to bully me. I was, though, the only kid in class who was Chinese (or any non-white for that matter) and I was aware that I was the only person they told these jokes to. I also have several memories growing up of watching my mother, who still speaks with a strong accent, being ignored in a store, being told to leave, being yelled at because the clerk didn't think my mother could understand her. At times I felt embarrassed, angry, even ashamed that we were seen as so undesirable. As a child, to watch your mother be mistreated feels worse than to be mistreated yourself, because you know it is wrong and yet have no power to do anything about it.

These experiences affected me in that they showed me that often racism is perpetuated through subtle, aversive means that are so damaging because there is very little that can be done to confront it at the time. We were the ones who were made to leave the stores, we were the ones who had to wait to be served, we just had to suck it up and be left to seethe. It also affects me now in that I want to make the voice of the oppressed stronger, loud enough so no one can ignore it. Yet I am also at times pessimistic, cynical, and guarded because of that very same experience of being ignored.

MONIQUE RIEKE

I was 12 years old and wanted to go ice skating. We had to go off of the reservation to skate since we did not have an indoor skating rink. So, my friend, her older sister and I all went skating at the white skating rink in town. Their father dropped us off and was picking us up at closing time. We were skating and laughing and having a good time. Then, unfortunately, three boys arrived between the ages of 13 and 15. They began skating quite fast around us, ignoring us at first (or so it seemed). After their fifth round, however, the tallest boy—who was about 15 years old—began to cry out war-whooping sounds when he went by us and did the tomahawk-chop motion with his arm. They did this for about five rounds around us and forced us to the center of the ice. I guess our reactions (or lack of any) were not enough for them because they began pushing my friend back and forth between them on the ice. I stepped in and told them to STOP! They did not stop and instead threw me (the smallest girl of the group) into the throwing contest. My friend's sister ran to get help but none was available. The one person running the rink apparently disappeared when this all started up. So, we basically just got off of the ice and sat in the warm-up area until closing time.

It did not end there, however. The boys harassed us for about 15 minutes before my friends' dad showed up. By that time, I had jumped one of the boys and was bashing the sharp part of my skate blade into his head on the ground! I had had enough and resorted to violence. I had three older brothers, so size and age were not obstacles to my show of strength. I was able to keep that boy pinned down, bloody and crying, until my friends' dad arrived. My friends were afraid of the zone I had entered when I began to hurt that boy. I felt satisfied that I was going to gain a reputation of not being picked on just because I am American Indian and a woman. (It did not work, by the way—another new place, another new time—I was picked on for being American Indian again!)

DENNARD CLENDENIN

There are so many instances where I have been a victim of racism, each and every one of them profound. Upon my separation from the Marine Corps in 1971, I had to take an exit psych evaluation. The white counselor asked me if I had any concerns regarding my experiences. I mentioned that it was difficult to serve in a rifle platoon with fellow marines who brandished confederate flags and were avowed members of the Ku Klux Klan. His reply was, "I understand how you feel, but after all you are a nigger." I wanted to kill him. After all, I'd done a lot of killing in Vietnam.

Toni Adams

I was 11 when my father decided it was time for me to go with him to visit his home state of Texas. I remember clearly he purchased a .38 policeman special to ride along with us (of course everyone drove in those days instead of flying). We were restricted in the places we could stop for the night, so my dad drove nonstop for many hours. When we finally arrived in Austin, Texas, where my great-great-grandfather founded the first Negro Baptist church, we were like small-time celebrities. I remember everyone coming over to visit and meeting for the first time the young children of my three adult brothers who remained in Austin.

I have a cousin who is close enough in age, so it was with her that I spent a good deal of time. My dad gave me shopping money and allowed me to go out with my cousin—something he never would have allowed in California. Shopping went well, although I was somewhat put off by the downtown white-only drinking fountain and used it anyway. But when it was time to go to the movies we purchased our tickets from a different booth and were directed to the balcony. Of course in California, this was a privilege restricted to teenagers (that is where all the necking occurred), but here we were required to sit in the balcony. I couldn't understand how the store owner readily took my money but restricted where I drank water and where I could sit in the movie theatre. I cannot tell you today which movie we saw. I do remember throwing popcorn down on those white folks who didn't want to sit near me. When I asked my dad why, he really had no answer except to tell me that is why we traveled with a gun—he knew his California child would not understand. The fact that 50 years later I so vividly remember the experience tells me it did have an effect on me.

Jim Peal

My white fourth grade class sang "Big Black Jim" to me. I will always be on guard.

Wayne Downey

As a child, perhaps in fifth grade, I can remember being called "piss yellow." I didn't know what it meant, but I knew it was not complimentary. Unfortunately, the offending party was Latino, whose ethnic and cultural background was intact, unlike my own. To this day, I still don't feel like I have a sense of belonging. If something cataclysmic were to happen, I don't know where I would go. I know that if I were to have children with a white woman, there's a good chance that my children could pass for white and not have to experience the hostility and animosity that was common for me as a younger person. This is a sad commentary.

Genny Lim

I can't say there was a single experience, but rather a plethora of experiences which shaped my understanding of racism. One incident was having an entire bucket of water poured on me when I was about six or seven by my white, Italian neighbor kids out of their second-story window. They were constantly shooting us with slingshots and hurling pebbles at us, but this drenching touched off all-out warfare. My older sister hightailed to the boys' home with a broom and the mother threatened to call the police when she answered the door to my outraged sister. The harassment by whites continued throughout childhood and I grew as wary and mistrustful of them as they were of me.

Racism comes in all ages, shapes and colors and shares one common theme: ignorance. They have hurt me and so many people with their reckless disregard for human beings that it is often hard for me to forgive their essential helplessness. Deep inside, however, I know it only stems from fear.

Chimi

A kid asked me if I lived in a teepee and hunted with a bow and arrow. It hurt my feelings because they don't think we are regular people.

In third grade when they studied the Chumash, it made me feel like they were doing science projects about us. It hurt my feelings 'cause I didn't want to make collages about the Chumash when I was one.

Michael Leslie

I "eyeballed" two white policemen cruising by in a patrol car when I was standing on a corner at age 18, in Los Angeles, California. The policeman driving the car swerved up on the curb, jumped out and pinned me to the wall. They then proceeded to search me roughly, manhandling my genitals and demanding to know, "What were you looking at?" I did my best to look harmless and apologize for looking at them, and, after warning me never to "eyeball" a policeman again, they let me go and drove away. To this day, I try not to look at policemen when I see them driving by, and I remain afraid every time I see a police car either approaching or in my rearview mirror. I would say that I am afraid of all police and public security officials.

Coz

When I heard the song by Bob Dylan called "Hurricane" about Rubin Carter, it made me realize how badly black people are treated. Since then I have always wanted to stick up for black people and Native Americans like myself.

Razia Kosi

In thinking back to a profound experience with racism, I'm remembering an incident when I was about six years old in elementary school. The assistant principal came into my class and asked to talk with me. Back then, and perhaps to some extent today, the assistant principals only came to talk with you if you were in trouble, so all the kids hissed, "Awwww, you're in trouble." I went outside with him and he said he wanted to ask me a question. He asked if my parents and I had a "Green Card." I had no idea what a Green Card was. My immediate response was, "No, we don't have a Green Card," thinking that it was something bad. He then explained what it looked like and asked if I had seen it. My parents never talked about a Green Card with me nor showed my Alien Registration Card, so I again answered that I didn't think we had one, again believing it was a bad thing, and I didn't want our family to get in trouble. He let me go back to class, and the whole day I felt uneasy about the whole interaction and scared our family had done something wrong.

When I went home I told my mom about the incident and she said that we did have a Green Card and I should have answered yes. She was visibly upset, and as soon as my father came home, we both told him about the incident. I said that when the assistant principal asked about the Green Card, I proudly said we did not have one. My father became very angry with me and said I should always answer "yes" if anyone asks me about a Green Card. He then took it out and showed me what it looked like.

In thinking about this as an adult, it's interesting to me that my father's anger was projected at me instead of the assistant principal for questioning a child about the documentation status of my family. My father, who had come to this country on a student visa for his master's degree, and was then employed and sponsored by a well-known engineering firm, still felt threatened by the fragility of being "welcomed" or "accepted" in this country. This incident is profound for me because the racist actions of the assistant principal impacted the trust and relationship within our family. I felt I had somehow put my family in a bad light by not answering the question correctly, and I could tell by my parent's anger and fear that what I had done could have very negative consequences for our family. I was instructed by my father to go to the office the next day and to tell the principal that we did have Green Cards.

As an adult and a parent now, I can't even imagine asking my six-year-old to go to the office to clarify the matter. At this point if one of my children were questioned, I would be in the principal's office enraged that my child was questioned illegally about their documentation status.

DAVID LEE

In the mid-1960's, driving through the country, my parents stopped for food at a drive-through joint in Tennessee. They refused to serve us so we drove off hungry. My mother cried. I was 4 years old. I don't go to fast-food joints, and I sense a continual level of anxiety, anticipating unfair treatment at any service counter.

JESSIE EWING

This happened just the other day, and after 19 years of living in this world it was one of the best moments of my life. I was at a gas station in a predominantly white area. There were two other women there. One was white, the other black. The black woman walked inside followed by the white woman. The white woman came out and started pumping her gas. Then the black woman came out. She headed towards her car then towards the white woman. And in a respectful, calm voice the black woman said, "While we were inside you cut me and it felt very rude." I couldn't believe it. I had gone to high school in that area and I had been cut too many times to count by white people, but this woman said something. The white woman rudely and defensively replied, "Well I'm sorry!" She knew she was being accused of being racist and I loved it. That's not to say I think it's fun to see people calling others racists, but I love it when people get called out and/or have to think about their actions and the effects they have on other people. I couldn't wipe that smile off of my face for hours. I will probably never see that black woman again, but she is an inspiration. She may not have gotten through to that woman but it was a start, and it made me think that if I use my voice too, meek as it may be, and others use theirs, then maybe, just maybe, things could really start to change.

Kye Lockhart

When I was around ten, playing ball in the front yard with my brother and sister, laughing and being excited, just being a kid, I guess the neighbor across the street thought I was being too loud, so they screamed out from their front door, "Shut up, nigger!!" I was stunned and hurt to say the least. I told my father and saw him go across the street and address the problem. He spoke with a firm voice and an intelligent mind. I never had a problem from those neighbors again.

One final incident I'll speak on was when I was a teenager. I had a really cool custom-made jeep. I was pulled over by a black cop. When I asked why I was pulled over, he mentioned it was because my windows were tinted. I, in return, told him that tinted windows are not illegal. He then said, "Well, how about if I take your black ass to jail?" and began to laugh very wickedly. I was more shocked than anything. He ran my license and found out that I had a clean driving record and no previous offenses. Assuming that he would find something wrong, but didn't, he came back to my vehicle a completely different individual. Being very cordial, probably thinking that I may tell his boss what he said to me and why he pulled me over.

J.C. Eaglesmith

At about four years old, my white mother's mother tried to "scrub the dirt off" my dark-tanned body (my father was American Indian), as I was "dirty" compared to my white cousins. As an eight-year old boy I was called a "bastard" by the teacher because my father was American Indian and mother Euro-American. Seems that state law in North Carolina prohibited Indians from marriage to whites.

I was hired to teach Native American history in public school, then fired for "Anti-Christian, anti-white attitudes," "dressing inappropriately" (wearing bone chokers and an eagle feather in my hat) and "co-habitation with an older white woman." (True—my biological widowed mother.) And this has affected me in that I am dedicated to teaching and being worthy of being a "culture carrier," promoting the integrity of human beings as Earthpeople and members of the Star Nation. Somehow, someway, it has not made my heart beat with hate. For this, I am grateful.

CAROLYN BERNARD

The moment that really crystallized things for me was when a boy in my high school math class went around labeling everyone in the class as "white" or "not," supposedly to point out how easy it was to tell. This was, keep in mind, a person who thought that Spain was not in Europe, because he thought that Europeans were "white" and Spaniards were "not." So, not the brightest bulb for sure. But he turned in his seat, pointing out each person in class and labeling them, and when he turned around to point at me, he was silent for a second, his finger poised. And then he said nothing, turned around, and started pointing out some other people. I am mixed, and of ambiguous appearance, and he just couldn't find a box in his reality to fit me in, so he conspicuously ignored me, as if I didn't exist. I had always realized how off the grid mixed-raced people were, especially those not black/white. But I think it was then that I realized how we could be simply invisible to those who did not want to see us.

Andrea's Story

I would like to start with my earliest memory of racism. I was thirteen years old and had been studying dance quite seriously at a studio that was owned and operated by African Americans for several years. Since I'd decided I wanted to have a career as a professional dancer, I realized I needed to move to a studio that focused solely on classical ballet if I was to be prepared to compete at a national level. I enrolled in a predominantly white ballet studio. During the registration meeting I was given the list of "appropriate" dance attire and requisite protocols. On the list, pink tights, pink ballet shoes and hair in a bun were clearly stated. After purchasing the tights and shoes, my mom and I went to a hair supply store and found a "fake bun" to pin at the back of my "Afro-centric" hair (that was neither long enough nor straight enough based on white standards of beauty).

When I arrived at my first class, I quickly noted that all of the students in the class I had been placed in were much younger than me. When I approached the instructor, she told me that my body type really wasn't suited for ballet and I would not be able to keep up in the more accelerated class. I didn't really know what she meant about my body type until we started the barre exercises. She kept telling me to "tuck in my behind" even though I had "tucked in" as much as was humanly possible. I also noticed that the pink tights and pink shoes blended quite nicely with the pinkish skin tone of the white girls in the class. Against my dark skin, there was no blending; simply starkly pale pink. Uncomfortable and humiliated, I quit after one lesson and found an African American studio that taught classical ballet. The requisite attire was skin-toned tights, skin-toned shoes and hair pulled off of your face. I observed a class while I was there for registration. Dancers had successfully dyed their tights and shoes in the myriad shades of brown from tan to dark chocolate. Woolly Afro puffs and head bands over tightly-kinked short hair lilted next to ponytails and braids. During my first class, the teacher told me to lift my abdominal muscles to elongate the derriere. I'd found a place where my "body type" and skin tone and hair texture were accepted and incorporated into the range of normalcy as I continued on my quest toward a professional dance career. That incident caused me to actively pursue a black aesthetic as an artist as I came into adulthood and eventually motherhood.

When my first child entered kindergarten, my husband and I were challenged to find a public school that met our needs as a family. We settled on a magnet school in downtown Detroit called Burton International. It was a wonderful K-8 school with a dedicated staff and seemed suited to our needs. At the same time, we enrolled our two-year-old son in an independent African-centered school, Aisha Shule, which was run by a dear friend of our family. Having prided ourselves in remaining culturally black by deliberate practice, a year later we were faced with a dilemma. Our two-year-old was not ready for organized schooling and needed to leave the pre-school, and the drive to downtown Detroit from our far northwest neighborhood was no longer feasible. The "choice" Detroit public elementary schools were either too far away or did not have any openings. We made the difficult decision to leave the city and move to the white suburbs.

For the first time in my life, I was confronted with the realities of the work involved in maintaining a home that is decisively, culturally black. I had to surround them with cultural artifacts and commit to rituals that would keep them culturally grounded in what it means to be black in the United States. We continued to attend our Afro-centric black church in the city. We continued to celebrate the seven days of Kwanzaa along with three other families every year. We lovingly quizzed our children, "Who is the godfather of soul?" "Why did they call Nancy Wilson 'the Baby'?" "What is the Chitlin' Circuit?" Our kids ate fried chicken, greens and macaroni and cheese using grandma's recipes. And when the white adults said they could call them by their first names, we said, "Sorry, in our culture children refer to adults with a handle. You can be Miss Nancy or Auntie Nancy but not just plain Nancy."

Our home life and cultural positioning was challenged once again when we moved to the white suburbs of Chicago. We were so far away from a black community that we couldn't even find a black church. There were no more relatives close by who could assist with the cultural grounding and we felt totally isolated from our roots. Additionally, we were faced with outsiders making assumptions about who we were culturally—confusing the entrapments of economics with a racial/cultural framework. All of a sudden, my kids "talked white," "weren't ghetto enough," and we had "sold out." As a family, we circled up and became even more diligent about having conversations with our growing young children, who were encroaching upon the teen years, about processing the world through two lenses: their cultural lens as black people and the lens of white folk. We also found a black community (although dispersed) in the surrounding suburbs through organizations like Jack and Jill. As my children have become young adults, they have held onto the legacy of black culture on their own. Interestingly, we are often still questioned about our family choice to live in a predominantly white community by black folk and by white folk.

I am an administrator in a predominantly white, affluent suburban high school. I work tirelessly to navigate the white system while maintaining my culturally black self. It is difficult to speak out and not be labeled the "angry black woman" or the "P.C. police." I have come to seek out white allies along with the few people of color in our district to help me process the world, recover from micro-aggressions and try and avoid race fatigue. It is fascinating to watch my peers glare at me in disbelief when I recount yet another incident in which I have felt isolated, profiled, marginalized. "But you are so articulate"; "I don't see you as black"; "Everyone has so much respect for you."

This media-proclaimed "post-racial" America is not only a fictitious dream, it is a nightmare! If we as a country remain in disbelief and confusion about the reality that our policies, practices and experiences are racialized, we will never be able to honestly address the invisible barriers that impede true progress and equity in our society.

ANDREA JOHNSON

David's Story

As I approach middle age, I have already accumulated volumes of stories, told and untold, of racist experiences—some from which I endured unspeakable pain, harboring decades of resentment and hopelessly unresolved. The worst perhaps wasn't the time during the 1960's, after the passage of the Civil Rights Act, when, traveling with my mother and father and baby brother through Appalachia, we stopped for food but didn't get served. I remember the feeling of confusion and sadness as my father finally drove away, and as I tried to comfort my mother, who began crying.

Perhaps it wasn't the time library workers ignored me while I waited with books to be checked out, and never came to help until a white student came to the counter, only to check out his books first. And then having the worker accuse me of being mentally unstable for bringing up the injustice. And perhaps it wasn't the time on the Berkeley campus when a young man among his group of fellow students yelled, "Let's kill the Chink!" as they followed me for a couple of blocks on Telegraph Avenue.

One of the more vexing ones for me could very well have been something out of a hackneyed comedy skit. This was the laundromat incident, actually one of many, where again someone comes up to me with an armful of laundry while I'm doing mine, thinking I work there. While taking my clothes out of the washing machine, a woman with a bag of clothes came up to me. Holding back my exasperation, I explained to her that I didn't work there. Suddenly I hear a man laughing. I turn and see him, my partner, holding his stomach and laughing. I felt the years of sharing, explaining, and teaching about racism wasted. In his clueless privileged world, he remained. And I began to leave.

DAVID LEE

On Colorblindness

We are not the same.
We do not breathe the same air.
Mine is contaminated with loathing—undeserved loathing for all that
    I am and all that I think and all that I do.
Doors do not open widely for me.
I push my way in through the cracks.
I play a role that's less intimidating—less me.
I dance the dance and sing the song that will make you feel safe.
All the while—knowing my own vulnerability to your judgment and
    your power.
We are not the same.
I see you but you do not to see me.
You see me only as you desire me to be.
Stubbornly, insisting that I am only like you:
Human. American. White-washed.
You don't see color.
You don't see my victimization, your role in my victimization.
You choose what makes you most comfortable.
And leave me to adjust to the discomfort you've created.
You don't see color and that makes you complicit in my suffering.
If you could see that Racism is about you and not just about me,
That would make us the same:
Equally responsible for unlearning our bias and self-hate.
Equally transformed by the experience of the "other."
But instead, you choose not to see.
You distort me into an (un)intimidating figment of your imagination.
I am the same when I wear the mask.
A threat, when I rise from the shadows.
A threat, when I speak my life's truths:
We are not the same.
Racism is real.
We have not arrived.

I (and so many others who look like me) am still living a different reality—one
    with greater risks for sickness and education gaps, incarceration and poverty.
We are not the same.
Your blindness enslaves me,
Subjects me to your uninvestigated stereotypes and bias and fear.
We are not the same.
My world is under your influence.
And you prefer me as an illusion.
You prefer to live without truth, without authenticity.
We both live crippled by what you refuse to see.

CAMISHA L. JONES

CHAPTER FOUR
UNLEARNING RACISM
WHAT IT WILL TAKE

TALKING TO WHITES

When talking about racism, what opens you up and what closes you down?

DENNARD CLENDENIN

Nothing opens me up. To date, I've never heard a white person say, "I'm a racist." When and if that ever happens perhaps I can open up.

JEAN MOULE

I am opened up when someone wants to know more so that they can make a difference. I am closed down when I sense that people want me to share... but then they nod their heads...and do nothing. Like in *Last Chance for Eden*: I relive it so some white person can "get it" just a little. I hate this part of the struggle we are in. The victims just get victimized again and again while the oppressors try to figure out a way to not take on ANY of the real work.

CAROLYN BERNARD

When talking about racism, it opens me up when people listen and when they are willing to examine themselves. What closes me down is when they use those dismissive phrases—you know what I mean. "The race card. Those people. But stereotypes always have a grain of truth. But I know people like that. I have a black friend. Reverse racism. You're too sensitive. I'm color-blind. You're just trying to be offended. Anything can be racist if you pick at it enough." And so on and so forth. It closes me down when white people prove that they don't really want things to change.

KYE LOCKHART

I'm always open to the discussion of racism, especially if it's something new I can learn. Just the fact of talking about racism opens me up. The feeling of being closed down comes from NOT talking about racism. Being ignored or being accused of hating white people really hurts.

What would it take for you to feel safe enough to tell
the truth about race/racism to white folks?

KYE LOCKHART

If I knew for a fact that a white person would do something on a daily basis to counter racism, then I, along with the rest of the world, would feel much safer in speaking the truth about the problem. A discussion about race/racism can only go so far. The action that takes place after the topic is discussed is what is truly paramount.

DENNARD CLENDENIN

To be flippant, I would have to be independently wealthy, with no reliance on white people whatsoever. More seriously, I would need to not be the only one speaking about my experiences. I would need other persons of color who could relate to my issues and share their own as well. In a perfect setting, I would love to have white people back me up as well; however, even well-meaning white folks on occasion can be part of the problem.

HELEN YE

An interest and curiosity, and openness by whites to REALLY want to know my truth, my story, and other people of color's truths and stories, without retaliation, feelings of guilt. I just want whites to HEAR MY STORY FULLY without judgment, without fear, but with curiosity and search for truth and clarity and honesty.

To be okay to express my anger, fears, frustrations, resentments; and for me to be able to hear whites' fears, anger and frustration, and questions.

GENNY LIM

Reassurance of no retaliation. Institutionalized racism is notorious for having ruined the careers, lives and health of many talented individuals. Instead of being rewarded for your integrity and honesty, you're punished for your "unprofessionalism" and "attitude," plus a host of other negative pejoratives associated with whistleblowers. I would have to feel there was a possibility of open communication and commitment to real dialogue and change. If the discussion happens in an unsafe environment, where confidentiality is violated and judgment is placed on those who speak out, there is little constructive purpose in such a half-hearted, meaningless gesture. Many institutions have engaged in attempts at diversity training and the like to no avail because the earnest commitment wasn't there.

Coz

If someone to protect and stand up for me was near.

J.C. Eaglesmith

Strong application of "our" constitutional and civil rights as written. I have been prosecuted for speaking out, telling the truth in the professional academic world. This has resulted in my being a homeless single parent twice. What would it take to feel safe? Another lifetime of just and fair treatment.

Camisha L. Jones

It is difficult to feel safe telling white people the truth about race and racism. Talking about racism always comes with some degree of risk and vulnerability for me. I can do it in the context of retreats and structured dialogues where there are norms and talented trained facilitators looking out for the safety of participants. I can do it to a lesser degree outside of those settings within a group when I know that a few white allies are present with me who believe racism to be real. On the rare occasion, I have attempted to reconcile one-on-one with someone I believed to have exhibited racist behavior. It is easier to do that when I know the person I am talking to is someone who is engaged in self-reflection about the issue of racism and isn't afraid of the discomfort of addressing racism. Having white allies who would be willing to speak or act on my behalf if a conversation goes badly is also helpful, particularly when conversations occur within the work setting.

Chimi

I would want to know if they would be upset or angry and not become violent.

Carol Walsh

In a perfect world, an acknowledgement of the emotional pain and fear that I live with daily would make me feel safe. I weep over the helplessness that I feel with regards to my children's experiences of racism, both real and perceived. I feel pain from the disrespect and disregard I experience because of my race.

I can't even get to the multiple wonderful parts of me because I must first deal with the reactions, both good and bad, to my blackness. Realistically, I would be content with a genuine acknowledgement of the realities of racism, institutional systems of oppression, colonization, and most importantly the acceptance and belief that their impact is alive and well today. Acknowledging the reality of my pain means you acknowledge the depth and realities of me. You don't joke about it, laugh about it, make light of it, or simply choose to turn a blind eye away from it because it displeases you, saddens you, or upsets you. Joining with me in the acknowledgement of my pain means that I can find true friendship and alignment in the fight against the "powers" that are fighting against us, which no longer need to stand between us. However, this will require that you do your work and acknowledge your own pain and fear that you have experienced because of the existence of racism. What have you done to become aware of your own white privilege and the existence of racism and sexism without having it be on the backs of people who look like me? What work have you done with your white peers to help them see their role and their part in the perpetuation of racism, both consciously and unconsciously? Have you seen us all as victims of systemic "isms" and oppression, or have you excluded yourself from the struggle and the conversation? Too often whites come "in peace" without doing any of their own work and either expect me to help them to "get it" or want some congratulatory medal because they dated, lived around, went to school with, or worked with a black man or woman. When you can truly join me by acknowledging my truth and identifying your own, then can I feel truly safe to engage with you around racism.

JIM PEAL

It will never be safe to tell the truth. Don't expect it to be easy. It will always be a risk...a risk worth taking.

What do you see as effective ways to bring up issues of race and racism with white folks?

RAZIA KOSI

The way to bring up issues of race and racism with white folks effectively is to have honest conversations with both sides sharing a desire to listen and be heard. When both whites and people of color have sat in the presence of each other's stories, seen the pain in both's eyes, heard the fear in each other's voices and witnessed how their bodies contain the sorrow in their hearts, it becomes difficult to allow the barriers of prejudice and stereotypes to continue to keep individuals from forming a human-to-human connection. Connecting with each other and each other's experiences is fundamental to entering the conversations about race and racism.

TONI ADAMS

I belong to a multiracial, multicultural, multi-everything church with a black female pastor. I have found that Rev. E. just tells it like it is (she is 80) and no one blinks an eye. When she talks about being undereducated in Florida because there were no books or schools for children and how the Bible was the only source of knowledge, folks recognize that racism is still playing a role in her life. That is why she is such an effective minister—all she knew was the Bible. She teaches us regularly not to run and hide from what is reality. Our motto is, "Everything in my life, I create, promote or step in." If there is an issue, it is the individual's issue and they need to deal with it.

MARY WEEMS

By initiating open, honest, and non-judgmental dialogue and conversations whenever possible both in and outside formal settings. As someone who has been working against racism in the university and in the community at large, one of the problems I see with most diversity-type programming is that most of it stays on the politically correct, blame-the-white-man level that usually silences white folks while people of color share their innermost feelings and experiences.

Using tools like readings, films, ice-breaking, community-building activities that create a space for white folks to make up their own minds often works to help them begin exploring these issues. Last, what's needed is time. White folks are socialized from birth to believe that non-whites are inferior, and learning to think and feel differently takes time.

Shawn Patrick

I find it to be more effective to bring up these issues by asking questions. Here I believe there is little difference between the person who is white and the person of color—everyone wants a chance to have their story heard and understood. So in asking these questions, my purpose would be to find out that person's point of view, to hear their story without passing judgment. Then I could have a chance to introduce a different idea, or explore similarities, or broaden their experience to systemic levels. I also believe that allowing people to have their stories heard diminishes defensiveness and the need to "prove" one's point.

Eric Lackie

I am still trying to learn effective ways to bring up issues of race and racism with white folks. My tendency has been to raise issues that directly pertain to the person I'm talking to rather than discuss general or philosophical race ideas. However, this often makes white people feel uncomfortable and defensive. I think many whites want so badly to be on good terms with people of color that they can't endure the guilt of hearing when they have been hurtful. This reaction often manifests into invalidation, denial, projection of blame, or even retaliation. For people of color, speaking truths that white people don't want to face or aren't ready to hear can come with painful ramifications. As a result, I am afraid to disrupt the white illusion that everything is okay between us because I am afraid of how they will treat me after I expose them to the truth. I want white people to know this and to learn to accept or even periodically request constructive feedback or criticism from people of color.

It's really hard for me to tell white folks about the comments or actions they make that feel hurtful or offensive to me. It seems as if so many white people want to defend themselves instead of having to listen and care. Most white people I have confronted seem to convey a message that I shouldn't feel hurt or I should just get over it.

My mom and I had a conversation with a white college student who had been a missionary kid in Zaire. He proceeded to tell me and my mom that Africans are like children, not to be trusted, and don't know how to be responsible. We both told him that we felt offended by his comment. Instead of assuming accountability or expressing genuine empathy for our concern, he tried to establish himself as an authority on Africans because of his residency and upbringing in an African country. I scheduled another time to talk with him about my feelings and he automatically went into a flurry of explanations about why he isn't racist and how he has always had good relations with black people. He even wondered why my mom and I, as African Americans, would be concerned about his views on Africans.

I have experienced these types of difficult conversations many times and with a multitude of white people. I think many white folks won't hear or validate my pain because of their fear of being considered racist. As a result, when confronted, they feel compelled to prove their racial innocence to people of color. What these white folks don't seem to understand is that listening with an open mind will help me to trust and appreciate you. On the flip side, not allowing yourself to feel, hear, try to understand and appreciate my cultural pain is what causes me to conclude that you are contributing to racism. I wish white people would see that listening and caring is a first step to unlearning racism.

INEZ TORRES

I would tell whites the same things I tell people of color. A clear definition is no more helpful than clear historical illustrations. It isn't enough to talk about how the children of color and their day camp were expelled from the Philadelphia swim club; we must talk about how the mental illnesses of internalized privilege and internalized inferiority were first formed in the history of these United States. I might give them the book *Lies My Teacher Told Me* or *When Affirmative Action Was White* and we would walk through these books slowly, compassionately, perhaps having each person journal their heart responses.

CAROL WALSH

I don't think I have ever brought up issues of race or racism unless the situation called for it. Unless I was in a consultation, training, a classroom, or engaged in a conversation where these issues (or peripheral issues related to race like Hurricane Katrina and the remaining desolation of much of New Orleans) arose, I would normally not bring up the issue.

HELEN YE

Some of my more recent truth-telling about racism has been difficult, but has resulted in positive outcomes. After some colleagues left my workplace, I spoke up at a staff meeting with my personal observations of perceived patterns of treatment, hiring and promotions in the organization. I also included a review and summary of a research article on racism in the United States.

Instead of just venting and mulling my frustrations in private like many other people feeling trapped or stuck in similar situations, I decided to speak up and make suggestions to help change some of the patterns observed in the department while also findings ways to support the department's and organization's goals. As a result of my speaking up, I now lead the department's work on diversity and cultural competency and am supported by the department's leadership as well as the larger organization's leadership.

CAMISHA L. JONES

Bringing up issues of race and racism always involves risks. I do it whenever I deem the situation demands it. Sometimes I do it because a white person has made a comment that reveals a blind spot they have. Sometimes because something has been said repeatedly that makes me uncomfortable. Sometimes I speak simply to "be me," to be true and vocal about what I think and believe. I prefer to do this when I know a white ally is present who would back me up but it isn't completely necessary. It always feels like I am laying myself on an altar. It is a sacrifice, usually a painful one, with no guarantee of effectiveness.

YUKARI TAKIMOTO AMOS

As Katz (2003) recommends, whites need to confront white racism without minority folks. With the presence of people of color, whites get busy defending their whiteness and never make progress. A white-on-white workshop is ideal. Also, with the presence of people of color, it is they who need to teach whites, and whites don't like to be taught by people of color.

CAROLYN BERNARD

It honestly depends on the white folks in question. Some people need to be approached very carefully and never head-on because if they feel disadvantaged in a conversation, they will become too defensive to hear anything I am saying. It's difficult to speak to these folks, but I find the most effective thing to do is to try to explain the difference between institutional racism and individual bigotry. The biggest hurdle, in my experience, for white folks in discussing racism is for them to understand racism as an institution. Once that hurdle is jumped, they can begin to see how that institution is omnipresent in all our lives.

There is a tool called the "racism bingo card." There are many versions out there on the internet, but they all depict a number of common denials heard from white folks in discussions of racism. It can sometimes be effective for a defensive white person to see a bingo card, because when they recognize their own tired objections in the card, they may begin to realize that they are in fact a part of institutional racism, and that their denials are neither unique nor powerful arguments.

But I think the most basic effective way to bring up issues of race and racism with white folks is to let them know how it affects your life. Our lives. White folks need to see that racism affects the people around them, people they can see and hear, people they can reach out and touch. It is not a vague concept or a thing of the past—it is right here in our lives, in our daily experiences, and we need them to acknowledge it.

CLAUDIA SHIELDS

I teach classes on racism to students studying to be marriage and family therapists, and the majority of my students are white. I guess you could say that I tell whites the truth about racism for a living. Over the years, I have had many beautiful, stimulating conversations with whites about the topic, and many times they seem to be appreciative of having had the truth told to them and they seem to appreciate being able to ask me questions about it. Many also tell me that the class has changed their lives.

Now, that being said, I have to also acknowledge that telling the truth to whites about racism in a class is a bit different because they don't get to "walk away" from the conversation because their grade depends on it. I hold the power—which is often not the case when a person of color talks about racism. That means they may stand to lose something just by having the conversation. Even in my classes, often my students become extremely angry at me for what I'm teaching them. I consider this angry phase part of the developmental process on the road to becoming multi-culturally competent. One of the greatest hurdles is to convince them that they can acknowledge that racism is real, without feeling that they are being personally accused of it. Once I can move them from the defensive posture, they can begin to listen. This requires moving them to an understanding that what we are talking about is a racist system that is centuries old, rather than necessarily suggesting that there is any individual act for which they are responsible.

This helps a bit, but as they begin to understand that they have benefited from this system, then comes the next phase. It's characterized by feelings of guilt and shame for just being white. From what I've been able to tell from their descriptions of these feelings, this seems to be akin to survivor guilt. Once I can move them toward a position of grace toward themselves, the conversation begins to change. I think that the fact that an African American person, who is clearly concerned about racism, would take the stance of moving them toward a position of grace and self-forgiveness makes a powerful impact. It is such an unexpected message. They often come into the class assuming that I am there to accuse them and to hastily give them a failing grade if they exhibit one ounce of racism.

Once they understand that this is not the case, they begin to become less defensive, open their minds, and the learning begins. This is also a very painful process because they begin to see that the world can be profoundly unfair—not at all the "level playing field" they thought it was. They then experience a very painful awakening and they become angry—not at me now, but at the educational process that has previously failed them. After weeks of being presented with factual information and compelling personal testimonies of students of color in the class or in the book of essays I use, they often say, "Why hasn't anyone told us this before?!" These are graduate students—many of them over 40—and they are appalled that they are learning this for the first time. It is as if at that moment they clearly see how systematic, macro-structural racism has even impacted the educational system. At that moment they begin to understand that they lived in a "world" that insulated them from some horrible and very present truths and, often, they begin to cry. I look at their tear-streaked faces and remind them that because they are beginning to see that world and to feel the pain of it, they are on the path to being able to develop healing empathy for their clients who "live there."

——·—— WHAT WORKS ——·——

In order to unlearn racism, what do you need or want from white folks?

GENNY LIM

I need respect, honesty, openness and integrity. Without respect there is not even a glimmer of hope. Without honesty and openness there can be no real dialogue, only superficial conversation. Without moral integrity, there is no basis for social change or self-transformation. Without self-transformation there can be no social transformation. The one informs the other and vice versa. The microcosm has to reflect the macrocosm. Our intentions have to reflect the greater goal for social harmony and equality. The process of unlearning racism requires astute and often painful self-reflection, self-criticism and self-honesty. There is so much denial about racism that the first step is to understand that racism does exist. Once that is understood, the next step is to see where it rears its ugly head. Sometimes it is much closer to home than we care to admit. Once embedded in racist structures, then it is always going to be a one-way street of frustration and resentment.

INEZ TORRES

I need them to do their own work so that they can retrace the history of this country with some authenticity and truth. I need them to go into themselves and get in touch with their own feelings of broken-ness and abuse—because they were abused when they were given all of those lies. I need them to learn how to hold those pieces with compassion. I need them to name their pain. The more recent arrivals—those that love to say their grandparents never owned slaves or shot an Indian—I need those to count the loss that was forced upon their predecessors when those first arrivals let go of their own roots for the ability to become white and privileged.

DENNARD CLENDENIN

I would need a total unconditional commitment from white people to go beyond hearing me. By that I mean it's one thing to hear something that is being said. It is another thing to actually listen and comprehend what has been said. And it is important to me that they believe in what I'm saying. My experiences don't come from a vacuum. These are things that have actually happened to me, by virtue of the color of my skin.

I want white people to suspend judgment to the extent that they can, and listen with open minds and hearts. I want them to "hang in there," and listen to some uncomfortable things. As a friend of mine once said, "The cure for the pain is in the pain." White folks need to step out of their skins and stop getting defensive. When I say white people do this, or that, they must not take it personally. I do not qualify my stories by making exceptions of the whites who are present, and I don't feel that it is my responsibility to make them feel comfortable.

WAYNE DOWNEY

White folks are going to have to take on the task of teaching themselves how to not be racist. Whites have to be responsible for policing their own racist behavior. I want whites to begin to do some of the heavy lifting because this job is too exhausting for the limited number of educated people of color. If whites feel like they are not up to the task because they've never had to do this before, and I'm asked to continue to educate, I have several requests. I want $1 million per year to include a full staff. I don't ever want to pay taxes again for a system that does not have my best interest at heart. Two months paid vacation per year at a destination of my choice to include psychological rehabilitation, physical rehabilitation, and current reliable data about the behavior of those who identify as white.

CAROLYN BERNARD

I want white folks to listen to people of color. I want them to stop trying to define racism for us. I want them to use their eyes and their ears, to see us and hear us and to know what we experience. I want them to unpack their privilege and take a good, hard look at it. I want them to stop patting each other on the back and to start paying attention to the institution of racism.

ERIC LACKIE

I wish that white folks would get in touch with their ideas about what racism is and maybe even gather the courage to explore these ideas with people of color. How can we even begin to unlearn racism if we are not clear or in agreement about what racism is?

Also, I'd love for white people to replace their claims of being non-racist with a deeper awareness of the fears associated with what it feels like to be considered a racist.

1. What are you afraid will happen if a person of color does consider you racist?
2. What do you think is the best response to a person of color who accuses you of being racist?
3. What do you think is the best response to a person of color who feels offended by a racially insensitive comment you made?
4. What do you think is the best response to a person of color who tries to explain the intricate ways that racism creeps into the beliefs and behaviors of "well-intentioned" individuals, groups, organizations, or communities?

Johnny Lake

In conversations about race and racism in mixed-race groups it is always interesting that with best intentions I am always asked by white people what is it that I want them to do. Interestingly it is not often asked by white people what they expect of people of color. It seems that my duties respecting racism are already clearly defined. But for white people it often seems important that I function in some way to tell them or inform them what to do about racism. This gets very tiring.

What do I need from you? EVERYTHING.
What do I want from you? NOTHING.
I want nothing from you unless it is something you do without my request, demand or coercion, without blame or guilt.

What do I need from white people? I need for you to STOP—just for a moment—STOP BEING white and just be a human being. RECOGNIZE that your destiny, your success, your well-being is directly tied to mine.

ADMIT that you always choose—as if there is really a choice—WHEN, WHERE, HOW and IF you will even SEE ME—much less truly listen to me, hear me or RECOGNIZE that my very painful existence in this racial context is the consequence of YOU BEING white—and refusing to STOP.

You have a CHOICE—even as it gets narrower and narrower—to CLAIM an existence totally separated from me—while my VERY LIFE depends on you and the CHOICES you make.

What do I want from you? NOTHING.

What do I NEED from you? EVERYTHING.

I need everything that you are as a human being, not as a white person claiming some privilege, to choose to be in this difficult space with me. I need you to be willing to listen and share in the pain we carry, to feel it, to know it, to understand it and then to help, to be courageous, to be willing to work with the ones who are trying to deconstruct the terrible inequities that we both have inherited, but which have benefited you the most, while destroying others.

I do NEED you. And you NEED me. We cannot succeed without each other.

"If you would stop being white I could afford to stop being black."
James Baldwin

Shawn Patrick

I would tell them that racism kills whites just like it kills the person of color. That every white person who is allowed to continue telling the racist joke, supporting sexist dialogue, or perpetuating homophobia hurts whites just as much as me. And I do mean "allowed." I would add that people who are white can do something about this, that it's not just about having a "kind and accepting" attitude, but that you could stop racism if you really wanted to. If every white person decided right now that they would no longer laugh at a racist joke, no one would tell them any more. Most white people tell me they feel "powerless" to act; the irony is they are the most powerful to get anything done about it, if they would choose to hold each other accountable.

Camisha L. Jones

I would urge white people to really look at themselves, to listen to the voices of people of color and then take an inventory of themselves. Racism is just as much about white people as it is about people of color. I'd like white people to stop exempting themselves from the challenge of overcoming racism. I would like white people to stop seeing people of color as the irrational enemy just because what we say and do about racism makes them uncomfortable. Racism makes people of color uncomfortable every single day of their lives. To achieve professional success and for doors of opportunity to open, people of color bend to the rules, standards, processes and procedures that make white people feel comfortable. It will take mutual discomfort to have the difficult conversations, to change our behavior and to make the decisions which will ultimately lead us to better ways to address racism.

What do you think it will take for whites to truly embrace diversity?

Camisha L. Jones

For whites to really embrace diversity and inclusivity, they will need to be willing to be transformed by the truth of people different from themselves. They'll need to get comfortable being uncomfortable, because their growth and the opportunity to cultivate a better world are embedded within that discomfort.

Shawn Patrick

I think if they can truly get how racism damages them as much as it damages people of color; if they can learn that difference is an asset, not a liability; if they can realize that we're not "out to get them," then maybe diversity will be embraced. But, at the same time, I think it will take something very different. The irony is that I teach classes about diversity all the time, and during the semester I will see amazing movement in students. Yet at the end of the term, I am always afraid to look ahead to see who really takes on the ideas, and who lets them all go now that the grade has been assigned. I do believe that no one will embrace diversity if they think they are forced to.

Gia Overton

When whites become the racial minority and the socioeconomic minority, only then will they understand what it is to be like us, and hopefully then they will embrace diversity.

De Andre Drake

I think whites do embrace diversity to a certain extent but on their own terms, by their own rules and beliefs, by telling us how we should feel, think or react to race issues, and if we do it the way they deem it should be done, then everything is okay.

Ijeoma Nwaogu

It will take a white male to tell other white people the truth. White people will not believe it if it comes from a POC.

Genny Lim

The day they realize that the odds are no long in their favor and that by not letting go of the reins they are only going to be dragged by other forces beyond their control. The global economy is contingent on foreign collaboration and our national economy is contingent on racial harmony. You can only oppress people for so long before the situation explodes. Until whites face the truth and reality of white privilege and its historical roots and stop perpetuating its pernicious cycle, diversity will only be a motto or vision, rather than a fact.

J.C. Eaglesmith

To allow the power of silence to lead to the journey through the "Hoop of Respect: Knowledge, Experience, Understanding and Wisdom."

Razia Kosi

They would have to trust that the people who have been subjugated to lower status will not treat them in the same inequitable or inhuman manner as many whites have done to groups other than whites. This would mean letting go of fear, entitlement and privilege in today's society. I think many people are ready to embrace diversity. Unfortunately, there is still a group of people who stay rooted in fear perhaps because they have the most to lose in embracing diversity. They need to hear and believe from other whites that they haven't lost anything by embracing diversity and have instead gained more in their lives by doing so

C. Spencer

Death of the planet as we know it and a start over from God.

Carolyn Bernard

I honestly think that until people of color are well represented in the media, whites will continue to ignore, dismiss and stereotype us. I can't give every white a person of color to be friends with, and I wouldn't wish that responsibility on any person of color. But movies, television and the news reach so many people at once. If people of color were represented with the kind of frequency, variety, and prominence that white folk are, I truly think that whites all over would start to embrace diversity.

HELEN YE

I think whites need to feel safe and need to be told the truth about history and current events in an open and honest conversation. The sharing of deeply personal human experiences from individuals from all backgrounds can be the common ground. Perhaps they need the additional reinforcement that retribution towards them will not occur.

JIM PEAL

White people need to learn from people of color how to be respectful of people who are not like them.

WAYNE DOWNEY

When their livelihood, their ability to function and survive in the world depends upon their ability and willingness to embrace diverse experiences, when it gets to the point where whites understand that they will die unless they embrace diversity, I believe they will choose to live.

How can white people help raise issues of racism when many whites like to believe that we have "transcended" race divisions and inequity is a thing of the past?

SHAWN PATRICK

I believe other white people can bring up the issues just by challenging the idea that we've transcended all divisions. Acknowledging that some progress has been made can be useful, but a white person could add that there is still more to be done. Pointing out that one or two highly public examples of a non-white person achieving success (e.g., President Obama) doesn't mean that every person of color in the country is suddenly on equal footing. Others can point out that for every story like the president's we see hundreds of similar stories about people who are white. How many stories like President Obama's need to be told before people no longer need to point out that we have a president of color? Or perhaps pointing out that in order to be seen as an equal, a person has to achieve the status of president in order to be recognized. These types of challenges can be done in a way that doesn't disrespect the other. But I think it's more important for a white person to realize that when these challenges come from someone who is white, that challenge has a greater chance of being heard than when it comes from a person of color.

CAROLYN BERNARD

White allies are important to the fight against racism because they can use their own white privilege to be heard where we are not.

ERIC LACKIE

You, as white people, can try looking back on fixed beliefs that you once held and recall how someone else tried or succeeded in helping you to change your thinking. How did they do it? Did they talk with you once or over a series of discussions? Did they argue with you, call in others to reason with you, recommend to you a movie, book, class, or an event? Consider how the same methods which helped to change your thinking may also help to raise issues of racism with whites who believe we have transcended race divisions. Also, when I encounter whites who discount my concerns about racism with counter-beliefs and counterarguments, I typically share those experiences with my supportive peers and family. This is where I can get validation and brainstorm new ways to raise issues of racism with unreceptive whites.

RAZIA KOSI

White people are critical to raising the issues of racism especially since many whites believe we have "transcended" race divisions and inequity. Challenging the conversations that increase racial divisions and inequities will be ripe in spaces exclusive to white folks. In those spaces, whites who want to create a new future need to share their voice and vision so issues of race and inequities are truly of the past.

CAROL WALSH

Whites need to learn to find real-world and current situations in which racism is the only possible response to the question posed. Whites don't experience racism, so seeing it and believing it will be difficult for many. Even those who believe it have no idea of the magnitude of its current existence and the impact it has upon people of color. However, real-world examples can help whites to stop "debating" the issue and begin to see that we, as a people, have never transcended race, but rather suppressed it.

YUKARI TAKIMOTO AMOS

Present statistics of inequality and inequity such as income gap and achievement gap between whites and people of color. Show pictures where poor people of color live. Show pictures of the rich community and have them analyze what kind of people live there. Have them analyze these inequalities and inequities without having them say, "...because people of color don't want to work. They don't have a good work ethic." If whites are prohibited from attributing inequality and inequity to an individual effort, they are forced to think other ways, more from a sociological viewpoint.

INDIGO VIOLET

I believe whites need to educate themselves and help to educate others. I always recommend the PBS documentary, *Race: The Power of An Illusion/Part III: The House We Live In,* as an excellent film that makes clear how past practices of racial discrimination have led to present-day disparities. It helps to dispel the "we've transcended race" mythology because it shows the structural, material, and economic benefits that have been officially granted to whites to the detriment of peoples of color.

What makes a white person "safe and reliable"?

CAROLYN BERNARD

White people can help raise awareness about racism by interrupting comments implying that we have transcended race divisions and by sharing examples of their own experiences with racism. They can talk about the stereotypes they have held, how they became aware of them and what they are doing to unlearn them. They can talk about the fact that it is possible to be a "good person" and still have racist beliefs and practices. They can share statistics and institutionalized practices that reveal current-day injustices that people of color endure. They can take the time to learn about the contributions of people of color and tell their kids about them. They can put themselves in the position of being a minority every now and then by attending events attended predominantly by people of color. They can ask good questions. They can ask for feedback. They can listen.

Knowing that they understand how race affects the both of us and that they are committed to being anti-racist makes them safe. Knowing that they will speak out against racism when they encounter it makes them reliable.

MARY WEEMS

My knowledge of their willingness to work against the white-dominant status quo in this country for equity and justice. As Lisa Heldke points out in her essay, "On Being a Responsible Traitor," white folks who take this position are often considered traitors by other whites who don't understand why they refuse to conform in a country that was founded by white men for white people.

WAYNE DOWNEY

A person who is vulnerable, who is willing to acknowledge their shortcomings, who is willing to be very open about his concerns and fears about race. He has a willingness to have fear, to be afraid that he might be misperceived. He has a willingness to get down in the trenches as some of the rest of us are put in positions to do on a semi-regular basis.

ERIC LACKIE

I respect white people who advocate for racial equality and social justice even when there are no people of color around to support them. I know a high school track and field coach who is white and who openly acknowledges many of the challenges that people of color and disadvantaged white kids face. In high school I remember him being very forthcoming with me about his perceptions of the racial sensitivities or insensitivities of other white faculty. It felt enormously validating to have a white adult be so honest with me about things I already knew to be true. Bob frequently reminded me of my strengths, provided opportunities for me to succeed, and appreciated my view of the world developed largely from my ethnic background and unique cultural experiences. Most of my life it's been unlikely for a white person to validate my feelings as an African American, let alone advocate on my behalf or for other people of color. Bob went out of his way to make sure that students of color were treated with the same level of respect that any human deserves. I've always known that I could trust Bob to listen, care about what I have to say, apologize when needed, advocate on my behalf, and be transparent and honest with me. I have the utmost respect for Bob.

Toni Adams

A friend is a friend without regard to race.

Travis Smith

One who understands that they've been used to push the agenda of the bankers and the oligarchy, and has decided to fight against it, I would deem semi-safe. Aldous Huxley wrote in *Brave New World*, "A really efficient totalitarian state would be one in which the all-powerful executive of political bosses and their army of managers control a population of slaves who do not have to be coerced because they love their servitude." I think it is imperative for a "white" person to know how they've been and are being used to further the agenda of the few who erect the policies and finance white hegemony! If they're against it, cool! But if not, then I know where they stand! Once they understand how they're complicit in white hegemony, consciously and/or unconsciously, then we can establish something and secure a relationship. I'm secure in knowing that you know what's going on!

Carol Walsh

One who accepts me as I am. Someone who treasures my contribution (as a person) to their life. Someone who can talk about these issues (of racism) openly and honestly. Someone who admits their ignorance and their desire to learn and grow. Someone who seeks me out and doesn't require me to "bow" in gratitude and humility because they dared to acknowledge me or grace me with their presence. Genuine and authentic people without agenda, motive, or plan are safe and reliable to me.

Camisha L. Jones

I consider a white person "safe and reliable" when they are actively unlearning their bias, when I see them putting themselves on the line, and taking risks to have honest conversations about race, and taking action in addressing unjust situations. I consider a person "safe and reliable" when they are open to receiving feedback on ways to become more inclusive and aware. For instance, I once had a supervisor who used the phrase "tar baby" in a meeting. He had learned the phrase growing up as a way to refer to a sticky or complicated situation. I, however, knew it as a derogatory way of referring to a black person. I was in complete shock when he used the phrase because I knew him to be an ally. I worked up the confidence to talk to him about it. He said he sensed that something was wrong during the meeting, listened to what I said and apologized for the discomfort he caused. He had never known that the phrase had a derogatory meaning. He then offered to follow up with the rest of the staff to address the situation. After the meeting he did some research on Brer Rabbit and the phrase "tar baby." He later let me know about what he learned. Ultimately, he thanked me for introducing him to the new information. He is someone I trust because I know even when he falls short, we can talk about it and he'll be open to receiving the feedback.

Indigo Violet

When they do their work to undo racism and stop projecting wacky desires for approval on to me.

Yukari Takimoto Amos

Let me give you an example of my husband's behavior. What I like about him is the fact that he actually listens to my opinion. Whenever I tell him my experience as a minority, he tries to understand it from my point of view, instead of saying, "No, you are thinking too much. That has nothing to do with race." A white person needs to seriously listen to the ideas of a person of color, instead of always producing alternative interpretations which deny the possibility of racism and white privilege.

What can a white person do to alleviate racism?

Erin Yoshimura

Believe. Believe that racism exists without needing constant tangible proof and work on challenging their own layers of racist and stereotypical beliefs—we all have them. This means that this is a lifelong journey. It also helps if white people become acutely aware of how they benefit from racism.

Standing behind a "shield of good intentions" does nothing to alleviate racism and basically lets white folks off the hook. White people need to step out from behind the shield and become more responsible for their impact. Just like if you rear-end someone with your car. You didn't intend to hit another car yet are responsible to pay for damages regardless.

Another way for white people to alleviate racism is if they witness a racist incident, then say something! They don't realize by "minding their own business" that they're indirectly condoning the racist act.

When my son was six or seven years old, we went to the dry cleaner's in search of my favorite sweater that I misplaced, hoping I forgot that I dropped it off there.

Upon entering the store, I noticed the drop-off line was really long and the pick-up counter was empty and, without much thought, went to the pick-up counter. After learning that my sweater wasn't there, I turned to leave when the clerk who just helped me said, "Next." A white woman walked up from the drop-off line and sneered at me, "This is the way we do things here in America, we take turns! If you choose to live in this country, you should learn that!"

I didn't realize that there was one line was for both pick-up and drop-off and, although I made a mistake, it was automatic that my race had something to do with it. Even though my great-grandparents immigrated here in the early 1900's, I'm still seen as a foreigner.

Out of 15 white people in the store, not one person said a thing. That would have been a perfect time for a white person to say something in my defense, but they all stood there quietly. And, yes, they all heard what was going on because the place was small and quiet.

Sadly, this exchange had a negative impact on my son. He was shocked, scared and embarrassed. I was sad that he had to witness such blatant racism at such a young age and probably learned that no one will stick up for him in the future.

Toni Adams

Have a black child or grandchild who is subjected to racism. Gives an entirely new perspective when it is a loved one.

CAROLYN BERNARD

The number-one thing a white person can do to alleviate racism is listen to people of color when they talk about racism. The number-two thing that a white person can do to alleviate racism is to examine their own privilege and attempt to eliminate racism from their own words, actions and thoughts. And the third thing that a white person can do to alleviate racism, once they have done (or are doing) the other two things, is to speak up against racism when they encounter it. They can do this by supporting anti-racist causes, by calling out the people around them who perpetuate racism, and by continuing to educate themselves about race and racism.

SHAWN PATRICK

A white person can challenge expressions of racism whenever they appear, whether that is a racist joke, an expression of ignorance, or a blatant stereotyping. These challenges do not have to be highly confrontational, either; it can be the simple yet direct approach of not laughing at the joke, offering counter-information, or posing a question. For example, if someone tells a joke and no one laughs, the joke won't be told anymore. This is how we shape norms in society, how we let others know what we will accept and won't accept. We do this all the time in our interactions; white people can choose to alter their interactions to make racism an unacceptable behavior.

A white person is not powerless to change racism; in fact a white person holds the most power in being able to change these norms. If a large group of white people came together and said, "We're not going to tolerate this from anyone," the norm of racism would have to change.

SONYA LITTLEDEER-EVANS

There are many things that white people can do to help alleviate racism. First, however, must come the awareness of how they are advantaged by racism. Once this awareness exists, then comes the accountability. To help alleviate racism, a white person must be accountable for the times that they benefit from racism and try and make a change to those circumstances. They must be accountable in front of other whites for receiving such benefit and help point out to other whites how they benefit from racism. Whites must also be able to see their own biases when dealing with racism and set those aside as appropriate. It is hard to admit that we all have biases, but it seems most often that it is harder for whites to admit this, especially in front of other whites, because racism is so prevalent. But even though this is hard, it is the work that must be done, because every time this type of accountability is taken, it is one step closer to the walls being broken down, one step closer to whites holding other whites accountable, one step closer to a person of color being able to believe in whites, and perhaps one more person becoming aware of their own role in the disease of racism. Once these steps start in motion, we are all on the path to alleviating racism.

Razia Kosi

If the white person can acknowledge that meritocracy is currently unavailable to every single person in this country, then we can have some honest conversations. A white person can also alleviate racism by speaking up in circles when people of color are not present. White people will say things to other white people that they would not say in front of people of color. White people who want to alleviate racism must speak up about racism, ask a question about a racist comment, inject another voice and perspective from a white person's perspective who does not want to have a passive role in perpetuating racism. Working to change policy, laws and practices that have benefited white people would be the next steps in the progression to end racism.

Yukari Takimoto Amos

Color-blindness is actually a type of racism (Bonilla-Silva, 2003) that completely ignores the social hierarchy embedded in various racial groups in the United States. Whites need to recognize that it is possible for any whites to participate in racism without their being racist themselves.

Carol Walsh

First, admit racism continues to exist today. Second, educate themselves on institutional racism and systems of oppression that are still very much present in our society today. Third, become an ally in this work. This does not mean they need to leave/end their friendships or remove themselves from their positions of privilege, but rather use these positions and friendships to educate their constituents and discourage racist practices. They must constantly remind their white colleagues why the alleviation of racism is not just the passion of a person of color but is a requirement for those who are in the majority dominant group.

Eric Lackie

A couple years ago I watched a television documentary in which high school youth were taught about the history of racism in the United States. Many of the white youth expressed shock and disbelief that anyone could be so hurtful. I remember appreciating the empathy expressed by the youth, yet I also felt a desire to educate them further. For example, while many whites seem appalled when hearing reports of the insensitivities and prejudices of others, they also seem largely unaware of their own racial insensitivities and contributions to racism.

White people can alleviate racism by first unlearning the racist thoughts and behaviors that exist within themselves. I feel more encouraged by white people who discover and admit their own contributions to racism than by those who hide themselves (and hide from themselves) by projecting criticisms onto other racist whites. I believe that whites who successfully work through their own racial fears and prejudices are in a much healthier position to alleviate racism in their families, at their schools and jobs, or in areas such as politics and religion. The opportunities are endless.

How do you think whites can be effective allies to people of color?

Indigo Violet

By doing their work to unlearn racism and in supporting and challenging other white people to do the same.

Helen Ye

Whites can be more effective allies to people of color by speaking on their behalf when someone says something that is inaccurate or wrong about an individual or group of people. They can also advocate for more political and financial inclusion and monies towards work and services for people of color, and to include people of color in decisions affecting our/their communities. And whites can be more effective allies by intentionally seeking out direct experiences with people from different backgrounds and striving to engage in cross-cultural endeavors.

GENNY LIM

For one thing, they need to take a back seat and listen before always trying to take charge. It is truly disturbing to see how whites habitually take over the leadership roles of every organization they join. So many have that "me first" attitude that allowed them to forge ahead and conquer the West, but they really need to take a back seat sometimes and stop driving the car. This compulsive egomaniacal approach to political and social organization is counterproductive to building community and coalitions across differences.

Whites often have a hard time really listening. I often think they only listen selectively for things that will reinforce their own thinking and agendas. I've worked with so many who typically want to be the center of attention, or they become petulant, despondent and negative. The spoiled-child syndrome is the net result of an upbringing of privileges. Some never quite outgrow this self-centered tendency and if tolerated by people of color it can eventually derail group cohesion and cooperation. If they want to be effective allies they need to learn that leadership is not always a top-down hierarchy. In fact, hidden leadership is more characteristic of communities of color, where elders are given more respect than others for their experience and wisdom. Leadership is more often an earned seat of authority, where the individual has proven themselves though acts of courage, generosity and fairness. Whites have much to learn about alternative models of leadership.

WAYNE DOWNEY

Whites need to go out and fall in love with a person of color and have children. Once whites have gained the first-hand experience of being treated poorly because of their associations, i.e., family and children, the dynamics of this conversation will change.

CAROLYN BERNARD

Above all, whites need to listen to us if they are going to be effective allies. They need to listen without getting defensive, without fighting, without denying. Then they need to speak up. They need to speak to other white people. They need to break the silence, and they need to be serious about it. They need to stop defining racism for themselves and hear what people of color are saying. People of color have voices, and we are talking about our experiences, but white people continue to not listen.

Razia Kosi

In order for whites to be effective allies they would need to examine what a world would look like if they were not in a power position or did not have access to privilege above others. They must be willing to create a society that values each person's individual gifts and talents. Trust is also a critical factor for both whites and people of color to become allies in ending racism.

Gia Overton

Ask questions. Take the time to get to know us. Share your assumptions with us so we can correct or confirm them. We are all human beings, regardless of our skin color, ethnicity, socioeconomic level, sexual orientation, religion, age or gender. Let's work together and make OUR world a better place!

Eric Lackie

Many of my white allies are supportive of any concerns I voice about the racially insensitive acts of other whites. However, I believe these allies also prefer that our friendship would exclude them from being confronted should I have any concerns about their racial insensitivities. Since my goal is to combat racism wherever it shows, I hope that whites will increase their ability to accept critical feedback, even from people of color they feel close to. Your ability to accept my feedback will increase my respect for you as a white person and deepen my consideration of you as a true ally.

$$\text{---} \cdot \text{--- OUR FUTURE ---} \cdot \text{---}$$

What do reparations look like for you?

CAROLYN BERNARD

I think it would be impossible to effectively pay reparations to people wronged by racism. The most meaningful reparation, in my opinion, would be to both acknowledge the contributions that people of color have made, willingly and unwillingly, to the foundation and success of this country, and also to actively work towards a future of equality.

RAZIA KOSI

I can't fathom a monetary value for all that has been stolen from the people who were kidnapped from Africa and then enslaved to build this country. If my children were stolen from my arms and enslaved to work for their entire lifetime, I can't imagine a payment for their future great-great-great-great-grandchildren that would make up for the horror, loss and trauma caused us. I don't think reparations would stop at a monetary compensation alone, nor do I think a formal apology would be enough either. I honestly do not know what would make amends for the wrong that was done.

MARY WEEMS

They don't look like anything because while, ideally, I can certainly understand why many black folks of note believe we deserve them and often use the precedent-setting argument that many of the Japanese families with family members who were forced into American concentration camps during World War II received reparations, I don't believe they will ever be awarded. If they were, how much money or anything would be enough to even begin to compensate black people for slavery and the post-slavery reality of racism all of us continue to live with each day?

WAYNE DOWNEY

There are certain systems and agencies that are designed to prevent or address or investigate allegations of race-based animus. Ones that are actually utilized in practice and not just on paper would be a clear indicator of reparations. An opportunity for people to go to college regardless of who they are would be an excellent example of reparations. I don't know that varying income ratios would be appropriate, but I'm sure that a Negro could argue that because they are experiencing some social animus, having a lesser tax bracket would not necessarily be adequate compensation for being inconvenienced. Enforcing the laws that pertain to civil rights, taking allegations seriously of racial animus as opposed to dismissing them would be excellent examples of reparations. And there has to be some public acknowledgement that if it wasn't for the exploitation of African people, these American people, this country would not be in the position that it is in today as being one of the largest global influences on the planet.

SHAWN PATRICK

I am not so certain about reparations. I can speak better to the idea of forgiveness. I say this in terms of forgiveness being a relational process, where both sides have come together with the victims wanting to forgive and the offenders wanting to be forgiven. I also believe this to be an ongoing process; in other words just saying "I'm sorry" is only a start, not a finish. For some non-dominant groups, so much has been taken away that I don't know if there is a way to give it back. But perhaps it would make a difference if the stories of those who have been offended against could be told in their own words. When these stories achieve the status of dominant voices, then I believe work can be done to create a different society based on equality. I think reparations would need to be forward-thinking as opposed to only making up for past wrongs.

TONI ADAMS

Since we never received our 40 acres and mule, it looks like "fantasy."

TRAVIS SMITH

I can't see any offering that can repair what's been done to my people! There was a student at Tuskegee Institute in Alabama who went to a filling station about a block off Tuskegee town square. While there, he used the "white men's room." The owner, in his rage and ignorance—backed only by his "privilege"— shot and killed him. He was acquitted by an all-white jury. That young man's name was Sammy Young, Jr. How do you repair the damage that's been done to his family? By giving them the store or the county? None of which will right that wrong! He's only one of too many that has been murdered in the name of white hegemony and ignorance!

Do you know how many women jumped overboard with their babies rather than finish out the dreadful journey into slavery? Do you know how many died as a result of being cramped in a hold, 18 inches in diameter, at the bottom of a ship for a 9,000 mile ride? No animal has ever been brought out of Africa under such conditions! When you've lost a language you've lost a memory, a transmission of wisdom from those who've come before you!

So to answer your question, I'm not sure what it would look like. I know you can't explain the modern world without talking about slavery! And I also know that no matter where I look in the modern world I find my people at the bottom and those who identify as white at the top. When the poorest people in Colombia, the United States, Brazil, Jamaica, Haiti, etc...are those of African or indigenous descent, and the offspring of the colonialist and colonizers are living well—something must be done!

I don't think a lot of us (Africans in the Americas) feel that it's going to happen, at least I don't! Not on basic human terms where we'll talk, negotiate and produce fruit. I'm sure it's the last thing on Obama's mind! It's not "politically expedient," or it's "too divisive." What I do know is if we let whites dictate the outcome there will be no outcome! As Frederick Douglass noted, speaking in terms of whites, "They'll always do wrong by choice and right for necessity." My guiding premise is we must do something for ourselves! I'm not expecting anything from you but more hard times!

YUKARI TAKIMOTO AMOS

In the film, *The Color of Fear*, a Chinese man said with a determined voice, "All I want is justice." I totally agree with him. No money, no apology, but I want justice. When we saw this film in class, a white male student yelled in anger, "What does that Chinese man mean? What is he talking about?" Justice means that we don't have a person like him who even questions what justice means.

CAROL WALSH

The institutional system that is set up to privilege whites should be reconstituted to advantage others. This would take the form of monetary, educational, and systemic/political/industrial power. There should be funds and land provided to African Americans, not in the form of a check, but rather in trust and endowments. Educational opportunities, since they were denied African Americans for centuries, should be provided at the top institutions free of charge. Finally, for real reparations to take place in perpetuity, systemic/political/industrial power must be vested in the minority population of people of color. This will allow policies and large-scale decisions to be made that would always benefit and advance people of color.

CAMISHA L. JONES

Reparations must involve more than financial compensation. If there are to be reparations, they must take into account what was stolen through injustice. For instance, I think reparations would need to be designed to rebuild business and work opportunities in poor neighborhoods to address the deliberate destruction of thriving black neighborhoods and the ways that racism has led to a link between poverty and race. Adequate reparations might be to provide incentives for businesses to open in red-lined neighborhoods and for them to offer youth internships and job training programs there. It would not matter if people who were not racial minorities could access these opportunities, the point would be to offer more job opportunities than those for unskilled labor in those neighborhoods. Additionally, as a way to access the incentives, perhaps the leaders of the businesses that open in those neighborhoods would need to take a course in the history of that neighborhood to encourage honoring its diversity. Another way reparations could address what's been stolen might be to research instances in which land was stolen from people of color or places where people of color were run out of town. Whatever they owned before these situations (or comparable financial compensation or credit) could be returned to the descendents of those families. Reparations would also need to address the ways that the justice system unequally punishes people of color. Given the ways that racism has impacted the economic well-being of people of color and the connections between poverty and crime, I think reparations could include a stronger program of prevention and rehabilitation within the justice system, particularly for young offenders. Again, it might be a good idea to connect such opportunities to neighborhoods whose history includes racial injustice and a high concentration of people being sent to jail. So prevention activities and re-entry support programs might be located in these neighborhoods.

MICHAEL LESLIE

The equivalent of 40 acres and a mule today, paid in cash or in kind to every African American today. In kind could translate as free mental and physical health care, free pre-K through higher education at the best institutions in the country, and quality subsidized food, clothing and shelter for all African Americans.

INDIGO VIOLET

Economic equality for all people of color—African Americans, Puerto Ricans, Chicanos, Native Americans, Chinese and Japanese Americans, along with all recent immigrant groups of color—revitalization of and investment in people of color communities including neighborhoods, schools, and job creation, re-negotiation of sovereignty and land usage for Native Americans, school curriculum that is actively anti-racist and fully multicultural, a sustained national dialogue and healing/reconciliation around race, ethnicity, and culture, an end to anti-immigrant policies and attitudes, and full affirmative action to ensure ongoing equality of opportunity.

ERIC LACKIE

BELIEF

I believe that a first step to making repairs is to acknowledge that damage has been done. For example, will you believe me when I tell you that as a person of color I have been hurt by whites who were either insensitive or actively racist and that I have not yet recovered from my injuries? Will you believe me or will you be surprised and deny it if I tell you that you are behaving or have behaved in ways that contribute to my injuries as a person of color?

UNDERSTANDING

A doctor's ability to determine a cure is enhanced by what they know about the nature of an injury and the extent of the damage. This information or awareness also applies to repairing emotional hurts in human relationships. For example, are you willing to step out of your comfort and hear my pain as a person of color, or is that too much for you to tolerate? Can you see things from my perspective? Can you step into my shoes and understand the pain and anger that would come from being mistreated as a person of color? Do you understand the logic behind why I am hurting?

RESPECT

The act of being respectful requires different attitudes and actions for different situations. There is no one way to show respect that applies to everyone. Also, what may seem like common sense or common practice to one group may not be so common to another. Do you plan to treat me with the kind of attitude that you think is respectful, or are you willing to learn the comments and behaviors that actually make me feel respected?

WILLINGNESS

An important factor in making repairs is a person's willingness to do the work. Simply acknowledging that your spouse or partner is hurting or that you have done something to hurt their feelings is only a first step. Relationships have more potential to thrive with each person's active participation in the healing process. Some examples of this participation can include spending more quality time together, honoring emotional space, going to counseling, and being more helpful around the house. With regards to culture, how willing are you to become a more active participant in the process of promoting the unlearning of racism?

What signposts do you keep an eye out for that signal the overcoming of racism in our society?

SHAWN PATRICK

It might be a simple signpost, but I find it remarkable when people have honest conversations about racism. Not just conversations that identify the problem, but conversations where everyone involved is able to state their own participation in racism or expressions of privilege. Also conversations where everyone can put defensiveness aside and start to hear the experiences of the other, even if those experiences are contradictory. In other words, I find it encouraging when people can put their own fears and injuries aside and empathize with the other, even if it means hearing difficult things about members of your own group. I think this is progress; it may even be an expression of equality—that my story carries as much value as yours.

CAROLYN BERNARD

Honestly, I keep my eyes on the media. It sounds superficial, but I truly believe that what we consume as entertainment both reflects and informs current attitudes about race in our society. The media is a distillation of what is going on in society, and you can see race relations reflected there, and you can also see how the media influences race relations. So I look for people of color in the media, and I look at what people say about them. What parts are available for actors of color? How are they received? I feel that when I see as many people of color in the media as I do whites, I will know we are getting somewhere good. There is still such a paucity of non-white faces, particularly in Hollywood and on American television. People of color are still getting the stereotyped, supporting roles. When a film or television show defies this trend, I feel hopeful.

ERIN YOSHIMURA

I can't think of any signals of overcoming racism in our society—more like we're becoming more inclusive and mindful of accurate portrayals mainly in pop culture. I'll never forget the first time I saw someone who looked like me in a commercial where she was the main spokesperson and spoke perfect English. Wow, I exist! That was about four years ago.

Today, I'm starting to see more Asian American actors on TV and in movies break with the stereotypical roles of the geek, geisha or martial artist and playing more roles that more accurately portray that we're in every segment of society.

TONI ADAMS

More and more inter-racial marriages and their progeny.

MARY WEEMS

I am encouraged any time I hear about an individual or group of people who is actively seeking to get this country over the racism at its foundation. For example, the Facing History and Ourselves organization's *Choosing to Participate* travelling exhibit currently on display here in Cleveland at the Western Reserve Historical Society focuses on some of the history of racism and what individuals have done and are doing to struggle against it. The election of President Obama as the first African American president and his efforts to put in place a federal government that is diverse in terms of race, ethnicity, gender, and political perspective. Artists in film, theater, poetry, dance, and music who use their art as a way of speaking out while arguing for bringing us together, including the recent project Playing for Change. Any time I facilitate, learn of, or participate in an open and honest conversation about race, any time I observe whites and people of color spending time together in public by choice—I'm encouraged.

WAYNE DOWNEY

Well, I do have to admit that the election of Barack Obama was a huge milestone. However, I don't know that it would constitute the finish line. I believe that when everybody is involved in eliminating behaviors that are prejudicial or cumbersome for people on the basis of skin color, that will signify that we are reaching a place of overcoming. I can't see racism ending in that our fabric, our very DNA has been predicated on the notion that preference is granted on the basis of skin color. I don't know how 400 years of attitudes and evolution can be reversed. But fairness, equality, access, money, housing, jobs, the ability to take care of oneself, the ability to take care of one's family regardless of the color of your skin, the ability to create a comfortable life, the ability to have basic needs met, and so forth, will be indicators of moving towards a more race-conscious society.

ERIC LACKIE

There is still too much evidence confirming that racism occurs at all times of the day, every day, all across the nation, and all over the world. However, I think one sign of the overcoming of racism in our society will be increased testimony made by oppressed groups and individuals about the overwhelming support from individuals and groups of all ethnicities, but especially from whites.

RAZIA KOSI

The signpost that I keep an eye out for that signals the overcoming of racism in our society is true equity in our neighborhoods, schools, workplace, media and society. This would have to be evident across the nation, from east to west, north to south. I live in a very integrated area and feel very comfortable going with our multi-hued family anywhere between the metropolitan area of Washington, DC, to New York City. I know we may still encounter racism, but this has not been the norm in our area. A signpost for me would be that we could travel in any part of our society, without questioning whether it would be a "safe" area for our family to travel. Another signpost would be for all people to stop talking about racism not existing and actively taking action to stop racism. This would be a critical signpost for me.

TRAVIS SMITH

When I find it a rarity that the average white person is so easily manipulated by benevolent politicians and the media. When I find a complete education provided by the school system, one in which the average student of color isn't left wondering after the 4th grade, "What have my people done," or, "Where do I fit?"

Langston Hughes wrote, "I, too, sing America. I am the darker brother. They send me to eat in the kitchen when company comes, but I laugh, and eat well, and grow strong. Tomorrow, I'll be at the table when company comes. Nobody'll dare say to me, 'Eat in the kitchen,' then. Besides, they'll see how beautiful I am and be ashamed—I, too, am America."

Yes, we are at the table today and in some cases at the head of it. But our conversation is in your language, we're wearing your style of clothing (under the guise of professionalism) and your names, and we're speaking on issues that either concern you or make you feel comfortable.

I look for signposts that are written in a person of color's language. And I don't mean Spanish, which is European as well. I'm looking for the days in which whites will have to learn to contextualize the world through a person of color's thought system and cultural expression. I'm looking for an America without an "underclass" held down—by political machinations—in black ghettos, brown barrios and red reservations.

CAROL WALSH

Obama's election and Michele Obama's popularity as a beautiful, intelligent, dynamic "partner" to the president was an overwhelming victory. For me this signaled that our younger generation (the majority voters in that election) may be more on the ball than many of us have given them credit for. Gaining a greater understanding of their thoughts and views on racism and becoming allies in the fight against racism may indeed be a great starting place.

Yukari Takimoto Amos

Many of my students would answer, "When everyone is color-blind, when there are no more quotas and affirmative action for black people, Hispanics, and Indians, when bilingual education is done away with, and when poor colored people are not given money by the government to have more babies, then we will have overcome racism." My answer is, "When the institutional aspects of racism such as the powerful association of race and poverty cease, the massive over-imprisonment of people of color begins to lessen, when the profiling of these same peoples by the police ends, when the de facto segregation of U.S. cities no longer exists, and with it inferior schools, and dangerous living conditions, then and only then will racism begin to be overcome. With strong economic prospects for people of color, good schools, access to high-quality health care, and adequate institutions of public safety, these negative conditions would begin to be replaced with safe neighbors, healthy social conditions, and more people of color living productive, self-fulfilling lives. Racism would begin to become a past tragedy of history, not to be forgotten, but overcome."

Michael Leslie

When we achieve parity in both graduate and undergraduate education across the board; when we are represented proportional to our numbers in business, education and politics; when our salaries and health statistics are on par with or better than those of equal qualifications in the dominant white group; when our employment rates are equal to those of whites; then I will believe that we are making progress toward overcoming racism in our society.

Camisha L. Jones

A signpost that will indicate to me that we are serious about overcoming racism in our society is honesty. When it is standard behavior to hear our leaders and most respected role models telling the truth about racist practices in our history and how those things continue to manifest themselves in our present reality, I will know that there is hope to see racism end. When our main concerns are justice and truth rather than reassuring the white folks and making them feel comfortable, I will know we are getting somewhere. This is what inspired me the most about Barack Obama's campaign for presidency. When he spoke about racism, he spoke honestly about it and America embraced him.

Of course, we also allowed (and continue to allow) so much hate speech and imagery related to him. As a country, we will be on our way to overcoming racism when we have a common understanding of what racism is, when we no longer think of it only as lynching and calling someone the "n" word but also characterizing a black man as a monkey and inciting fear in people's hearts. We'll be able to overcome racism when we take responsibility for the fact that our country was built on racist practices and beliefs and it will take more than laws to undo that legacy. It will take each of us doing the hard work of changing our hearts and our beliefs.

SECTION TWO:

FOR WHITES

CHAPTER FIVE

TELLING THE TRUTH

—·— GOOD/HARD TALK —·—

What's good and what's hard about talking about racism?

ROBERTA WALLITT

What's good about talking about racism is that it allows white people to engage in a conversation we have been taught to not talk about. By expressing our fears and (mis)perceptions out loud, we have an opportunity to examine them with others and come to a better understanding of ourselves and how we've developed beliefs that limit us in so many ways.

What's hard is actually doing it. Recently I have participated in a group of white people who came together to talk about race and racism as a way to better serve as allies for people of color. I have been struck by how easy it is for white people to get sidetracked into other oppressions that we have experienced—sexism, anti-Semitism, homophobia. Anything to avoid talking about racism. I have also noticed that some white people have trouble even saying that they are white and owning the privilege that comes with that identity. White people want to talk about their position as economically struggling or how their immigrant grandparents pulled themselves up by their bootstraps —without acknowledging how whiteness affects our opportunities to improve our circumstances.

What makes talking about racism especially hard is the fear of many white people that by talking about racism, their own racism will be made visible. When people are insecure about what language to use (Is it "people of color or colored people?") they are afraid to open their mouths. When the group is mixed, that fear is compounded.

In my early years of learning about my (unintentional) participation in a racist society, the hardest part was how it affected my self image. Having always thought of myself as "good" person—and, even more, a "good" teacher— I struggled with information from a friend of color that I was not meeting the educational needs of my students of color. It undermined my identity and I didn't know who I was if I wasn't that "good" teacher. While it was devastating at the time, it was the best thing that could have happened to me, as it pushed me into a new journey.

One of the other things that makes it hard to talk about racism is the tendency for white people who want to continue thinking that they are "good" (as I did) to present their credentials. This just happened to me yesterday when I was talking to someone I had just met who will be teaching in a new charter school. I asked if he had had experience working with a diverse group of students. He first told me that his parents were Holocaust survivors who had worked for civil rights. Then he told me he had grown up in a diverse neighborhood. He told me he was committed to social justice. But he never answered my question. I have learned that when a white person begins a conversation about racism by presenting their credentials, they really are avoiding talking about racism.

ROBIN DIANGELO

Good: In our white-central society, for white people to talk directly and honestly about race is personally, intellectually, and emotionally challenging and filled with potential growth.

Hard: So few whites understand racism as a system that privileges us regardless of intentions. We don't understand how much of our conceptualization of race functions to hold racism in place. So we arrogantly plunge ahead, discount and debate the perspectives of people of color, defend ourselves, take great umbrage if our views are challenged rather than affirmed, and generally work to maintain our superficial understandings rather than deepen them. White arrogance and sense of entitlement to comfort, along with our resentment and anger towards people of color that is barely below the surface, make talking about race with white people maddening.

AMY C. ORECCHIA

White people talking about racism is good because it's pretty rare. It's good because by talking about it, we are acknowledging it, which just might be the first step towards doing something about it. It's hard because there are still many communities where whites are able to live their day-to-day lives without noticing racism. Whites don't notice racism because they are not being directly affected by it. If you are acutely aware of something—if it's right in your face every day—you're going to find a place to talk about it. If not, then you're going to be talking about the latest reality-show drama or the price of gas. What is hard for me personally in talking about racism is that I have very strong and mixed emotions about it. I lived most of my life in a predominantly white, sometimes overtly racist, world. It makes me feel guilty, yes, but also actually angry that there are all these other perspectives and life experiences that I didn't discover until I was an adult. It makes me angry that there are so many other whites who have this same experience, and maybe don't even move beyond their comfort zones after they become adults.

Sara Krakauer

I think it's important to talk about racism because if we don't acknowledge it, we can't fix it. The first step has to be understanding the realities. It can be hard to face the fact that life isn't fair. Even though we are told this when we are little kids, there's an American value that says that hard work yields success. It's hard to admit that our privileges are not earned. Even after admitting this, it's even harder to figure out what can be done about it.

John Alexander

Deepening my understanding of racism and the many ways I benefit from it has been central to my growth as a human being. But that growth is hard because life is hard when I strive to be conscious, accountable and genuine. Becoming aware of the privileges I have as a straight, white, middle-class, able male has been a daunting challenge because society has not asked or rewarded me for being conscious of those privileges. So talking with other whites is hard because they often get impatient, as though I am making too much of the privilege. And talking with folks from other races and ethnicities can be hard because neither of us wants my education to come at their expense.

Eileen Kugler

What's good in talking about racism is that we are honest with each other. We can have real, meaningful, valuable conversations. And we develop friendships that are deep and authentic.

What's hard is being forced to be painfully introspective. If it doesn't hurt, we're not really getting at anything. I believe this applies to everyone. What do we expect of people when we first lay eyes on them? How is that informed by the color of their skin and the shape of their eyes and the length of their nose?

BETSY PERRY

What's good is that you simply can't change without talking. If you won't talk about it, it will be as it is. What's hard is that I want forgiveness; I want the person talking to me to say, "Of course, I don't mean you," and "I understand," and "You're doing such a good job of trying to change!" This is bullshit. It is not the job of POC to console me, and in fact, sometimes they do mean me, and they understand that the situation sucks, and trying to change isn't the same as changing. There is no forgiveness to be had. There is, maybe, acceptance. There is the continuing struggle, every day, to change my heart.

JANET CARTER

I grew up in a white liberal family where racism was something that bad white people did, while a good white person wasn't even supposed to notice race. So it is a relief for me to be able to talk about racism. An African American man once asked me, "What do white people say about race when there are no people of color around?" My first answer was, "They don't talk about it much, if ever." If we do, it is usually in very limited ways. Talking about race or racism on the personal level, i.e., how I feel about my race or another's race is taboo. So, that makes it hard. Even in situations with white people who "get it," there is still an edge. We want to tell each other stories that show how we do get it, not about how confused we might be or how a painful situation just happened that we feel awful about.

To have a genuine conversation where race is talked about in a real way is so refreshing. To have a deep sharing of experience is even more rare and precious. The hardest thing is feeling my own vulnerability and staying open to the other person's experience at the same time.

TOM MOORE

The good part about talking about racism is that it gets things out in the open. In silence, we're left to our imaginations on what others are thinking. The hard part is just finding a way to bring up the subject. It's a lot like religion and politics: When is an appropriate time? How will this person react? Does this person want to talk about it?

CRAIG MORFITT

I think many white people are uncomfortable talking about race and racism because they worry that they will say the wrong thing and upset someone. Perhaps there is also a fear that, in talking about race, some of their prejudices will be exposed. There seems to be a real fear amongst white people that they will be considered or labeled a racist, and that may contribute to a reluctance to get involved in discussions on race. It's hard for them to take that first step.

Those who are willing to take the first step and begin to discuss race in depth may be pleasantly surprised by the reaction they receive from people of color— even if they do expose their prejudices or past behavior. I have found groups to be extremely forgiving and embracing when they see that someone is honestly trying to participate. The good part is that by discussing race and racism, and by attending workshops and lectures, white people can quickly become more knowledgeable about race and the attendant issues. That improved knowledge leads to a greater understanding and less chance of "putting their foot in it" with inappropriate comments. The payoff for their effort will be meaningful relationships with persons of color and a new insight into the world around us and how it is experienced by others.

It can be a particular challenge for a white male involved in facilitating workshops on race because we tend to enter the arena without any obvious credibility on the topic. Persons of color speaking on race and racism are presumed to have some knowledge of the topic, and therefore some credibility, but not so for white men. We have to prove to the audience that we know what we are talking about, but it has been my experience that people of color will embrace and respect a white male facilitator once that credibility has been established. So, whilst getting involved can be hard or challenging, the rewards make the effort worthwhile.

JULIE WOULF

The best thing about talking about racism is feeling connected: to myself, to other white people, to people of color. I feel less crazy and confused. Our conversations get less vague.

The hard thing about talking about racism is the visceral sense of guilt, fear, embarrassment. At least when I was being a "good white person" there was a place to hide from the pain of knowing that so much of how I move in the world is connected to oppression.

WILLIAM MCGUIRE

I grew up during the early stages of the civil rights movement and inflicted verbal racial slurs on the quiet people of color (blacks, Hispanics, Asians and Native Americans) marching near my hometown of Mobile, Alabama, for their equal rights. I had learned from my peers that the people marching were taking away rights from whites like me.

Fortunately for me, there was an older black man working as a janitor in my high school (the high school had an all-white staff and student body) that began to talk to me about my values and beliefs and how they might influence my life decisions. Over a period of time this man became my mentor with respect to racism and helping me to understand how hurtful I had been.

He would also tell me that "if I didn't talk about it, I couldn't fix it" (meaning the racism inside of me). He would quietly tell me about how he was treated as an older black man by younger whites. All I needed to hear to trust his feelings were sincere was the slight quiver in his voice. I saw how hard racism was for him to talk about and suddenly realized how much harder it was for me as the oppressor to admit I was really a racist.

I believe racism is more alive today than it was when I was a young high school boy back in Mobile, Alabama. The murder of James Byrd in Jasper, Texas, the events in Jena, Louisiana, with the alleged Jena 6, the hanging noose on the door of a female black college professor at Columbia University, the swastika painted on the door of the Jewish professor at the same university, Hurricane Katrina, the murder of young men that have "come out" as homosexuals in the U.S. military, and hundreds of other racist incidents have all convinced me to fight racism. Back then, I was the one listening to the people I had a part in oppressing. Today people of color are listening to me as I share what I learned from what I had inflicted many years ago. I am a long-time diversity, inclusion, and equity champion working in the U.S. Department of Defense influencing many others to share their stories. I don't know where I would be today had I not learned early in life how to treat others with infinite dignity and worth. Racism is alive and well today and I plan to continue to do my part to fight it. Racism is not just an issue for me to cure as a white male. Racism impacts everyone and must be defeated. I'll do my part and then some; what will you do to help me in this global endeavor?

JIM LANGEMO

Talking about racism is good because it gives me new insights into my privilege. These conversations are most effective when they don't make me feel embarrassed or ashamed, but rather help me see how I can use my insights into privilege to help me make change in my environment. The insights translate into different ways I speak, think, act and look; they translate into different ways I don't speak, think, act and look. They also help me dive deeper into my own wiring by asking such questions as, "Why do I think like I do?" "Why didn't I see what just happened?" By pursuing the answers to these questions, I begin to rewire my thinking, which helps me become the person I envision. Talking about racism also makes me hold up a mirror to my own actions. I could give the cocoon of privilege some of the credit/blame for the hurt I have caused others and the ways in which I have supported the status quo, but that wouldn't be correct. Knowing more about my privilege helps me to understand some of the root causes, but I have to take personal responsibility for my actions. Conversations about racism help me take that responsibility and make a renewed commitment to creating a different kind of world.

Frank conversation about racism is also healing. I have seen on countless occasions healing take place when people can tell their personal stories and they are listened to and validated. What's more, a sense of kinship and brotherhood emerges in the best of these conversations. Those who are victims no longer stand alone; those with privilege now feel able to do something—and both feel united.

Another reason these conversations are good is that they are educational. Our current education system, as well as the media, does very little to correctly inform and teach. This leaves many of us painfully ignorant of our nation's past. We need the conversations to help us wake up to the real history of our nation.

These conversations are hard because they take people of color back to the place of the pain. Each one has to give and give, and the costs are dear—sharing the hurt, the anger, the sense of helplessness. When done right, seeing the pain it costs people can inspire EuroAmericans to educate themselves. These conversations are also hard because there are a number of preconditions that need to exist before they can really happen: There needs to be trust, safety and mutual respect in the room. These can be difficult things to achieve and either way they take time.

—·— DENIAL —·—

What percentage of your life is impacted by racism? Why or why not?

Amy C. Orecchia

I would say 100%. It's not an acute or very personal impact. I might go days without even noticing. However, because I am living within a racist culture, all aspects of my life are influenced by racism. In my work in counseling and social-work settings, I've had many clients who mistrusted me before I even spoke with them because of bad experiences with other white professionals or the system in general. When I drive through a predominantly black or Latino neighborhood in this city, I notice that road work seems to take four times as long to finish as it does in the white neighborhoods. I see bouncers at a club with a dress code kicking young black men out for having hats on when there are white men inside that are wearing them. I notice that the flyers in the waiting room of a predominantly African American–run community agency that serves mostly African American clients have pictures of only white families in them. On and on and on...it all affects me now that my eyes are open for it.

Laura K

Very little—five percent or less. I live in a city with a smallish community of color, in a state with even fewer people of color. My life is impacted when ignorant undergraduates hang an effigy of Barack Obama from a tree (by the neck, no less) and I am ashamed to be part of my institution. My life is impacted when the cops kill someone and the black community responds differently than the white community and the cops do, and I wish people understood why. My life is impacted when I teach on racism and the students of color are conspicuously silent and I don't quite know why, but I don't want to put them on the spot or make them tell their horror stories AGAIN… My life is impacted when I walk into my church and it's mostly white folks. My life is impacted when my colleagues refuse to attempt to pronounce "foreign" names correctly.

Amy Fritsch

I think a significant portion of my life is impacted by racism in that the interactions I have with students, colleagues, friends, strangers, and employees are informed by racism. All too often, as a white woman with white children and a white husband, it is convenient or easy to think that my life is not impacted by racism, but that is dangerously false. There are friends I did not have because my racist father would not allow those friends to come to my house. There are words I do or don't say based on fears of racism or racist assumptions that affect others around me. There are students who I'm sure I don't connect as well with because of the racial divide between us—students who, if I were better at being an anti-racist, might perhaps learn better in my class. There are colleagues whom I misunderstand and who misunderstand me because of racism. There are friends I don't have now because of racism and the divisions and assumptions of society. There are brilliant and funny and interesting people of color who do not participate actively in my favorite hobby due to racism from others who participate (and, likely, from me), and I am the less for their absence. There are employees in stores or restaurants to whom I may make carelessly racist statements or who make statements or actions to which I may respond inappropriately due to my lack of knowledge of cultural differences. It goes on and on. My impact on the world around me impacts my life, impacts how I am treated and perceived, and impacts the entire world as well as the individuals I encounter.

In what ways have you been able to avoid talking about or dealing with racism?

Robin DiAngelo

In every way. The only time a white person has to talk about racism is if they are pushed to participate in a workplace diversity training or something similar. But even in that setting, many whites can and do remain silent. Of course whites talk about race all the time in implicit and coded ways (discourses on schools, neighborhoods, safety, jokes, etc.). But I have been able to avoid honestly talking about race by being socially rewarded by other whites when I avoid race, and penalized by other whites when I bring it up. For example, I will rise in my career much more easily if I remain silent and don't challenge other whites. If I do challenge them or our practices, policies and procedures, I will likely be labeled a troublemaker and avoided. As for avoiding dealing with race, segregation makes that fairly easy for me.

Jim Miller

Often it hasn't hit close to home. It's been much easier to just live my life and not think very much about it. I discuss it quite a bit with friends, but more in a theoretical frame of reference. Very rarely, it comes up when there is a situation at work or (much more rarely) in personal life that raises the question, "Are we judging this person's performance (or actions) partially because of racial stereotypes?" I sometimes am tempted to overlook or excuse what I think is unsatisfactory performance, because of what I feel is a person's background, something in that person's environment that made achievement more difficult (when maybe it didn't).

Amy Fritsch

I have been able to avoid talking directly about racism with my children as much as I would have to, in order to try and keep them safer, if I were a person of color. I've been able to focus on other issues of oppression that have affected me more directly and personally, such as issues of domestic violence, sexual violence, and gender inequalities that I have fought on my own behalf. As such, I've used energy I might have spent on racism on other areas of oppression, and those have distracted me from seeing the bigger bogeyman of racism. I've also spent a great deal of my adult life focusing on my own traumas and have filled up the time where I might have been thinking and learning about and dealing with racism with personal and family issues.

Daniel Cohen

I have avoided talking about race by not feeling. This has been a real cost for me as a white person. There has been a literal and psychological gulf between myself and people of color. They were "the other." Therefore their pain was not my pain. My hurt was not theirs. I was an individual working hard and succeeding, growing up in a predominantly white community 25 miles outside of Chicago. Whenever I walked into a room or sat in a meeting I felt totally entitled to speak. My voice mattered as Dan, the individual, not a part of any group. What happened in their communities did not outrage or connect to me emotionally. When African American children were being shot and killed at a record pace in Chicago when I was growing up, it was not my problem. I did not feel the pain of their classmates, sisters, brothers, mothers and fathers. I chose not to.

I am skillfully practiced (over 30 years) at not seeing and not feeling. That is how embedded it is. In my mind I was a sensitive, thoughtful young person; this is how my community perceived me growing up. No one sat me down and told me not to feel the devastating loss or feel compassion for the families; I simply did not. Those were "dangerous neighborhoods" and "things like that happen there to those kids." That is what I was taught and no institution explicitly challenged those statements. There was no sense of compassion and empathy and therefore no sense of community responsibility. Sure I felt pity and sympathy, but not empathy among equals. And because of that gulf and that distance I could not be fully authentic and honest with myself or in my relationships with other white people or with people of color. My ability to feel deeply for others has been damaged by racism. This has been a real cost to me of racism.

—·— GUILT —·—

How does guilt keep you from dealing with racism?

BILL PROUDMAN

Guilt can be an enormous barrier when it pervades and takes control of my actions and behavior over the long term. Staying stuck in guilt and having it drive my actions is not a healthy or sustainable platform. Operating from guilt will not help me to strengthen my voice or partnerships over the long term. It will only make it more difficult for me to have vibrant partnerships where I can bring my full self knowing I have something valuable to contribute.

My behavior, when derived from prolonged feelings of guilt, can diminish my own personal power and limit how I show up in partnerships with both people of color and other whites. Operating from a place of guilt can close off my efforts to investigate others' realities as well as better understand my own self interest.

Conversely guilt is sometimes helpful. When I am able to recognize and call out feelings of guilt in the short term, I can get in touch with many feelings that I might otherwise suppress. Noticing when I feel guilty helps me stay in difficult conversations because it lets me reassess my stake in the conversation beyond feeling guilty.

However, if I repeatedly operate from a place of guilt, I find I invalidate my role in being a vital cog to finding common ground or new ways of behaving/interacting with others. Sometimes guilt for me in racism is linked to my defending my innocence. When a lot of my energy goes into trying to convince others that I am not the culprit or in defending my "good guyness," I often miss opportunities to more fully understand how racism is impacting the quality of the partnerships I have.

HOLLY FULTON

It makes me confused so I balk or stammer or stay silent because I'm afraid of people of color judging me. I sometimes still choose to stay quiet to protect myself; it's a fear-based automatic trigger.

JIM MILLER

Mostly the awareness of how racism has benefited me may keep me from responding to a minority person in the same way I would a white person. But it's complex—I might tend to give a black person the benefit of the doubt in a question of promotion or award, figuring that even if their superior performance is doubtful, they had to put forth more effort because of bias against them.

LAURA K

I find myself unwilling to tell stories about my own racism because of my shame about the things I've done over the years. As a "well-meaning white person," it may be harder for me to confront the persistent racism deep in my heart than for someone who is openly racist to do so. I keep thinking, "Dang it, I've been teaching about this stuff for 10 years or more, and confronting racism in myself for 20 years or more—ain't I done yet?"

SARA KRAKAUER

I certainly feel guilty about my race and class privileges. By addressing racism, I am acknowledging my privilege. It's a lot easier to forget about it. Nobody is there checking to make sure that I work against racism. In fact, society encourages me to keep my mouth shut. White people don't like hearing about it, and people tend to think you are being politically correct if you try to talk about race. Doing the right thing is actually discouraged by friends and the media.

AMY FRITSCH

I feel guilty that I do not have my thoughts and assumptions all together in a non-racist way and that I have the potential to do damage. I feel guilty that I benefit from a racist structure and that some of the good/positive things I have are at others' expense. I recognize that as a citizen of the U.S., much of what I have is at the expense of others all over the world and I feel guilty about that. I feel guilty about not thinking too much about it, even knowing that it would send me into a spiral of self-loathing if I were to think about it extensively, knowing that I cannot, even through my own futile actions in terms of purchases and gestures, help set the balance to something fair.

BETSY PERRY

I keep trying not to think about it. It's that simple. I have, before all the bingo cards, used the bingo-card arguments: It wasn't me; I mean well; I'd listen if only you weren't so confrontative. The bingo cards are there for a reason: They outline the easy arguments I and many other people use to avoid thinking about their own hearts.

TARA RONDA

There is an episode of Seinfeld that sums this up for me—Elaine is dating a man who she thinks is part black and he thinks that she's part Hispanic (neither of which turns out to be true). But when they begin talking about their misunderstanding she says, "Should we be talking about this?" Through a comedic lens, the show addresses the guilt and discomfort that people feel when discussing something like race—in other words, I (and many others) have this vague feeling whenever I talk about race (even in a neutral or positive way) that I'm doing something wrong because it's something that shouldn't be brought up or mentioned. I believe this comes from the old view of "diversity" in which we should all be "color-blind," which of course is neither possible nor useful. I find, however, that I don't feel this guilt when I'm joking around with a friend of color or someone I know well—then it doesn't feel so taboo or "underhanded."

BARBARA IMHOFF

My guilt is primarily based on my laziness around dealing with racism. I feel some generic guilt for being white, but, more than that, I feel a personal guilt for not investing in dealing with racial issues enough. I have attempted to correct racism when I see it, but I've never taken the time to do anything further. And the longer I wait, the guiltier I feel. And the guiltier I feel...

MELISSA SWEENEY

For me, it is less about guilt and more about embarrassment that keeps me from dealing with racism directly at times. I'm embarrassed that after all the time that I have already invested in "unlearning" racism that I still catch myself in moments that I am not proud of. For example, not long ago, I saw a black man at the end of the street I was walking along. Automatically, I assumed he was homeless and was going to ask me for money. When I passed by, I realized this man was only waiting for food he had ordered as take-out from a restaurant. Upon this realization, I felt ashamed and embarrassed. "Damn it!" I thought, "I did it again!" Rationally, I know it is inevitable that when one grows up in a racist society we become automatically programmed with racist thoughts but that still doesn't make me feel good about those thoughts—no matter where they came from. I have learned to keep what I call a "second movie reel" in my head for editing purposes; one reel plays all of what I have learned to-date, the other lets me create a new version of truth based on my own critical inquiry and tough lessons learned. I prize my second movie reel and will always make it a point to use it to "unlearn" white supremacy. But, that doesn't mean that people of color don't pay the price along the way. For that, I do feel guilty.

How do you think you benefit from racism?

JANET CARTER

My ancestors were among the Puritans who colonized this country. I have benefited from centuries of control over land and resources, opportunities for education and entrepreneurship, and cultural acceptance available to white people at the expense of people of other races, as well as European immigrants once deemed "not white." I grew up in a white liberal New England family, proud of my heritage, without understanding the unearned privilege it gave me. I was raised to be a "good white person" who would not ever want to benefit from hurting others. The process of waking up to my privilege and to the brutal history I never learned in school has been both painful and exhilarating.

One of the biggest benefits that was hard for me to understand—and is really hard to communicate to other white people—is that I don't have to think of myself in racial terms. I choose to look at it now in my life, but having that choice is a huge privilege in itself.

I carry an ingrained sense of entitlement that often works, whether I exercise it consciously or unconsciously. Even when I am afraid in situations involving authority—a cop, a doctor, the unemployment office—I have a magic cloak of "legitimacy" to hide in. Society reinforces my successes as personal achievements, even though I am lifted up by invisible helpful hands. Whether I succeed or fail, I am not seen as an "example" of the white race.

SARA KRAKAUER

As a white woman, there are so many situations where I can look cute and get what I want—assistance from strangers on the street, tips on getting deals from realtors or people at stores, and trust from potential employers. In my job, I easily earn the trust of white parents of my students. I was also born into a family with inherited wealth, and white privilege likely is connected here.

BARBARA IMHOFF

I benefit all the time from the assumptions that people make about me based on the color of my skin. I'm white, so (people assume): I probably didn't rob the corner store; I probably will do a better job than the African American woman that applied at the same time; I've probably got a good education; I probably can afford that car I'm looking at; I can probably read; I probably won't harm your family; etc. I am not good, smart, educated or kind based on my skin color. Nor is the reverse true. But people make assumptions and comparisons every day that harm or denigrate people of color. In reality, I probably do make more money, have a better education, a better job, more and better toys than the person of color next to me. But it's not necessarily because I deserve these things more than they. And it was probably a lot easier for me to attain these things than for them, simply based on other people's assumptions.

BETH ELLIOTT

I benefit from racism because I am part of the majority culture. There is privilege in knowing the rules of the dominant culture and looking like people in the dominant culture. It could be that I am acknowledged first in a store or restaurant. It could be that I am listened to more than people of color. My experience of the way I benefit is very subtle and is often denied by other white people.

BETSY PERRY

I have the unmarked condition. When I walk down the street, into a restaurant, into a job interview, I am "normal." I don't stand out. Nobody thinks, "Oh, the black person!" They think "The person!" I don't have to compete for jobs with the brilliant black people in my field (computer science) because most of them have been weeded out by societal racism. (Note: I say "black" here because Asian-descended people are commonplace.) When I talk to a policeman, I am never afraid that he'll treat *me* like the criminal.

I also have the accumulated advantages of my race and class. I got to go to a prestige college. That meant that when one of my kids applied to my alma mater, she had a step up over kids whose parents didn't go there. When one of my kids got into a fight in school, he was treated like a good kid who got into a fight, not like a troublemaker.

Jim Langemo

I benefit in myriad ways: I have better chances at low interest rates on home loans or car loans; I have a better chance at jobs; I have a better chance of being paid more for the same job; I have a better chance of being heard, seen and respected.

I know my family history: My family didn't have their name changed at Ellis Island or Angel Island; my family wasn't given their name in plantations in the South. I know what areas of Europe my ancestors came from. My history wasn't so completely ripped from me as my African American friends who can only identify the continent they are from. Shoot, for some of my heritage, I can name the city. I could probably find the farm if I tried.

Most marketing and advertising is done to cater to me; the models look more often like me; the print is in language I understand. I don't have to take an extra step in translating why something may or may not appeal to me. I have few hurdles to climb to just get through the day without being reminded of my race and/or skin color. I am not often followed by store security. I am rarely asked for two forms of ID. I rarely receive looks from people that I don't belong. I don't see consistently negative portrayals of me in the newspaper or on TV. I don't hear of reports like the recent report in Philadelphia of black children being kicked out of a swimming pool.

Laura K

I use a film about South Africa in one of my classes, Long Night's Journey into Day. In it, one young, mixed-race South African says, "Nobody has apologized to me yet, either for oppressing me directly or for happily benefiting from my oppression." I should feel guilty because none of my brothers are in prison— no male in my family is. If any of them were a black man, at minimum they would have been stopped by the police unjustly, if not imprisoned unjustly. I benefit from racism when I can manage a homeowner payment, when I have a full-time job, when I got to pursue advanced education, and nobody ever once said I couldn't or shouldn't be able to because of my race. I benefit from racism when someone serves me in a public place—nobody looks past me or waits on somebody else first because of the color of my skin. Nobody has ever crossed over to the other side of the street because I was walking by...I'll leave it at that, I think.

Tara Ronda

It took me many years to realize that I did benefit from racism. It wasn't until I was an undergraduate taking an African American Philosophy course that I learned where I stood and how I benefit from being white. Things started to look a lot different for me then. In my daily life, I realize that I don't often find myself in a place where I am the minority (in fact, like many white people, I actively try not to put myself in that position). I don't have to worry about people following me through a store, a landlord considering me an undesirable tenant, or people not understanding (and often not wanting to understand) my perspective. As a step-parent, I don't need to worry that my child will one day be bullied or berated for being of color, or that my child might one day be falsely accused of a driving infraction or more serious crime because of her color. Every day, I take for granted the fact that people largely accept me for who and what I am, and although I've often been marginalized as a woman, it's not quite the same thing because women's rights was in many ways a more successful struggle than civil rights. I also think it's more acceptable to be racist than sexist in our society.

Amy Fritsch

I think I benefit most from racism by the fact that my name, my face, my appearance, and my choice of dress frame me to anyone looking at me—in person or on paper—as part of the white mainstream. I am of combined British and German descent, and have the look of your standard English-German farm girl. Add to that that I am relatively pale for a white person, and have the blue eyes of those of Northern European descent, as well as a pair of blond-haired, blue-eyed children whose appearance would have been coveted by Adolf Hitler for model "Nazi poster children" and it is clear that I will be perceived as fitting the desired norm of appearance.

From my name and appearance, therefore, I code in our culture as non-threatening: I do not "look like" someone who will be "different" or "difficult" or ask hard questions or take a stand for issues of minorities. Unlike "scary brown people," I am "safe" and not a threat to a shop's inventory, someone's child on a playground, someone's sense of superiority as a white person who might feel challenged by a person of color's competence.

As a child of natives in Southern Illinois, I grew up with a mild Southern/hick accent until I was nine and in fourth grade. I observed that the children of university parents, who tended to have a more Midwest-neutral accent, were taken more seriously, and I modified my own speech based on friends' feedback and, ironically, Dan Rather's (non-Texan) reporting voice. Since I was largely successful at acquiring a mostly Midwest-neutral accent myself, I have the additional advantage of not sounding Southern (often an attribute that is perceived as a "black" sound in the North where I now live) and thus being given more credence when I speak.

DENTON MITCHELL

I realize it is not right, but I am sure that I do in some measure benefit from racism. If I became aware that I had benefited—say in a hiring situation—I am not at all sure that I could "do the right thing" and "step aside." Two reasons: First, the interviewer is not bound by my decision to step aside and hire the "person of color" and may well go to the next available "white." And second, I have never been in a position to be able to turn down a legitimate offer—my family has become accustomed to eating at regular intervals and also to "living under a roof." Altruism is great— but often comes at a very real cost: one that I might be willing to pay on my own behalf, but not on the behalf of those that depend upon me for support.

MAC SABOL

As a white man, I have definitely benefited from racism. For starters, I have had opportunities opened to me not because I may be smarter or more gifted than others, but because of the color of my skin. From an employment perspective, the color of my skin has also meant that I am probably going to be placed in a "preferred" category by a lot of decision makers.

It is important that I state this: I think that I have benefited from racism, but I do not ASK or DESIRE to have this benefit. In a diversity training seminar many years ago, I was confronted with the question, "When did you become aware of your whiteness?" That question just stunned me. I had never considered that I was part of a "privileged class," especially since my family was very poor. Yet, I know that I AM part of a privileged class. The sad part is that nonwhites know it too, because they have experienced the non-privileged part.

MELISSA SWEENEY

I benefit from racism in every possible way imaginable. It is because of racism that my white self has had the opportunity to live in safer neighborhoods, go to better schools and make a better living. What is ironic to me is that I have used my white-skin privilege to dismantle the very thing that has put me in this power position—white supremacy.

JOHN ALEXANDER

I don't think I benefit from racism; I know I do. And I sympathize with whites who don't yet understand this benefit even as I feel frustrated and angry at their willful ignorance.

I taught a mixed-race class for eight years that focused on healing from racism and other cultural traumas. It generally took the whites about half the semester to fully accept the reality of the privilege that society granted them. I've frequently talked with colleagues of all races and ethnicities about how hard it is to teach and for white students to learn this basic truth. And even though almost all the students of color were painfully and consciously aware of their lack of privilege, they also were learning during that first half of the semester, as they became more aware of how racism works for whites and how pervasive and omnipresent the privileges are.

As I've talked with colleagues who also teach about and are aware of these systems of privilege, I always ask if anyone has a technique for making this system more visible, more accessible. So far, I've yet to find someone who can make this a teachable moment in less than two months of standard classroom time. That strikes me as a powerful, persistent system that I benefit from with every breath I take.

TOM MOORE

In an absolute sense, I don't benefit from racism at all. I can't benefit from any system in which some people are of lesser status than others, in which there is fear between groups, and in which some people have limited opportunities. The alienation of any part of society diminishes me; walls through society mean that we are all separated from the whole.

—·— FEAR —·—

What are some of the things that you are afraid to say to people of color?

LAURA K

I am still afraid to speak about some of the worst episodes of my own racism, such as the time I falsely accused a black man when I knew the one who broke into my car was wearing a blue windbreaker with stripes on the sleeves, and this guy was wearing a blue raincoat with no stripes on the sleeves. He was in a mostly-white neighborhood early on a Sunday morning, and my brain said to itself, "What are the odds that there are two black men in blue coats in this neighborhood at this time on a Sunday morning?" I'm afraid that episodes like this one will invalidate all the work I've done against racism.

TARA RONDA

I don't believe in affirmative action. I have a hard time admitting this to other feminists and women as well, because it's often a tool for female advancement, but I think it's a poor system. I have watched several people of color at my job get promoted to very high-paying and high-power jobs although they were absolutely inept at doing their previous jobs. While I believe everyone should be promoted on their own merits, I think affirmative action is both a useless system and offensive to those who benefit from it. I wouldn't want to get a job just because my bosses need to fulfill a female-to-male quota. I am angered by affirmative action because, to me, a person's ability to effectively do a job is far more important than his/her color, and if we provide the types of educational opportunities and other early support to children of color that they would need to become successful, then we wouldn't need such a system. So let's educate our way out of it.

I am also tired of being the bad guy. Just because I'm white doesn't mean my family owned slaves (in fact, I'm descended from a long line of Quakers who opposed slavery) and we honestly need to move past it. I know that many black families have been and will continue to be affected by their history of slavery and that's important to recognize—we should continue to teach our young people about the lessons learned therein and about the social and economic fallout from slavery that continues today in the urbanization of blacks, inherited poverty, lack of educational opportunities, consistent civil rights violations. But let me be involved in the solution and stop acting like all white people should pay reparations—to me, that's just a weak way of trying to financially benefit from your family's misfortune.

Barbara Beckwith

There are other questions I may want to ask, but don't. I am now so aware that I need and want to listen very carefully to people of color when they share their experience of subtle or overt racism, that, at times, I hesitate to express any reservations I have, which makes me feel dishonest. I can, frankly, empathize with David, the obtuse white guy in The Color of Fear who, because he himself felt no tension in his relations with people of color—who were, by the way, his employees—was sure that there was no real black/white problem. It took a roomful of men of color days to get him to put aside his experience and believe the experience of other men in the room. I saw his obtuseness but I also struggle with the question, in racism-related situations, of how do I believe your experience and stay honest to the lingering "but—but" questions in my mind? It's tricky, stretching my mind while keeping my integrity.

I struggled with this when a fellow National Writers Union steering committee member and diversity committee activist wrote to our local newspaper about students taunting her with verbal insults at various middle and high schools where she was a substitute teacher. (She is a Korean American adoptee.) She described how, despite the school system's professed "zero tolerance" policy on racial insults, with comments ranging from "what are you?" to ching-chang-chong sounds, to "go eat pork-fried rice" to "slant-eyed bitch," only one principal took immediate and effective action, suspending a student who called her "Chink." The principal of one school, when she complained of veiled threats, said, "Kids will be kids," and took little action. Students from one school flooded the newspaper with letters counter-attacking, saying that some comments my colleague considered racist were not so. We discussed each comment: Is "Konichiwa" (Japanese for "How are you?") insulting, or was it a friendly gesture from a kid who didn't know Korean from Japanese? She may have been right or wrong about specific words being insults, but anti-Asian taunts clearly weren't being dealt with effectively. In the end, I realized that my forthright colleague had named a problem that Asian students and parents were well aware of and disturbed by. I had to ask my questions and express my qualms, to get to the place where I could appreciate her courage as a whistleblower.

Finally, there are "tell me what you think" questions I don't ask out of respect. During strategy discussions in the organization I'm active in, I want to ask my colleagues of color, "What do you think? What are your perspectives, your advice?" But I don't necessarily ask these questions because I know that, for a person of color, there may be more risk to speaking your mind: less assurance that you'll be heard, that your perspective will be seen as pertinent, that your opinions will be viewed as cogent. And I know the stress this causes.

What do you think keeps people of color and whites apart?

Amy C. Orecchia

I definitely think segregation keeps us apart. This is starting to change—even in places like Minnesota and Wisconsin—but it's still very apparent. Affluent suburbs still tend to be mostly white. It's a source of great tension that many inner-city neighborhoods are getting "gentrified" to the point where, with property-value increases, the people who used to live there can no longer afford it. Stereotypes keep us apart, especially when we see things or meet people that confirm our stereotypes.

Laura K

Fear and laziness. It's darn hard work to get to know folks who are different from us, and to confront our stuff and to return repeatedly to the same conversations and to stretch our personal boundaries. Much easier to sit at home and eat Cheetos. And for some, it's too painful to be confronted by our stuff, so, "Better to stay with the troubles we have than to flee to others we know not of," as Shakespeare would say.

Marie Doan

Habit. Unconsciousness. As with most suffering, the fear of what we imagine rather than the acknowledgement of what is. Fear, ignorance, and lack of compassion for someone different than one's own self.

The often unconscious historical pattern of always looking to POC to lead on the topic of race has created some very dysfunctional organizational dynamics. It remains rare that a white person, let alone a white male, is publicly leading organizational diversity efforts.

Almost all chief diversity officers in Fortune 100 companies in the U.S. are either POC or white women. Many white males who are members of a diversity council in an organization introduce themselves to me as the "token white male" council member. We need to begin to think and practice diversity so it includes all of us.

What keeps us apart generally falls into any of three categories: fear of saying or doing the wrong thing (offending/hurting others), trying to fix a problem I don't fully understand, and defending my innocence or "good guyness." Being politically correct has taken a toll on our partnerships because people, especially business leaders, have a lot at stake to show any confusion or messiness publicly. There are many examples of white public figures saying or doing the wrong thing: the 9/11 firefighter memorial about what faces should be on the statue, the policemen in the recent Gates incident, Don Imus, Joe Biden's reference to Obama during the presidential primary, etc. These missteps become public land-mines that reinforce in the minds of whites that any misspeak about race is fatal. Its effect among whites is to lessen their courage and lower their engagement in any public dialogue about race.

Some of the ways I have witnessed people in organizations unconsciously keeping whites and POC apart are as follows:

- An all-white leadership team abdicating their power to their predominantly people-of-color and white-female diversity council until the council makes a decision that the leadership team cannot (for whatever reason) support.
- Whites looking to POC directly or indirectly to back them up when they notice a race-based dynamic in a meeting (either by looking for confirmation or positive affirmation).
- When white men are engaged as full diversity partners, their authenticity is sometimes questioned by others not used to seeing them authentically engaged.
- Confusion by whites over whether they should ignore skin-color differ-

ence and just treat everyone the same or focus on the difference at the exclusion of the similarities. This sameness/difference paradox is rooted in the myth that one option cancels the other instead of being simultaneously color-blind and color-conscious.

- Whites thinking that every instance of mistreatment across race (white to POC, POC to white) is racism, thus misunderstanding and misusing the term until its meaning is lost and muddled.
- Asking and/or expecting POC to speak for their entire racial group as well as all people of color.
- Fatigue from POC who are repeatedly asked to sit on every committee and board in their community because the white community is looking for "diversity."
- Whites reluctant to provide feedback to POC for fear of being labeled racist or non-supportive of diversity efforts. One ramification of this is having a white supervisor withhold constructive feedback to a POC when that same supervisor would not hesitate to provide tough feedback to a white subordinate.
- Whites hiring or promoting a person based on their skin color instead of skill. This negatively impacts POC, who have the added burden of feeling they cannot make a mistake in order to prove that they are qualified or capable, especially when they are the first or one of few from their group in a position at work.

DOUGLAS DETLING

Fear, especially in the current economic climate.

AMY FRITSCH

I think people of color and whites are kept apart by the anger and fear that I can only imagine must be present in so many people of color as "good" white people fail even to see the dire nature of the situation of so very many Americans of color. The fact that so many white folk are actively and vocally racist (see discussions of immigration, of "illegals," the language used in reference to President Obama, and so many other disgusting examples) cannot do anything but drive a wedge and leave the America of color feeling unsafe. I believe white folks feel threatened by the idea of losing their privileged status even when they don't recognize their status as "privileged" (see East St. Louis). I believe that most people of color in America have a level of either fear or resignation about the fact that people—and especially men—of color are less safe in America than white folks, and that fear on a day-in-day-out basis produces an ongoing trauma that is the same as living in an abusive family. If the United States is one big, abusive family, beating and belittling the "children" of color in the analogy, of course the people of color are forced to tolerate that situation with nowhere to go, with even the abuse denied and their reality and truth dismissed, and no safe house existing to which they can flee. There is no reconciliation without an acknowledgement of wrongdoing and a turning from causing harm.

ACCEPTING OUR PART

Where did most of your stereotypes about people of color come from?

How did those stereotypes affect your perceptions and attitudes toward them?

BETSY PERRY

They came from growing up in my society, pure and simple. I grew up in an overtly racist state; I heard versions of children's chants that relied on the N-word. I only had one black playmate; only one black family lived in my extended neighborhood. I never made any Asian friends. I didn't know POC as equals; they were Other. I am constantly shocked and ashamed of the stuff that wells up when I walk through an all-POC area, when I hear about a POC being arrested, when I encounter any POC at work. I stomp on it hard, but it's not ever going to go away. It's in the bones.

JIM LANGEMO

I got most of them from parents, grandparents, education and product marketing. I got them from what I heard AND from what I didn't hear. For instance, my family's immigration story is told—the reasons for leaving Europe, the struggle to get here, the struggle to find your feet. Those same learnings weren't juxtaposed with the Mexican immigration experience or with the experience Africans had when they were forced from their country into bondage. For another example, so much of the civil rights movement isn't taught in our public schools. If it were, we would be a much different country.

How has it affected my perceptions and attitudes? As Bob Dylan says, "All he believes are his eyes, and eyes, they just tell him lies." I have realized that my lens is clouded with the teachings of my elders and with the media and public education. My attitudes and perceptions have thus inspired emotions of fear or indifference. They have allowed me, in my ignorance, to perpetuate the myths by telling jokes and using offensive terms.

Robin DiAngelo

My family, my schools, my textbooks, the heroes and heroines I was given, my leaders, the media, the way I was allowed to be "just human" but always had people of color pointed out to me by their race. I learned it from being told all people are created equal on the one hand, and never having a person of color sitting at our dinner table on the other. I learned something very powerful by living in a segregated society and not being taught I had lost anything by this segregation. In fact, I was taught to measure the value of a space by the absence of people of color; the whiter the space, the more valuable I was told it was (think "good" schools and "good" neighborhoods).

Ken Hornbeck

I received a lot of mixed messages growing up, so my perceptions and attitudes about race have been complicated as a result. Nothing has been cut and dry. The messages I received from my father and great-uncle about black people in particular flew in face of my personal experience with my football buddies. My father to this day makes remarks about black people that upset and frustrate me. He was no doubt passing along what he had been taught by his parents, and those messages made an impact on me, whether or not I choose to acknowledge that fact. So, too, my great-uncle. He actually sat me down and "schooled me" about black people. He would say that all you had to do was look at a "colored woman" and you could see that her nose, ears and mouth were "just like those of a gorilla. Proof that they are inferior to white folks." He firmly believed that if the races were allowed to mix, we'd all be ruined, because of the influence of "black blood."

It's important to emphasize that these lessons were passed on to me by people I respected a great deal, especially my great-uncle. I thought that he hung the moon. He was not an evil man. He had a great love for humanity and for me in particular. I believed, as a child, that he knew everything, and could do no wrong. He shared his wisdom about race with great authority and passion. Who was I to doubt any of it, even though it went against everything I believed to be true inside my young mind and heart? I can say that his words and warnings caused me great confusion, especially as I interacted with my teammates and other friends who were different from me.

In terms of what lasted, I can intellectually manage what I was taught. I can edit and correct the misinformation. I can seek to understand the messengers and the reasons for the messages. And I can work on forgiving those who tried to teach me what they believed was right. The problem is that those lessons, those messages, get into us on an arguably cellular level. They become ingrained to the degree that they very nearly are beyond our control. There are times in my comings and goings, my interactions with people at work, on the subway, on the street, in a place of business, where I feel fear or guilt or confusion or indifference or any number of other negative feelings based on my records. Try as I might, educate myself as much as I might, those records continue to influence how I behave, what I say, what I choose. All I can do is keep working on it.

TARA RONDA

My perceptions of race come largely from the fact that I was raised in a very homogenous community—in nine years of schooling prior to high school, there were perhaps five black kids, a couple of Hispanic kids, and maybe one or two Asian kids in my school. We never discussed race except when we talked about civil rights in our history classes, but because our teachers were also largely white (I don't remember ever having a person of color for a teacher), we never really gained another perspective on those issues.

As an adult facing the fact that I had racist views and benefited from white privilege, it was genuinely difficult for me to accept the fact that my parents were racist—I always knew it about the rest of my family (and was never comfortable with that), but the more covert way it played out in the house where I grew up was in many ways more insidious because it took longer to recognize. And once I did, it made it difficult for me to respect my parents. I still have trouble with that and actively avoid conversations about race with them in many instances.

HOLLY FULTON

I was raised in a racist/classist household with enormous privilege, lots of money and comfort, and I believed my parents' messages about people with less than me: poor and colored folks. These perceptions and attitudes made me ignore them, judge them, avoid them, be scared of them, and believe that I was better than them.

DANIEL COHEN

Most of my stereotypes came from my father in his coded language and in his outright racism.

I was born at Michael Reese hospital in Chicago and I have never been back there even though I have lived in the Chicago area all of my life. Michael Reese Hospital is located on the Near South Side of Chicago in a predominantly black neighborhood. Whenever we passed by the hospital or when I asked about my birth story, I remember my father saying that the hospital is in a bad neighborhood. He never explained what "bad neighborhood" meant. I never asked, but I clearly understood that he meant the neighborhood was black and therefore dangerous, unsafe, and I should not go there.

After my parents married they followed a relatively common pattern of white people leaving the city of Chicago (white flight) and moving out to the newly-built suburbs. The neighborhoods they left were being labeled as "bad" or "not like they used to be," and the schools were "not good any more." Once again I deeply internalized that my parents meant that the neighborhoods they left were black neighborhoods and dangerous. We did not want to live there.

I remember just a couple of students of color throughout all twelve years of my schooling. One of those was Greg Williams, who came to Deerfield when I was in middle school. He was tall and muscular, and we all assumed he played basketball and that his father must be on the Chicago Bears. When they began to practice in Deerfield, it became a foregone conclusion that if you saw an African American man or there was a new African American student in school, they were part of professional athletics. On top of that I would hear racial slurs by my father, who would call blacks "shvartza," a Yiddish term for black people that has a serious derogatory tone to it. I knew he was using it to demean and to separate. I did not like the word or the tone and I did not like him at those moments. He thought he was funny; I found him ugly.

MAC SABOL

I grew up in rural South Carolina. My neighborhood was all white. Even though we were poor, we still learned that we were not like the people "on the south side of town". Most of my schoolmates in parochial school were white. When I had to go to the public school beginning in grade nine, I remember being so scared of people of color, because I had learned through my associations with my classmates and others in my neighborhood that all of "them" had this inherent hatred for white people and just wanted to hurt us all.

It was a shock to me when I entered grade nine that most of the people of color were just as wary of me as I was of them and that many of them had been told that white people wanted to harm them too. So, it was a personal struggle in grades 9–12 for me to reconcile my own stereotypes with my experienced reality.

I found that my own preconceived notion of people of color was just that—a preconception and not grounded in fact. I would also add that learning about what was "taught" versus what was "real" extended to my understanding of Catholic religion, to my understanding of sexuality/sexual orientation and to my understanding of many other "isms."

As I was drawn to uncover the truth, I grew further and further apart from my family. My journey was (and is) viewed by my family as somehow a threat to the fabric of the "family unit" and a danger to them. It has been a painful lesson for me to learn that, sometimes in the quest for the truth, the path less traveled will become very lonely, indeed.

AMY FRITSCH

Most of my views of people of color came from the media, from my family, and from my (flawed) observations of my classmates in public school.

I have talked in other places about my father and grandfathers' racist attitudes and unwillingness to interact with people of color—and especially black people—and my awareness of those attitudes, both conscious and unconscious. I argued with them about their racist attitudes and statements at the time, and remember being angry at my younger brother's internalization of an even more virulent and violent racism than my father and grandparents espoused. I was embarrassed by my grandfather's failure to update his language, as he persisted in referring to "colored" people all his life.

I wanted to emulate my mother (whose racism I was largely unaware of until recently), because she at least made an attempt in her language and actions to act out of a religious belief and an American attitude that "all people are created equal." Sadly, I know that her more subtle and insidious racism is that which I internalized and which I carry and attempt to extinguish.

In my town the "black side" of town was the poor side, and my church would bus young children to church to try and "save" them from their poverty, their godlessness, their blackness. These paternalistic attitudes were ones that crept under my skin in subtle ways, and I remember resenting that these little black children were not adequately appreciative of what the church was trying to do for them, that they were not adequately bathed or sweet-smelling, that they were not good enough at sitting still or behaving or being quiet.

I never managed to notice that the only students of color in my honors classes were the students of "good" color: Chinese, Korean, Indian, and mixed-race-who-looked-white. I did not see in the lingering aftereffects of such long segregation the limitations on learning that generational lack of education fostered. After all, I did not have a single grandparent who'd graduated from high school or a single parent who'd even attended college, and yet I was in the honors classes, right? I didn't process that there were no other students in the honors classes whose families were not affiliated with the university. I noticed that there weren't black students in my honors classes with me, but naively and ignorantly supposed it was because there simply didn't happen to be any black students at that level of academic ability (much like I was the only townie). I never moved past the American myth seen on *Sesame Street* and *The Electric Company*, that people of various backgrounds lived next door to one another, were friends, and hung out together. Although it wasn't my experience, I supposed it was most people's experience. Until a few years ago, I continued to assume that was a reality rather than an ideal or a wish.

I think some of the attitudes I've carried have leaned toward a certain desire for people of color—particularly black people—to assimilate better: to speak Standard English, to speak more quietly, to be less boisterous. I, like so many others, including my mother, considered Asians ("Orientals" at that time) to be "good" and "smart" and still remember—now with a cringe—my mother commenting in the 1980's that she'd never seen an Asian person smoking because "they're smarter than that."

JOHN LENSSEN

I learned in school that the white Europeans came to this continent and civilized the Indians. I learned from my parents who fought in WWII not to trust the Japanese. I learn from the media that black men are angry and violent. I learn from the media, when I do not critically de-construct this information, that Mexican people in the U.S. are illegal criminals. I learned from Walt Disney and sitcoms on TV the images of beauty and desirability—the images of white people—the images of blue eyes and blonde hair. I learned from all around me in the United States that white men are in the highest-valued positions and that of course we live in a meritocracy and so they must have merited these positions—and the logical uncritical conclusions would lead me to believe in their superiority over people of color—and thus, as a white male, my superiority over people of color.

I must work critically and consciously to surface and let go of these images and perceptions that impacted me as a young person and continue to impact me today, as I am so often unconscious of all of these influences. I must be honest in that, even as I work to oppose racism, I still have racist attitudes that impact me every day. I must have daily contact and authentic relationships with people of color who show me over and over again that the media, the schools, and my parents were wrong about the racist stereotypes and fears.

What part do you think you play in perpetuating racism?

ROBIN DIANGELO

I do my best to challenge racism in my daily life, but overall the part I play is my silence, my obliviousness, my ability to ignore racism and receive no social penalty, my investment in the ways that racism benefits me, my lack of urgency about it, my pull to maintain white solidarity and keep myself and other whites comfortable by not challenging our racism.

JIM LANGEMO

There are things I do, known and unknown, to perpetuate racism. I do this on one-to-one levels or small-group levels when I let a comment or joke pass by. I do it when I don't take a moment to help someone see a situation from another point of view. I do it on a macro level by how I spend my money, which companies I support, what TV shows I watch or who I vote for.

TARA RONDA

I am white and supported by the white-privilege structure, so in that fact alone I am allowing social and institutional racism to continue, even if only passively. I also know I have my own prejudices—in my job working with college students, I have on several occasions been encountered by students from various cultures with whom I was very uncomfortable. I would often do what I could to get them out of my office more quickly because I couldn't identify with them, maybe had trouble understanding them (many are international students), and was uncomfortable with their cultural habits. I am more conscious of it now and try not to do those things.

Laura K

I am not in a position of power for hiring or purchasing, but as a professor I have influence regarding whom I call on in the classroom and whom I mentor outside the classroom. My primary mentorees are women and Anglos. I don't go out of my way to work with students of color who are struggling academically so that we can redress the "beginning the race with inferior shoes" issue. I don't encourage my institution to accept international students, because I don't believe we're large enough to serve them well. I am the first person to say, "We need to enforce the required minimum TOEFL score for admission, because students who don't have good enough English won't succeed in this institution."

Amy Fritsch

I suspect that my personal adoration for and excitement over Shakespeare— and British literature in general—helps to perpetuate the White-Men-Only Club of The Canon as taught in my classroom. I make an attempt to include texts from various time periods by authors from different backgrounds, but everyone knows that Shakespeare is my favorite. I attempt to teach him in context and to point out the racist nature of his wording where it appears, as well as the racist nature of England and the English (then and now). However, I don't know if that is enough to overcome the cultural idea that white authors are more important and more valuable than authors of color, particularly since I cannot change that our oldest texts include no authors of color, as their work was not preserved by a society that did not value their contributions.

John Lenssen

I believe that, just by teaching at the University of Oregon in a system of institutionalized racism, I am supporting and perpetuating that structure that communicates white supremacy. My moments of anti-racism are small compared to the power of the system.

Also, when I do not address the multiple and complex factors—including white privilege on the one side and the need for white anti-racism on the other side—involved in my teaching diversity and equity classes as a white man in the university system, I communicate the message that white people are still the most credible sources (white superiority) to address the issues of people of color.

Sara Krakauer

As a white person, I benefit from race privilege. Whenever I take advantage of these benefits I am playing a part in racism. In some cases, I have no choice. I may get offered a job in which I have advantages because of my skin color. Since I think of racism as a system of oppression, I know that I live in this system. So, in some ways, by not actively fighting against racism, I am committing crimes of racism.

Do you believe that racism is a learned behavior and attitude? If yes, why? If not, why not?

Ken Hornbeck

I do absolutely believe that racism is a learned behavior/attitude. We are not born with bias. Children will notice difference, and may unabashedly speak of it aloud and with no shame. There is nothing inherently wrong with noticing difference. A child may ask aloud in a supermarket, "Why is that man brown, Mama?" That's simple curiosity. But it is these very adults, these Big People Who Teach Us Things, who pass on their often negative messages about The Other to young people. In most cases, what is passed on is precisely what has been learned, either directly from their elders, or subliminally through media and other forms of institutionalized racism. We end up teaching what we have learned. In many cases the messages are intended to protect the child, and are not seen in any way as malicious or hateful. We want our children to be safe, and in the pursuit of that safety we pass on messages about "the dangers of THOSE people."

Children also practice what they see in others, especially in parents, grandparents and other adult care providers. We often underestimate just how observant children are. We cannot kid ourselves. Children notice everything. They understand the subtleties of inflection, of a raised eyebrow and exasperated sigh. We may think that we are teaching tolerance to our children, but what are our actions really saying? If, as white people, we are interacting with a person of color and a child witnesses impatience, condescension or some other indicator of privilege, what message are we sending that child? Are we not signaling that this behavior is acceptable? Are we not perpetuating racism? If we consistently behave differently toward a certain group of people, our behavior becomes, in essence, a schoolyard, and we can be all but guaranteed a repetition of that behavior in the next generation.

John Lenssen

I believe that racism is a learned behavior and attitude. There is no evidence anywhere that beliefs and attitudes about superiority and inferiority related to skin color occur without the structures, values, and behaviors of racism.

Susan Dodd

Absolutely. Although children begin to notice racial differences by the age of three or four, these are primarily differences in skin tone. Children pick up on the attitudes of their caregivers and begin to adopt those world views at a very early age. There are many subtle messages that adults convey to children regarding people of other races and cultural backgrounds. I remember very clearly as a child the way my mother would lock the car doors as we drove through the only section of town with black people in it. She didn't have to say a word to me to let me know how she felt about "those people."

Laura K

Absolutely it's learned. When I was young, I asked my mom once why all the blacks were sitting in the back of the bus (this was long after the Montgomery Bus Boycott, mind you). She shushed me—so I learned it was not okay to ask questions about race. She would not give my brother any money for his prom because he went with an Asian gal—there exist only two very grainy Polaroid photos of him in his tux that day because mom didn't even want to be around before his prom. That's heartbreaking! We always used to joke that if I didn't want her to come to my wedding, the easiest way to ensure that would be to marry a black man. On the flip side, most of the energy I've put into learning about and teaching against racism comes from my guilt and shame about my parents.

JIM LANGEMO

I believe racism is a learned behavior. Children don't judge people by the color of their skin. I have seen it in countless children (or stories about children). They are curious about skin color; they find it interesting and beautiful. They don't shy away. They aren't afraid. What they don't do (and what they learn) is to attach stereotypes to the color of the skin. This is taught.

I also believe that humanity is messy (you may use the word "sinful" if you are Christian; you may use the words "ignorant" and "confused" if you are Buddhist). Racism is a learned behavior, but at its root is our fallible nature that is too often motivated by fear, ignorance and greed. That knowledge doesn't mean that we give up because it can't be overcome.

AMY FRITSCH

I believe there are aspects of racism that are learned and aspects that are innate to humans. Humans, like other animals, tend to fear that which is different and presume a level of predation from other animals. Chickens do not trust foxes, humans do not trust bears. Very small children and even older children seek out those who "look like them," and I believe there are studies with monkeys that indicate that they prefer images of monkeys are who are more similar in appearance to their family group. A fear of those who do not look like the family group, in an evolutionary view, helps to keep the young of that group from being eaten (literally) by predators.

I think that the studies of black children who feel devalued by a lack of visual role models in positions of authority, of girls who feel devalued by a lack of female authority figures, show that there is an inbuilt need to have "someone who looks like me" valued as the young person would like to be. My own daughter, at five months, had seen a number of small children, but saw a boy nine months older than her who shared her blond hair and blue eyes and reached for him, a worshipful look on her face. So, from this perspective, I do think there is some genetic encoding that has young people drawn to those who look like them and fearing those who look different from the family group.

That said, racism, especially in the current academic definition as a form of oppression perpetrated by a group with greater power than the group against which the racism is leveled, must, in my view, be a learned behavior. In order for someone to have racist attitudes and to take racist actions, that person must first go beyond an understanding of "those who look like me" as "safe" and move into a sense that those who have similar appearances are superior to and better than those who have different appearances. Certainly the idea of attacking and oppressing the Other, rather than fleeing it, as would be the norm in the animal kingdom, would need to be learned. I cannot see the notions of superiority, the notions of causing harm in situations other than direct threat, to be anything other than learned.

The idea that the institutionalized and ongoing racism such as we see in the United States might be "reasonable" or "innate" is nonsensical and must therefore be seen as a learned and artificially perpetuated paradigm to work for the benefit of those (whites, men) who profit from societal inequities that oppress others (people of color, women).

TARA RONDA

I've never heard someone claim he was the victim of the "racism gene," but I've heard many people say that they were raised with a certain set of beliefs. What's positive about that is that if it can be learned, it can be unlearned and changed—of course it becomes more difficult the older we get, but I truly believe it can be done.

Are there two Americas? Why or why not?

ROBIN DIANGELO

Firstly, I think it is important to acknowledge that America is a continent of which the country of the United States of America is only one part. This point was very well made in the film The Color of Fear.

As to whether there are two "Americas" within the U.S., I would say absolutely yes. I think there is the country that is perceived by many white "Americans" that is embracing and inclusive, and then there is the other "America" that is experienced by many people of color that is anything but embracing and inclusive.

To be considered "American" it seems that people must assimilate and conform to the stereotype of an "American." However, the holotype for an "American" is based on the white experience and white culture. We hear the phrase "as American as apple pie and baseball," but we don't hear such phrases embracing the cultural identities of non-whites.

DANIEL COHEN

Yes there are, and here is a story that highlights this. Back in 2004 my family was driving to the airport to fly from Chicago to Philadelphia. As my wife is taking our baby out of the car seat and I am unloading the luggage, I realize that in the rush to get to the airport I left my wallet at home. I am without any identification, there is nothing saying that I am the person on the airline ticket. After berating myself for my carelessness I simply look ahead and tell my wife, "Don't worry; let's go into the airport. We'll tell them our story, be honest, smile and we'll see what happens." And that is what we did.

At that moment I had full faith I would be believed and recognized when I went into that airport. In my America, from the moment I was born as a white, male heterosexual with wealth, I learned that my experience was normal, and I was entitled. Every institution in my America taught me this, and it also taught me to not even see this privilege. With this came a sense of safety and confidence.

I was taught that this world was mine to take. This sense of power runs deep in me. My America taught me that I will be heard and acknowledged. And that translated into having complete faith that the system would always listen to me, serve me and protect me. So in a post-9/11 world, where our nation's fervor for security has squashed our liberties and racial profiling is out of control, I know in my gut that I can walk into that airport without any identification and expect to be listened to, understood and perhaps get to board the plane. The possibility of being hassled in front of my family, humiliated, searched or even arrested NEVER enters my mind. We simply smile and speak our truth. And how does society continue to teach me this there are two Americas? We were allowed to board the plane and fly to and from Philadelphia.

Tom Moore

Yes. Just drive through North St. Louis, then head out to West St. Louis County and notice the difference. Or drop in on any of the local, state or federal detention facilities.

Mac Sabol

There DEFINITELY are two Americas, one for whites and one for people of color. No question about it. Even though we co-exist in the same space in this country, in reality we operate in two different spheres. Several years ago, I had a personal "two Americas" experience that really hit home. At the time, I was Senior Vice President of Human Resources at a startup company in upstate New York. We had made a conscious decision to hire our workforce using unusual criteria—we hired based on who people were, their values and beliefs, not based on what they had done, and we specifically targeted the disadvantaged south side of the city, where a large percentage of the poor and the chronically unemployed live.

The workforce concept was simple: hire for attitude, pay a premium wage, provide world-class training, and expect top-shelf results. Compensation was set at $60,000 per year ($75K with benefits). We used a prominent firm to help us design a mechanism to identify people based on attributes. The initial workforce consisted of almost 300 people, all of which had the attributes we desired, but few had advanced college degrees. Many of them only had high school diplomas. They were tasked to build the multibillion entertainment complex (as construction workers) and then, once completed, to run it (as the service employees). Top pay, top performance. We took many off the south side streets, gave them their hope and dignity back. We gave them a reason to believe.

One day, I needed to drop off some uniforms to one of our team members who owned a convenience store on the south side. Not thinking twice, I drove down to the store and went inside. Once inside, it occurred to me that I was the only white person anywhere to be found in the area.

I went to the counter and asked for the owner. When I identified myself as the HR VP of this particular company, the several people who were in the store heard me, stopped shopping and started to come toward me. Initially, I was startled, at least until they started patting me on the back and hugging me and THANKING ME FOR WHAT WE WERE DOING ON BEHALF OF THE COMMUNITY. I was overwhelmed by their genuine and sincere gratitude.

I will add that, when local city-council politics (led by the white majority leader) ultimately derailed the project (another "ism" at work!) and we had to lay off those people, the pain I felt inside was what sent me over the edge and into eventual rehab. I had been part of giving them hope and I was part of sending them back into despair. To see a dream die is an unbelievably painful experience.

Are there two Americas? Yes, and that ugliness is very much alive in the 21st century.

What does assimilation mean to you?

DOUGLAS DETLING

Assimilation is almost the antithesis of diversity; it is when groups lose identifying characteristics of their ethnic origins, cultures, etc.

ROBIN DIANGELO

Act white and we might accept a few of you.

ZARA ZIMBARDO

In the context of my family, assimilation is my Sicilian-American grandmother ordering her children to "speak American" only. It is beautiful names with many vowels that have been chopped to fit American tongues that don't want to be bothered to pronounce them. Assimilation is, as my father once said, "giving up everything but your food." It is the process of becoming digestible to dominant white culture. It is losing flavor and smell. The erasure of cultural memory and heritage in exchange for entrance into the privileged club of de-ethnicized whiteness with its shiny promises of upward mobility. A united state of amnesia.

I search for how this trade-off shows up in the lives of Italian-Americans, who have become increasingly white from the time of my grandparents' generation to my parents' to mine. Do we faintly sense phantom limbs of amputated names, identities, dreams, collective memories? Are we haunted in ways that we don't have shared language to describe?

Assimilation is learning what is "too much," "too strange," "too loud," knowing who is an embarrassing relative. It is being taught that one's own cultural traditions are backwards, limiting, a hindrance to moving forward. "Freedom" then equals freedom from the past, from connection to ancestors, land, and cultural history. In return, the relative freedom to be defined as an individual, free to be seen just for who you are, not as one of "those people," not a representative, free to be anybody, nobody, somebody. Through the lens of my family, I see the history of Italian-American assimilation as the transformation of ethnic identity from being a liability to an (optional) accessory.

AMY FRITSCH

I tend to use the word "assimilation" to refer to any individual or sub-group that modifies some aspect of itself in order to fit in more fully with the larger group. I assimilated my speech patterns—for the most part—beginning in fourth grade when I realized that the students and people who spoke with the Midwest-neutral accent of television were taken more seriously than those of us with the rural-hick accent that carried a Southern twang and a presumption of stupidity. I modified my speech and accent in a hope of gaining greater acceptance and attention from the wider society.

Similarly, learning English, the language of the majority, is something an immigrant or immigrant group may choose to do to fit in or to garner the benefits of greater fluency of communication and the opportunities that come with that.

I've thought about the name changes so common in the Chinese immigrant population, where most individuals will have an "English name" they use in society at large. I wondered at what those changes meant to someone's sense of self and sense of heritage. My colleague talked about how his name on his birth certificate was clearly Spanish, but that his mother had registered him for school in kindergarten with the English version of his name which he had—mostly—used ever since. He talked of how grateful he had been that his official school name had not been a "Mexican" name so that he had the ability to distance himself from his background, and how that has been the source of much soul-searching regarding identity and cultural pride for him.

It is when the things left behind as one adapts to a new environment are things left behind out of shame or are good things that would have been beneficial to keep that assimilation becomes a negative and often even destructive force.

Tom Moore

Assimilation, in the better sense, is assuming the modes of speech, dress and deportment that allow you to deal with the larger society around you. In the lower sense, it is the abdication of your soul and abandonment of your traditional ways of life so as to be accepted, camouflaged, rewarded, or treated with some shadow of respect by members of the majority.

What does diversity or multicuturalism mean to you?

John Alexander

Multiculturalism means profound respect for and attention to the gifts we bring from our varied cultures. If we can accept those gifts with respect and understanding, both the giver and the receiver will benefit.

Multiculturalism is the Silk Road where stories and songs are carried and goods are traded and bartered, where our goods from home find value and respect in another's eyes.

Tara Ronda

I am greatly annoyed by these words because they are cop-outs—they're terms used by policy-makers and educators to indicate our "willingness" to think about other cultures and bring them into the fold of America. What we're really saying when we say "diverse community" is a black/Hispanic/Asian/etc., community with problems we can't figure out how to fix, such as poverty, educational inequities and racism. And multiculturalism doesn't make sense to me either, because to me that means we embrace multiple cultures in America, but that's nothing more than lip service.

BETSY PERRY

Diversity means that we cherish people as they are, in their differences, that we welcome people as "us" who aren't the same as "us." It means that I treat a POC as not "just like me" but as a person with different experiences than mine. It means that I go out of my way to make sure that everybody on the downslopes of the kyriarchy—POC, the disabled, women, the poor—is included in public and private spaces. It also means that I respect POC when they want to be alone together; I don't insist that every single space they inhabit be mine as well.

BILL PROUDMAN

Diversity is the multitude of differences we as humans have from one another. All of us are diverse, not just some of us. Many people have bought the notion that white men are not diverse. There is no white-male monolith. White men are as different from each other as any other group. While we share some similarities based on how we have been conditioned to assimilate into white-male culture, we are all different. We gain greater freedom to bring more of ourselves into work when we notice our uniqueness and differences while acknowledging our similarities.

TOM MOORE

Multiculturalism is the celebration of, and learning about, people of backgrounds different from my own. It is the synergy of the huge variety of people with whom we share the planet. It is the honoring of each entire unique person. It is closing the gaps and spanning the walls that we have dreamed up among ourselves.

CHAPTER SIX

WORKING WITH OTHER WHITES

——— WHAT SEPARATES US ———

What are some of your fears in bringing up the issue of racism with other white folks?

TARA RONDA

I don't feel particularly fearful of talking race with other white people, although I am sometimes afraid of what I'm going to encounter if I do. I'm extremely uncomfortable with people who are overtly racist or even mildly prejudiced —I know I also have some of those prejudices, but when you hear it from other people, it just comes across as so much more abrasive and wrong (which maybe is also a reflection of how I look to others when discussing race). I've also noticed that when talking about race with other white people, it's usually a hush-hush type of conversation, where we are afraid to raise our voices for fear that someone else will hear us. There is this general fear that we will be perceived as racist (and even if we know we are, we don't want to be seen that way) by other whites or by people of color.

MELISSA SWEENEY

My biggest fear when I bring up racism with other white people is that my own pain will deepen because they won't care.

JIM LANGEMO

As for white people, I sometimes am afraid to bring it up because I am afraid I won't always know where to take the conversation next. Of course, every time I do things work out fine—or at least I feel like I was an ally even if nothing was accomplished—but the fear remains. I just have to step through it.

There is another fear I have with bringing up racism with any group. I have abandonment issues. It's my own baggage and I own it, but it is there and it has worked to silence me at times.

BOB GROSS

With other white folks: Although I've been on this path for a number of years, I still have a level of embarrassment about bringing racism up with whites when the focus of the conversation seems unrelated. I do it often—and mostly get a thoughtful response. But I still harbor a certain reluctance—as if I'm being impolite or self-righteous.

AMY C. ORECCHIA

It's scary to talk about racism with white people because they might be part of the group that "doesn't get it," and they have the power and the choice not to change. It's scary because it's often frustrating and futile.

SUSAN DODD

When having these conversations with white folks, I know I have offended people in the past. They very quickly felt like I was calling them "racist," even when that was not the case. It is hard for me to have these conversations while working through so many levels of defensiveness. I have often been told that I misunderstood the context of a racist joke or statement. I find it hard to gently confront people about their beliefs because I'm afraid my comments will be more offensive than helpful. This is especially difficult when speaking to older members of my family.

I have some relatives who are very dear to me that serve as an example. While staying at the home of these relatives on a recent occasion, the topic of race came up in discussion. My otherwise kind and compassionate relative uttered the "N" word and could tell by my expression that I was offended. He spent the next two days of our time together bringing up his racial beliefs and experiences as a white man who has lived in the deep South for nearly 80 years. He referenced President Obama's recent comments regarding racial profiling and stated that racial relations in the United States would not get any better until his own generation of white folks died off. To me, this is an excuse established to maintain his current beliefs without making any effort to accept an alternative world view. It also felt like the door was closed from having any further discussion. Where do I go from here? I can't conceal my feelings and an uncomfortable situation is created because the other knows I'm offended and has no idea how to correct it.

To a white person, being called a "racist" is as offensive as being called a bastard. You're either a "racist" or you are not, period. It is difficult to talk to white people about racism because there is such a misunderstanding about what racism is. Racism is viewed as individual acts of hatred, rather than a generalized world view. Many whites feel that if they "have some (people of color) for friends" or if they can vote for a black president, then they can't be racist, problem solved. These same folks, then, are most offended at any implication of being "racist" when they can clearly prove, by show of friends or voting record, that they are not. This is my challenge; this is my sticking point. How do I move past the defensiveness and a world view that has been formed and supported for a lifetime?

SARA KRAKAUER

I am often afraid to say the wrong thing. Recently, I tried to organize a diversity training for teachers at my school. Several people told me that I could do more damage than help if I didn't organize the training well. This kind of thing makes me discouraged. If I am always tiptoeing around the issues to avoid insulting someone, how can we ever have honest conversation?

EILEEN KUGLER

When I engage other white folks with comments about racism there will initially be an inquisition as to why I am asking them (white folks) about racism, followed by statements about my "buying in to how we have oppressed others of color." Then something will be said to ostracize me for not staying true to my whiteness, and possibly some form of physical retaliation. As I've grown older and in some cases wiser, I have learned when I can and can't engage white folks about racism. The bottom line is: Unless I am engaging people in a consulting role or as a seasoned facilitator in race-relations education and training racially diverse groups, I rarely put myself in a position to feel fearful when talking about racism. I believe deep in my heart that most whites really don't understand racism today and that they believe "talking about it" will lead to "talking to them" about the wrongs they have committed as the oppressor. This applies to discussions with anyone about race: There is the fear that the discussion will turn ugly with people making emotional charges without listening to each other. I'm never afraid to have an honest discussion with people. But I need to trust that the other person is willing to hear me, just as I am willing to hear him/her. I've learned over time that both parties to a dialogue need to be willing to change themselves.

Betsy Perry

With white folks, quite honestly, I don't want them to be mad at me. This came up at work: I was criticizing a piece of writing and somebody asked why. I said "It seems prejudiced to me," which didn't get across. Then a POC spoke up and said, "It's condescending," and I sighed with relief, because she'd said it better. The reason she said it better was that she was willing to confront.

Bill Proudman

With whites, my fears are largely focused around productively challenging and confronting white men. I find it more challenging to engage with white men about issues of race than persons of color. This tells me that much of my work is with other white men. I and many other white men have learned to go it alone and not ask much of each other.

I have much work to do to learn how to more skillfully challenge and support white men when I have been taught and rewarded by the dominant culture to "show no chinks in the armor" and "don't let them see you sweat." The conditioning I have received over a lifetime with other white men runs deep and is often unconscious and pervasive. Many white men and women have learned to look towards people of color for their education, coaching and mentoring about the dynamics of race and racism. We don't generally look to other whites for this. We need to do this more often. By continuing to look exclusively to people of color to teach us about the effects of racism, we burden and further fatigue them, while ignoring and discounting the very real work of engaging other whites in these critical conversations.

Relying only on POC for my learning about the dynamics of race is not only unsustainable, but ultimately not healthy for people of color who didn't ask to be my coach, mentor, or teacher. I know that sometimes when I attempt to engage other white men my overtures are many times interpreted as scolding or negatively judging. I've been labeled as the PC police, as lacking a sense of humor, then ignored or isolated. I need to be more persistent. To do this I need to develop a deeper support network of other whites, particularly other white men. I am slowly doing this.

As a white, straight, educated, physically able male, I am not the norm as a diversity consultant. I am often asked by whites and POC where my passion for diversity comes from, because (unfortunately) many straight white men are not expected to be passionate about diversity. My passion comes in part from being mentored 20 years ago by a man of color named Harrison, who I became totally dependent on for my diversity learning and awareness. When Harrison died unexpectedly of a heart attack at age 47, his death had a lasting impact on how I partner with other people of color and where I draw my learning from related to all issues of diversity. While I did not directly cause his heart attack, my sole dependence on him for my learning created an unbalanced partnership. And it wasn't just me. Many other whites were also dependent on him and other POC for their learning about race and racism. Asking POC to teach us whites about race and racism is ultimately not a sustainable proposition.

Harrison's untimely passing caused me to reflect deeply and build a sustainable passion to reach out and learn with and from other whites and particularly other white men. I now know more about what my self-interest is in creating equitable and inclusive communities and systems. I come to my partnerships knowing I have real value to give as I continue to learn. Much of my learning over the last 15 years has come from other white men as we break the cycle of dependence on learning about the systemic nature of race or gender from POC or women.

Amy Fritsch

I am afraid that in conversations with white folks I will have inadequate words or think insufficiently quickly in response to their challenges to be a good spokesperson about racism. I am afraid that I will not show white folks the clear facts of the issues and that my failure to have the right information or the right analogies or sufficient facts or responses will only further cement racist beliefs.

What do you need from other whites to feel safe to talk about racism?

Robin DiAngelo

I'd appreciate not getting the silent treatment from other whites when I name racism. I wish other whites would find the courage to engage in honest self-reflection and to put racial equality before their own needs to "look good."

Susan Dodd

In talking to whites about racism, it would help for someone to ask what I think. Instead, I think a lot of times white people will be very busy defending their beliefs or explaining all the reasons why they feel they are not racist. I don't get the sense that many whites are curious about racism. Instead it seems that many white people tend to hold on very tightly to their beliefs, rather than explore themselves as racial beings or looker deeper into racial issues in our society, such as why people of color may be sensitive about racial injustices. I think it is a very scary place for some people to explore because there is a fear of being blamed for those racial injustices. It is easier and safer for white people to convince themselves that they are not racist and therefore not part of the problem. If there is no responsibility taken for "the problem," then there is no obligation to help change our racist society. It feels very rare for other white people to be open to talking about racism, particularly in ways that we as whites can make a difference.

Zara Zimbardo

In order to feel safe to discuss racism with other white people, I feel a need for a minimum base of shared understanding of how privilege and oppression function in coexistence. It does not necessarily mean that we all need to have the same analysis and language, but at least a view that sees the operation of power in society, instead of a view that is wholly rooted in a blinding individualism, which can lead to proving that "I'm not racist" as the most important outcome of a conversation between whites. That type of conversation can be an escape from staying in tough places and entering deeper, uncharted dialogue.

I long for, and try to help create, an atmosphere of compassionate willingness to hold each other accountable for the ways we participate in a racist society with the ultimate goal of shifting our culture. I need some degree of openness to turning toward discomfort instead of away from it. This is why a shared understanding of structural racism and collective liberation is critical. Without it, why would anyone want to dive into profound uneasiness, pain, and fear of the unknown within? For me a commitment to social justice is the container that holds and gives purpose to the process of making racism and whiteness more conscious. What more powerful container can there be to strengthen courage, compassion and curiosity than to look at what we as white people have been socialized to not see or feel? How can conversations keep an eye on the ways we can use privilege to challenge racism instead of becoming mired in paralyzing guilt and a desire to be individually exempt?

Safety comes from a supportive space to think out loud with white people, to face anxiety of what may arise, to acknowledge the power of fatalism—"Racism has always been and always will be; it's useless to try to change. What can one person do?"—and help each other to creatively fight against that seductive demon. I feel most safe with other white people who experience racism as something that limits their humanity, and see their own healing as inseparable from healing our society.

One of my greatest fears being a white person trying to talk with other white people about racism is that bringing it up will serve to further increase defensiveness and an aversion to talking about it. This worry is so great that I shy away from bringing up race issues if there is not some basic layer of love and respect for each other that will support us to look at what we are structurally blind to in this society, to thaw parts of our hearts that we may not have realized were numb. In order to question our inherited beliefs about ourselves, about people of color, and the history of our country, I think that support can come from seeing that we did not invent racism but share responsibility for both its perpetuation and its dissolution.

Laura K

When I talk about racism with whites, I show *The Color of Fear*. Before we go into any general discussion, I ask, "What did these men do that was helpful toward reconciliation?" (I use it in a reconciliation course) and, "What did they do that was not helpful toward reconciliation?" Then I write those things on the board. Essentially, that then gives us guidelines for conversation. It was helpful when they owned their stuff, so it will be helpful if we own ours, as well. It was helpful when they validated one another's reality, so it will be helpful if we do the same thing.

Barbara Beckwith

I need other whites to drop their defensiveness. To get over their desire to prove themselves as one of "the good white people." Instead, to be interested in the topic—to be eager, or at least willing, to recognize the ways our skin color gives us automatic, unearned credibility, to learn the histories left out of our history books, and to look at the structural and cultural racism that's still pervasive. To understand racism's effects on all of us. And do so without self-absorbed guilt, or need for absolution.

Daniel Cohen

I am WHITE. This is my reality; I walk in this world with privilege and advantage and a deep belief that the system will protect me and listen to me. I am a by-product of the American way. I am not ashamed to have wealth because of where my parents were able to buy a house based on their race. Instead I am angry at the inequality and motivated to work toward real justice for all: justice that spreads my advantage to all, justice that changes a system so all can believe in it.

I need other whites to stand up and speak to our privilege as white people. Speaking our racial truth is essential in this struggle for equity. We must model this behavior not to elicit shame or blame or guilt but to be allies to each other (our white brothers and sisters). We need each other in this struggle. I can empathize with white folks' shame, and I will stand with them as they begin to be ready and willing to move to a place of collective responsibility and action.

Beth Elliott

I feel safe but uncomfortable sometimes. To feel comfortable I would need them not to be defensive or take the conversation personally. It's doesn't have to be about being wrong, rather about recognizing that the "elephant" really is in the room and taking up a lot of space and energy that could be used in more healing and productive ways.

Bill Proudman

I need other whites to visibly demonstrate their courage by speaking up and being real about race and its impact on their lives. I need them to work hard to see the everyday nature of racism without moving to distance themselves from it, minimize or invalidate it. I need whites to have more courage to publicly state what they know and don't know about the dynamics of race without being politically correct. I need whites to not get stuck in blame or shame and instead keep their personal power to show up in the sometimes difficult conversations and decisions that race elicits.

Many whites who view themselves as socially progressive on many issues often minimize or disregard their own collusion in everyday racism for fear of being branded as a racist or ignorant of the impact of race. We have got to get over that and start to examine more of the subtle forms of everyday racism that we as whites generally don't have to think about or experience. We have to move beyond feeling we will be labeled as clueless or the problem. Let's step up more often and initiate the needed conversation about the impact of race in everyday life.

I need whites to be more courageous in using their personal power to engage with me and other whites in meaningful conversations about how our whiteness affects our lives and relationships. Don't leave it to POC to continue to raise these conversations in and out of the workplace.

Finally, I need other whites to strengthen their curiosity while transcending any guilt or shame that may be triggered by any examination of the above. Work to better understand your self-interest in eliminating racism so you can hang in there when the conversation becomes difficult. As Gandhi once said, "You must be the change you wish to see in the world." It starts with you and me.

Betsy Perry

Sadly, I need to believe that they're on the side of justice. I SUCK at confronting or discussing racism in contexts where I'm not sure people will sympathize. Which means I'm leaving all the job of confrontation to POC. I'm trying to change that, at least online, but I don't think I can do it in person.

Denton Mitchell

When I have been engaged on a basis that denies that premise, I have always attempted to "set the record straight." Point in mind—living in the Bayview district of Milwaukee, I was approached by a neighbor who complained that the area was being taken over by [people of color] and how awful it was. My response was to cut him off and say to him, "You do know that my wife is Japanese, don't you?" There was a pause—then he walked away. Afterwards, I wondered if I had "done right." In the next few weeks, I came to understand that I had, indeed, "done right." When he saw me on the street, he nodded and smiled. And I never again heard him speak to me or any other neighbor in those terms. It may well be wishful thinking on my part, but I perceived that he became more accepting of others in the area, and seemed to be happier, as a result. I certainly hope that was actually the case!

AMY FRITSCH

I need to know that the white folks with whom I am talking are sincerely open to discussion and to thought. I need to know that they will listen and think and reflect, and see that the discussion is not about condemnation but about trying to have adequate knowledge to include everyone in a way that is, by their own definitions, "American." I need to know that, at any point in the conversation, if they find they are unable to continue to discuss or to take in more of the concepts and realities being discussed, they will be honest and say that they need time to process the discussion to date. I need to know that there is honesty and sincerity and a desire to listen, rather than a desire merely to prove their own points by finding ways to shoot down offered experiences, data, and research. I would like to know that people will discuss race and racism with an eye toward equity and fairness, that people I love and respect will not pretend that racism doesn't exist or isn't serious, because I would like to be able to continue to respect those people.

JOHN LENSSEN

I need from other whites their willingness to stay present with my emotions —my anger, my tears, my frustration, my hopes, and my compassion. I need from other whites their willingness to stay in the room even when it is uncomfortable and even when they believe that they are being attacked and blamed. In order for me to feel safe to talk about racism, I need other whites to listen to and to really believe the stories and experiences of people of color. In order for me to feel safe to talk about racism, I need other whites to stop defending their good intentions and to pay attention to the impact of their thoughts, words, and actions. I need for other whites sometimes to shut up and listen and I need for other whites sometimes to speak their truth even if it may be uncomfortable to people of color and other whites. I need for other whites to embrace conflict and to walk into what has been hidden, forbidden, and unspoken.

Why do you think many white folks don't identify as a group?

CRAIG MORFITT

I don't think we identify as a group because we've had the luxury of not having to. I believe that Western capitalist society was created by white men to primarily benefit white men and, to a lesser degree, white women. We have grown up in a system that was built for us and which has taught us that we are effectively the "holotype" or the norm. Perhaps, because the system is built around us and relates directly to our cultural identity, we haven't seen the need to identify as a racial or cultural group.

AMY C. ORECCHIA

We don't have to. We don't need the protection and strength that come from associating with a group. Also, we're not taught to. We learn about "non-white" cultures in school when we have a specific history month, or when "multicultural considerations" are tacked on to the end of a book chapter or article. However, we rarely learn about different European cultures or customs. "White cultures" are considered the status quo, and this is part of what perpetuates racism, because until white culture is seen as just another one of many, it will be kept up on a pedestal. I think this issue is more complicated too because if you are a recent European immigrant who would be labeled white, your specific culture and language are still very salient; however, by the second generation these families can blend in with the white-majority culture. Whereas immigrants who have phenotypes labeled non-white are kept outside of this majority culture just because of how they look, so they tend to hold on to their cultures of origin for more generations.

SUSAN DODD

I think many white folks consider themselves to be "just Americans" because they have been a historically dominant group who prided themselves on their independence. White people as a group have not had to bond together for survival.

BARBARA IMHOFF

We're conditioned to be competitive with each other from early childhood, so we think in terms of "I" not "we"—the cult of the "self" prevails.

We ARE the group. We're the primary culture, so we don't feel the need to identify as a group.

We have few fundamental commonalities. We are pluralistic in faith, in interests, hobbies, social groups. There's so much to choose from that we have few vested communities.

The extended family has become a lost tradition, so we don't learn to identify even at the root level of family. That breakdown of group identity manifests at the societal level.

MELISSA SWEENEY

(Un)consciously, white people perceive themselves as "human" and "normal." With this world view, they don't believe they need a further ethnic identifier because they already walk comfortably in the world. Whites perceive people of color as "other" and further classify them as "different" because people of color don't look like them, talk like them, dress like them, etc.; identifying people of color as "abnormal" makes it easier for whites to maintain a one-up position. When white people fail to connect themselves to their specific ethnic roots or embrace their lineage, they do not realize how they are dying inside because they lose their relationship to their ancestral memories and the knowledge of the struggles of their own peoples. This level of disconnect enables a lack of empathy and understanding of those that are classified as "different." And this lack of empathy allows for an easier maintenance of white power and a perpetuation of the status quo that "white is right." White is also "might"; after all, white supremacy is (un)consciously maintained with a stronghold of privilege in numbers. Why would white people in power want to dismantle their army?

ZARA ZIMBARDO

On one level, white people don't identify as a group simply because we don't have to. Of course white people form groups in all kinds of ways, but the whiteness of it largely remains underneath conscious awareness. On another level, I think that many white people do not identify as a group because that consciousness can be profoundly, stunningly uncomfortable. To point it out can be painful.

When I think of who identifies as a white group, what comes to mind are groups who are openly racist. No white person I personally know falls in this category. That being said, it is fascinating to me to reflect on how learning about white-supremacist groups in my progressive education as a child and adolescent was part of what helped to me to not see that I am white. It was easy to "otherize" those whites understood as evil, which served to reinforce that I was not them, and yet that also made white privilege and forms of white-liberal racism impossible for me to see.

Apart from those groups where self-identification as whites is equated with being white supremacists, there is another kind of distancing that occurs which makes many white people not want to identify as a group. What does it mean when one says, "Those people are really white"? It is not generally considered a compliment. To be glaringly white on a cultural level connotes a lack of culture, flavorless, being awkward in one's body, repressed, a sad lack of groove. Not the best party. No one I personally know would want to openly identify as white in that way either, apart from self-deprecating jokes. These are two examples of easy separation.

Less easy is to take Thandeka's suggestion to play the "Race Game": to simply name whiteness in casual conversation with whites and say for instance, "I'm reading a book by a white writer," "I visited some white friends," and observe the reactions. In my experience, to label whiteness in liberal white circles is often alienating at worst, dismissed at best. A subtle glaze over the eyes, eyebrows raised in confusion, nodding and looking away. Such a tiny intervention into language is an iceberg tip, touching on what she calls "the great racial unsaid." The absence of a racial signifier describing someone is usually assumed to mean they are white. What does this do to our psyche? What dis-ease comes from speaking it? It gets at the root of how privilege functions, by not being able to see itself as particular. It shakes the structures of denial and blindness. It can definitely sour a social interaction and make it squirm.

A core feature of whiteness is the universalization of experience: We are just people, just individuals and human beings. Privilege is a site of ignorance. White people are "free" to ignore race, "free" from having a racialized identity. To name that whiteness is in fact a racialized identity compromises this "freedom." A white group identity is experienced as being reduced. Liberal color blindness can make white the hardest color to see. Whiteness is defined as the unspoken norm, the standard against which others are made "others." Historically it has been defined as the beautiful, the good, the true, the fully human, an identity defined and upheld as superior in contrast to people of color. Reflecting on this is to come face to face with its ugliness. We wish to forget how we became white, an identity structured by absence of ethnic culture, presence of privilege and security, and violent contrast to oppressed racialized others. What glue holds us together? What holds us above? What holds us apart? To see ourselves as a group, in a group, deflates the joy of only seeing universal humanity and individuality, and may surface collective amnesia, shame and discomfort that we often do not have the language and support to face together.

Daniel Cohen

As a white person growing up I was aware that people of color have been discriminated against. Even growing up in Deerfield, a predominantly white community 25 miles north of Chicago, thirty-five years ago I knew there was discrimination and that must be really bad for "those people." I, as a white person, in no way saw myself as part of an advantage group. I did not even see myself as part of a white group. Everything around me was white: all my teachers, friends, coaches, etc. It took me years later after college to begin the process of seeing myself as advantaged and then also to see myself as a white person as part of a group that disadvantaged people of color. I was a good guy, working to end apartheid in college, fighting for AIDS funding; I was well liked—how I could be racist? Here is the crux for white folks: Most white people, me included, are invested in certain beliefs about themselves and this nation. To see myself as part of a white group changes all of that.

I went back to examine my relationship and inequities with my three sisters. As I recognized my privileges in relationship to women—my whiteness became crystal clear. I am a white person; I have been advantaged and privileged. I, as a white person, have discriminated against people of color, have stereotypes, have been racist, and am part of a larger system that perpetrated and perpetuates all of that too. I have internalized so much. Seeing myself as part of a white group meant I am no longer simply Dan the individual, or Dan the good guy, or Dan whose hard work got me where I am, but rather I am both Dan the individual AND Dan who is white and part of a larger system. I now have to make a choice as to how I must be in this newly-awakened system.

Amy Fritsch

I think that to identify as "white folk" would disrupt the desire to be part of a "special" group and force white folk to acknowledge that we are, as a whole, a group that truly already has special privileges, many of which we are unaware of and which have gone unacknowledged and been taken for granted. This, in turn, would require us to see that people of color have a legitimate special status of still being oppressed, and to have to question our own role in the act of oppressing and ways that we have benefited from that oppression rather than merely "made good" on our own merits, as the American Fairy Tale tells us we have.

BILL PROUDMAN

I believe there are a number of interconnected factors that contribute to why most whites and particularly white men don't identify as a group. One major influence is the impact of dominant and subordinate group dynamics. Dominant groups are defined as the norm in society—being white, male, and heterosexual. Being in the dominant group often makes the group identity invisible because the focus is almost always on the other. We see this play out in organizations as follows—when the issue of race comes up, it is almost always the experiences of POC that are focused on. POC are expected to lead and teach others in the organization about the dynamics of race. We never examine what it means to be white. That is the norm. Just the way things are. The same is true for women when the issue is gender.

The impact of white-male culture is another factor. White-male culture is the dominant and prevailing culture in most organizations in the U.S. It dictates organizational values and acceptable behaviors. White-male culture is most invisible to those who never have to leave that culture (white men).

One of the main hallmarks of white-male culture in the United States is rugged individualism. The focus on the individual over the collective is framed in our Declaration of Independence and Bill of Rights. For many whites and particularly white men, this rugged individualism has them see most situations from the individual lens. White men see themselves first as individuals and rarely see themselves from a group identity. As a result, many white men can often feel personally attacked when really the other person is talking generally about their experiences with the white-male group.

Another complicating factor is the tendency of white men to view most things through an "either/or" lens. It must be this or that, yes or no. To focus on their group identity, many white men feel they are being asked to give up or ignore their individuality. Like an either/or choice. Add to this the many current negative societal connotations of being labeled white male, you can begin to see why most white men would not likely stand up in a crowd and proudly claim membership in the white-male group. Until whites and white men start to examine their group identity (i.e., what does it mean to be white?), people of color will still be expected to educate us whites about the daily effects of racism.

BETSY PERRY

It's the unmarked condition. We aren't "white folks," we're just people. Why can't YOU (applied to any minority, not just POC) be "just people" too? Why are you forcing me to pay attention to your differences? Can't we all just be the same?

JOHN LENSSEN

Most white people in the United States, like me, are supported and conditioned to see themselves as individuals. We are exposed to the myth of the rugged individual, the platitudes of individual freedom, the stories of individual heroes. And we see people who look like us benefiting from this reality/mythology for white people. We are encouraged to compete and to win. We do our own work in school separate from other students and separate from our families and our community. Many of us grow up in nuclear families with the expectation that each child will grow up and leave the family home to make a separate home for themselves. We go to schools that never address the common experiences, the common characteristics, the common culture of white people in the U.S. We are directly and indirectly taught that the white European American experience is the human experience and that the human experience is mostly about individual white people. We white people often lack the foundation of connection and community with other white people (and also lack any foundation of connection or community with people of color), even with our own relatives.

Our individualism also serves as a defense against personal responsibility for the racism that exists, and as a way to clearly see the ways that we whites, as a group, every day benefit from this racism.

CHAPTER SEVEN

WORKING WITH PEOPLE OF COLOR

What are some of your fears to bring up the issue of racism with people of color?

TARA RONDA

I am afraid that by even bringing the issue up, I am somehow being offensive. Race is one of those things that we've had the fear of God inflicted upon us for addressing. I don't want to open old wounds for people or be the recipient of misplaced anger because, although I often feel misclassified by people of color, I understand that I am in many ways representative of all white people. Which I think is one of the biggest problems—perceiving individuals as representatives for their respective groups, which of course we can't really be.

MELISSA SWEENEY

When I talk about racism with people of color, my main fear is that I will cause more pain with what I say or do not say.

JIM LANGEMO

The biggest fear I have with bringing up racism would be taking people of color back to the hurt—a hurt that has four hundred years of history, but bleeds like a fresh wound. I don't like hurting people. I also sometimes fear that I may be perceived as trying too hard to be acceptable, to fit in. I notice this feeling comes up when I am a minority with women or with the GLBT community.

AMY C. ORECCHIA

It's scary to talk about racism with people of color because I feel like I really don't know what I'm talking about. I know this is a topic I am ignorant about, and I'm afraid of saying something that is my perception, but isn't accurate or is offensive to someone else. I have a couple of friends who lump white people into two categories: those who get it and those who don't. Empathy is such a big part of my profession (counseling) and my personal identity (something that comes quite naturally to me) that it's scary to think that my ability to accurately empathize is compromised.

Barbara Imhoff

I am fearful that I will discover that I am even more of a racist than I admit to myself. I am fearful I will say something to offend a person of color based on my ignorance or subconscious racism. I want to look good, which gets in the way of honest dialog. I feel that I "should" know more than I do about other cultures and about the subject of racism, which might keep me from openly communicating.

Sara Krakauer

I did a racism training and felt pretty attacked by people of color in the room. At one point, I asked how I could be expected to give up financial benefits that I have, and someone yelled at me that it's not about giving up. It's about treating everyone with a base level of respect. I get that, but racism is systemic, and not always interpersonal. So, I feel confused about how to address race from both levels—the institutional and the personal.

Eileen Kugler

One of my first fears when bringing up racism to people of color is that they won't have a clue how racism has impacted me personally and they will immediately attempt to challenge me versus listen to and hear what I have to share. I am the person identified as "the racist," as they have learned that racism is a white issue.

I beg to differ on that perception. I contend that there is racism in every group of people regardless of how those groups (or individuals) identify with race, ethnicity, creed, or national origin. In my experience, people just refuse to talk about it, especially if the people to do the talking are in different racial groups. I don't see this fear of talking about racism being eradicated in 2013, or even up to 2025.

I was in a situation where a black person was willing to excuse anything a black person said or did, but assumed the worst about what a white person did (in that case, the white person happened to be me). There was no opportunity for discussion or dialogue. That's the situation I fear.

BETSY PERRY

With people of color, I worry about asserting privilege, about saying, "Your job is to educate me," rather than, "You're a person I know, and I'm not going to treat you like an example of 'What POC Think.'"

BILL PROUDMAN

With people of color, I find myself sometimes hesitant to share my feelings or thoughts, particularly in charged situations. Some of my concerns emanate from family-of-origin patterns of wanting to avoid conflict and confrontation at all costs. I sometimes feel like I will be misunderstood even before I speak. It has been helpful for me to recognize that often when I am misunderstood, it is not about me but about the experiences the person of color has had with my group (other whites) and the accumulated fatigue of having to deal with whites who invalidate their reality. I can unconsciously trigger this myself by defending my "good guyness" or unconsciously negating their reality because I don't want to believe that their life is that hard on a daily basis.

Every time I confront one of my fears, by acknowledging it publicly I find a deepened reservoir of courage, that when combined with my curiosity keeps me coming back for more. I am less afraid of looking stupid, or being judged as clueless because I am authentically engaging in my own ongoing work. I remind myself that on many dimensions of diversity where I am a part of the dominant group, I am more confused now than before and that is okay. Being confused does not diminish my ability to engage with others. Instead I work hard to have my confusion feed my curiosity.

I attempt to let go of any expectations that my end goal is to sort all this out so I don't have any more questions. I now work for the reverse—to pull back more and more layers, even if it means I might be more and more confused. I have learned to better use my confusion and fear to keep me curious and engaged rather than convincing a person of color that I am not like other whites who don't understand the everyday effects of white-skin color privilege.

AMY FRITSCH

In discussing the issues of race and racism with people of color, I have great fear of mis-stepping or giving offense. I fear displaying my ignorance, of being less informed than I would have hoped to be by this time in my education. I fear using a term incorrectly or offensively. I fear being judged as lacking, being judged insensitive, being deemed unworthy of the conversation or unworthy of being "bothered with." I fear that I will frustrate people of color who, so very often, are asked to "school" white folk in issues of race. I fear being seen to ask for them to "speak for all people of color," no matter how carefully I word my requests for sharing. I generally ask, "Do you have time or energy to share with me your own perspective on or experience with this?" I have learned to use that wording to try and show respect for the fact that it is not the ongoing job of people of color to "school" me.

If you could say three things to people of color about racism, what would you say?

TARA RONDA

1) I am not the bad guy. I am trying to change the way I think.
2) I don't believe the "color-blind" theory. I will not pretend that you are the same as me because I know we're different. The first thing I noticed about you was that you were a person of color.
3) And now be open to knowing me and allowing me to get to know you beyond the surface.

JOHN LENSSEN

A. I have come to understand so much about the impact of racism on people of color through the generosity of their sharing their stories, their struggles, their pains, their challenges, their lives with me. And I am grateful for these stories. My life has been changed by these stories. Yet I do not expect them nor do I feel entitled to these stories.

B. I know that I can never fully understand the impacts of racism on people of color and yet I must understand. It is my responsibility to understand and to be responsible and accountable for my role as a beneficiary of racism and to take action as an anti-racist.

C. I understand that, as Victor Lewis states in *The Color of Fear*, racism is primarily a white people's problem. As a white person I must be committed to educating other white people about racism, about anti-racism. I must be committed to push them and to support them to not only see white privilege in their lives but also the ways that we white people reproduce and continue racism as agents of institutions that are racist. I will take this commitment on for the rest of my life.

What would be some questions you would like to ask people of color?

BARBARA IMHOFF

What was it like growing up for you as a POC? What can I personally do to alleviate racism? Are you willing to talk to me about racism? Do you resent who I am and what I have because I'm white? Could we ever be friends? Do you think I'm a racist, and in what ways? Would you prefer to not deal with the issue of color? Would you be willing to teach me about or invite me to participate in your culture/faith/traditions? Do you dismiss me simply because I'm white? What are your struggles in the everyday world? Do you say what you're really thinking (to me as a white person)?

MARIE DOAN

Would you like me better if my skin color were the same as yours? Can we be friends? Would you be willing to come to my home and invite me to yours? How do you feel about interracial marriage/dating?

AMY FRITSCH

What attributes of your heritage and culture do you find most valuable? What do you think white folks could stand to learn from your culture's values/ attitudes/traditions?

What are some of the most hurtful things you encounter or experience as a person of color? Why do those stand out?

What have been the most heartwarming moments that you've experienced as a person of color with regard to how a white person has behaved, included you, stood up for you or someone else?

Can you think of ways that a white person's words or actions have had a positive impact and that I might want to consider emulating?

HOLLY FULTON

What are ways you want white people to be allies that you don't see out there in society? What do you want to see whites doing to fight racism that they aren't? What do reparations look like for you?

JOHN LENSSEN

Can you tell when white people are just talking to say the right words?

What is your response when I reveal that I still have racist beliefs and stereotypes?

How do you feel when I acknowledge the times that I do not speak up for people of color and against racism?

Do you believe there will ever be a time when race becomes socially/economically/politically irrelevant?

ZARA ZIMBARDO

What do you see as effective ways to bring up issues of race and racism in the current discourse of "post-racial" America?

How can white people help raise issues of racism when many like to believe we have "transcended" race division and inequity as a thing of the past?

What frustrations do you have about white people who are attempting to be allies against racism?

What suspicions do you have of white people who claim to not be racist?

How can we distinguish between cultural appropriation and appreciation?

CHAPTER EIGHT

PERSONAL STORIES

When did you first experience racism?
What happened and how did it affect you?

ROBIN DIANGELO

I "experienced" it before I was born. Where I could be born—which hospitals my mother was allowed to deliver in (any), who delivered me, how my mother was treated by the doctors and nurses—all were influenced by race. It has always been there and isn't limited to a moment or incident.

AMY C. ORECCHIA

When I was in kindergarten my family moved to a small rural Midwestern town that was overtly racist towards the newly arrived migrant farm and factory workers. Although I was young, I heard the women at church whispering rumors about "those Mexicans" as well as my mother's sighs when I got head lice, likely from a "Mexican boy" in my class at school. I learned pretty quickly that being "Mexican" was not a good thing, but I was confused when other white kids taunted me for being this bad thing. Wrongly accused, I began to point out their incorrect interpretation of my physical features—"My hair is not black, it's dark brown!"—and showing the lighter skin that was covered by my shorts and t-shirt. They usually left me alone, deciding I only looked like "one of them" but my relief was short-lived. When I saw my Mexican classmates the next day, I felt guilty and confused.

As I reflect on this experience, first of all, I am very glad my family moved away from this community after I finished the first grade. Second, what stands out to me is what a powerful effect this one period of my childhood had on me. Without even being conscious of why, I insisted my hair was "dark brown" until my late teens. It is overwhelming to know that people of color endure similar taunting, suspicion, and stigma every day, without the privilege of being "left alone" after a few protests.

Susan Dodd

My earliest recollection of racism occurred when I was a young child in the Midwest during the early 1970's. I was at a department store with my mother and a sales associate offered to take me on a walk around the store so my mother could shop in peace. The associate, who was black, offered her hand to me. I felt okay about going off with her, but I remember asking her, "If I touch you, will I turn black, too?" She smiled and said "No," and I could see that my mother was somewhat embarrassed. I was only three years old, and there was a lot I did not understand about racism. But I did "know" at that time that somehow being black would not be as good as being white. In hindsight, I'm very thankful that this lady was so kind to me. My very first interaction with a person of color was a pleasant one, and I am sure that helped me to question many instances of racism I encountered from that point on. There was a time in my life when I felt guilty recalling that encounter, ashamed of how I surely offended this kind person. However, I now realize that she encountered racism on a regular basis and surely did not lose sleep over one toddler's blatant curiosity. I, however, gained a lot from this experience.

Melissa Sweeney

Dating interracially has brought to the forefront issues of race/racism into my white world. Growing up, I had been taught by my family that everyone should be treated equally, but when I brought home my first black boyfriend, I got very mixed messages. An elderly aunt that I respected had said, "How could you do this to our family?" Even at a young age, I had challenged her to be upfront about the underlying statement behind her question, and I remember responding, "How could I do 'what' to our family?" I never got a direct response but I certainly dug for it—wanting her to be accountable and to hear herself. It was disappointing for me to learn that the same people who loved me were not as open to loving others—even though they thought they were. Over time and by way of my family getting to know different men I have dated, they have grown more "tolerant" and even more open to the idea. Interracial dating, to this day, remains a hot-button topic. When I worked as a family therapist, I focused my clinical practice on work with such couples. Not only do interracial couples have the day-to-day challenges any partners face but they also have a community generally unsupportive of their partnership; of course, this poses additional challenges and makes the likelihood of these partnerships to be less successful.

Laura K

This is like the question my friend asked when she interviewed men and women about what they do to protect themselves against sexual violence. The women talked about pepper spray, not walking alone at night, checking the back seat before getting into the car...The men looked blankly at the camera and said, "Well, nothing, really—haven't really thought about it." My first experience of overt racism probably was when my brother went to the prom with an Asian gal and my mom wouldn't speak to him and refused to pay for the prom. I was the one who took those two grainy Polaroids so there would be SOME record of his having gone. I was ashamed.

Holly Fulton

As a kid: When my parents called Brazil nuts "nigger toes." I didn't know what "nigger" meant until later and I remembered my parents using it as a NAME for a NUT and thinking, "Oh my GOD, they were so RACIST!!" When I was an older kid (teenager) my father told a friend he thought there were too many blacks at Brown University, where he went to school. I was mortified and horrendously embarrassed.

Marie Doan

When I was an adult I dated a man from the P.I. It was painful. My parents were not happy and his family had preconceived ideas about the "type" of woman I must be since I was not from the P.I. At his family gatherings, the men and women would separate and socialize and then there was little old me sitting alone. Everyone spoke Tagalog and I was left out of the conversation—very uncomfortable to say the least. I didn't fit into either group—ladies or men. Years later his sister and I spoke about their former perception of me being "that" type of woman and how it changed as they grew to know me as a person and not a skin color.

I don't think my step-dad ever really accepted it. He was always too afraid of what the neighbors would think. My answer to him would always be, "Dad, I am sure that the neighbors are happy that I have a boyfriend that I love." That never went over well with him as one can imagine.

Mac Sabol

My first real experience with racism happened when I was about seven years old. I had developed pneumonia and ended up in the intensive-care unit of the local hospital. The person in the bed next to me (also about seven years old) was sick too. He was a person of color. I later learned that he was in the same room as me because the hospital was overfilled and there was no room in his "designated area."

As I got a little better, I remember turning his way and trying to say hello and introduce myself. I was STRONGLY told by the adults in the room that I was not supposed to talk to blacks, that it was inappropriate (I remember a nurse telling me that talking to "niggers" was no way for a "proper Southern boy" to behave). I remember we both looked at one another and he seemed to understand my consternation. He seemed to say, "It's okay," in his eyes, as if he was reading the puzzled look on my face. The next day, he was no longer in the room with me.

I have thought a lot about that boy over the years. The situation really became clear to me many years later when I was in a diversity training class and learned that people of color experience racism so much earlier in their lives than whites do. I am guessing that even at his young age, the person in that bed next to me had far more knowledge about racism and was far wiser than me.

Beth Elliott

The first blatant racism I experienced was when I was 18 years old. I dated a young black man. It caused huge drama in my family. My grandfather wouldn't allow me in his house and wouldn't be where I was. My parents supported me and liked the guy, so they were ostracized too. Some of my "friends" didn't want to be friends with me any more. It was shocking in many ways. Eventually the relationship with the young man ended and many years later my grandfather apologized. What really bothers me about this situation is that I lived 18 years without experiencing racism and people of color experience it as part of their everyday life.

Bill Proudman

One of my earliest memories came one hot muggy August afternoon in Pennsylvania when I was about 10 years old and our family was traveling by car to a relative's house. My family (parents, myself and my three younger siblings) was traveling through a predominantly African American neighborhood in an adjoining city. Many folks were sitting on their front stoops drinking lemonade and beer trying to survive the sticky summer heat. I remember vividly my mother turning around with fear, yelling to me and my siblings to roll up the window, sit up and look straight ahead. I remember feeling afraid while also wondering why we needed to roll up the windows, which was supplying the only cool breeze.

This moment instilled the notion that I should fear black people. I know this is just one of a number of childhood messages given to me by adults that reinforced this fear. I received tons of misinformation about people of color. It was pervasive and often subtle. Combine this with the fact that I had no close friends of color as a kid till I got late into high school and the pattern was set: Fear what I don't know.

I use this and other childhood memories as reminders that it is my work to unlearn these tapes, not just about race but also about many other issues of difference. I was taught to fear the most what I know the least. I have spent considerable time in the last 20 years unlearning these tapes. My response has been to be more curious, explore what I don't know or am anxious about.

It has taken me most of my adult life to remove this tape from my head. It still comes up occasionally—"A black man I don't know on the street; I must be afraid." Instead of acting on it, I get conscious of the old message and work to not let my reaction in the present connect to something taught to me a long time ago.

BETSY PERRY

This one happened when I was in elementary school. My parents sold their house to a black couple. The neighborhood made threats. My best friend was forbidden to play with me. That's the only part I remember. My parents remember the death threats and the cross burned on their lawn.

Note that the racism story I remember is the one in which I'm a victim and my parents are the heroes. THIS IS NOT AN ACCIDENT. I remember the stuff that makes me look good.

Amy Fritsch

I think my first conscious experience of racism was when I made—rare for me—a new friend in junior high when I was about 13. Her name was Valerie and she was quiet, sweet, smart, interesting. She was willing to talk to me while so many other students would only do so to taunt or belittle me. She smiled and was kind and funny. She was also black. Light-skinned, to be sure, but still black enough. I had not realized until that day the extent to which I was aware of my father's racism, and surprised myself when excitedly telling my mother about my new friend by inherently knowing I should mention Valerie's blackness and asking if I'd be allowed to have her come over to play. My mom, who, along with our religion, consistently said that the outward aspects of a person were irrelevant and that it was the spirit only that was important, asked if I thought that my dad would approve of that. It was unsettling to realize that not only did I already know that my dad would never allow Valerie to visit, but that my mom, who totally disagreed with his attitudes, would both support his racism and excuse him of it—as if that made it okay—by explaining that he "had his reasons" based in his experiences.

I stopped talking to Valerie, thinking that there would be no point in pursuing a friendship where we would not be able to spend time together outside of school, where we shared few classes. We would still smile and wave, but I wonder, now, if Valerie knew that I had not pursued her friendship because she was black. My mom always remembered Valerie, and told me when Valerie, in her mid-20's, was hospitalized for and died from the sickle cell I didn't know she had. I know I lost out on a friendship with a lovely young woman due to racism and my lack of courage to push the issue, defy my father's racism, and do what both my mother and I knew was right and be friends simply because I liked her.

Ironically, my friend Ila, who was an immigrant from India with two parents who were professors at the university, and who was ultimately the salutatorian of our class, was entirely acceptable. We were friends from third grade through twelfth grade, and she visited my house often. So I knew early on that people from different ethnicities occupied different levels of acceptability with my father.

John Lenssen

My most memorable early experience with racism was when my friend from school, who was African American and was bused from his neighborhood in the Central district in Seattle to my predominantly white neighborhood, came to my white friend's house in my predominantly white neighborhood to play basketball. He was the only person of color on my white friend's basketball court. As we were playing basketball, my white friend's father drove up. My white friend's father was my idol. He was the coolest dad. He was always nice to me. He gave me rides to places. He was interested in my life. He drove a new car. As he drove up he started yelling racial slurs at my African American friend and then started screaming at his son to get that "n…" off his property. This was the moment when my world changed. I was outraged. I could not believe my ears. The hatred coming from this man contradicted everything I had thought about him before. I could no longer think of him as a good man.

As I walked back to school with my African American friend I was shaking with anger and disbelief. It was then that my African American friend tried to comfort me. He told me not to get upset. He said it happens all the time. And I believed him and for the first time caught a glimpse of what everyday life—everyday experiences with racism—was like for him. The next day, my white friend told me that he would not be talking to my African American friend again. My life changed that day. My eyes were opened and I began to see what my African American friend experienced in school—the looks, the exclusion, the talk behind his back.

CHAPTER NINE
WHAT IS NEEDED TO UNLEARN RACISM

—·— OPENING UP —·—

What opens you up and what closes you down to talk about racism? Why?

Amy C. Orecchia

I think that racism is an emotionally-laden topic and I'm always more comfortable talking about issues that involve strong emotions with people I know better. One thing that closes me down is when people of color have strong anger towards whites when discussing racism. It's hard because I understand why they feel that way and I think I would feel the same. However, if I am part of who they are directing their anger at, I don't even know what to say, except to convey that I think I understand.

Robin DiAngelo

Opens: Whites being willing to be humble and sit in the face of not-knowing. Whites caring more about understanding how they collude with racism than they care about "saving face." These dynamics open me up because they create the possibility of insight and growth.

Closes me down: White defensiveness, arrogance, and unwillingness to expand their view. Nothing that people of color do closes me down, that I am aware of.

Tara Ronda

The times when I have been most open to real discussions about racism have been in the college classroom. As both an undergraduate and a graduate student, I've had multiple opportunities to examine my role in society as a white woman and to look at how people of color have been and are treated. It helps me to be in an academic environment because it feels like a safe place to dissect such serious issues. These classes have included people of color and I found that we could relate to each other on an academic level so it helped us get past those initial misgivings we might have had about talking about racism.

On the other hand, I close down almost immediately when I feel that I am being classified in some way. For example, in the African American Philosophy class to which I referred, there was a black woman who was very offended by the fact that we would even discuss racism as though we could ever understand it academically. At this point in my life, I think I understand a bit better what she was saying and why she was so angry and passionate about the issue, but I think it was the wrong way to go about it. In yelling at all the white people in the class who were genuinely trying to understand by asking questions and trying to relate in some way, she alienated a group of people who wanted nothing more than to connect with people of color. Maybe that connection is not possible, but I think it's important that we try at every opportunity. I don't like when I am automatically classified as being racist or imperialist or ignorant or all-powerful just because I'm white. I think that kind of racism is also completely unproductive in helping us become open to each other's experiences.

I just need people of color to withhold judgment as much as they are able until they know my actual stance on issues—I often feel that just by being the white person in the room, I'm "that person with privilege and power." That may very well be true, but I don't believe I carry myself that way consciously. I don't revel in the fact that I don't have to be concerned about the same kinds of things as people of color, but I often get the sense that people of color think I do just because I'm white. Also, I need people of color to be open to talking with me about their experiences and feelings—without openness on both of our parts, there is no genuine attempt to understand each other. I need them to believe that I really want to understand as much as I can where they come from and what they face every day. I want them to know that I try to work towards equality in so many ways every time I leave my house.

LAURA K

When someone assumes that because I have white skin I do not understand even one bit, I might shut down. When someone assumes that because I have white skin it doesn't matter that I teach on racism or think I'm sympathetic because I really can't be, that would shut me down. I hate to say it, but it's easier for me to have conversations about racism with people of color whose anger is not directed at me, or even who don't appear outwardly angry. Do I think they're entitled to their anger? Absolutely. Do I want to be present or be the target when it's unleashed? No, thank you.

BARBARA BECKWITH

When I mention to fellow white people that I lead a grassroots workshop called "White People Challenging Racism: Moving From Talk to Action," they often respond, "Good for you!" followed by a change of subject. Or they tell a story of when they stood up against racism. Or tell an instance when they felt unfairly criticized by a person of color. The first response shuts down conversation, the second shifts the issue of racism to "we good white people" vs. "those bad white racists," and the third focuses on anger that's often a response to racism, not on racism itself.

MARIE DOAN

If someone else is brutally negative toward my race, then I feel defensive. Why? I am trying so hard to understand humankind and that kind of negativity closes me down immediately. I don't have coping skills to effectively handle putdowns.

BETH ELLIOTT

What opens me up to a conversation about racism is anyone who will talk about it. What closes me down is being ignored or discredited when I think that the conversation is important and other people are uncomfortable having the discussion. There are times when it feels like people think that I am making a big deal out of nothing and they just won't talk about it. It is very frustrating and sad for me when that happens, but I just keep working on it quietly and relentlessly.

BETSY PERRY

What opens me up is kindness. What opens me up is honesty. Sadly, I need some mix of the first and the second. Reading Avalon's *Willow and The Angry Black Woman* is invigorating, but I also need people like Ta-Nehisi Coates, who can say, "That's where you're at, but you've got to change." What change I have been able to make—and it's not enough—has come from people of color, over and over and over again, telling their stories, telling about how racism has affected *them*. I'm not good with abstract words like "racism." When women of color tell me over and over again, "Strangers ask to touch my hair," I am blown away, horrified. That makes the situation concrete for me, and that's just one example.

AMY FRITSCH

I open up to conversations about racism (and, in fact, most experiences) when people share their personal experiences, their emotions, and how they have been impacted by what they have seen and heard. I open up when someone trusts me enough (a huge step and a huge expression of trust, I know) to tell me what they have been through in enough detail that I can get a glimpse of the experiences I will never share.

I close down when I am called names, accused of being the racist society rather than being a part of it, like it or not. I close down when I am told that I am bad, when I am told that I should feel guilty (believe me, I do), that the actions of white people in history are my fault, that there is no point talking to me since I'll never be able to understand.

I have been told that discussions of race are not about me: I am white, and my position in discussions of race and racism should be that of a listener. I agree that in any type of discussion or community, it is incumbent upon the newcomer (me, as a white person in discussions of racism which I have not experienced) to learn as much as I can before joining the discussion. That said, for me to be an ally, there must come a time when I do join the discussion, both in interactions with people of color and in interactions with other white people. If I stay silent forever, I merely perpetuate the status quo. If, however, I am to join the conversation, I need to be able to check my understanding of terminology, of ideology, of history, of attitudes, of others' stories to make sure that, to the best extent possible, I am representing the ideas of anti-racism clearly and effectively. To be able to do that, I need to be able to be part of a discussion where, while it's not the "job" of a person of color to educate me, someone will listen to me and give me feedback. Being able to have such an open discussion is part of what I need, and part of what helps me open up rather than close down when I am myself shut out.

JANET CARTER

There are so many different scenarios for conversations about racism; it's hard to generalize on this. It makes a big difference who I'm talking to—my cousin, a co-worker, the handyman—and whether that person is white or a person of color. There are SO MANY pre-scripted conversations we white people can have about race ("I don't care if they're black, white, purple or green." "What about reverse racism?" "Look at Obama. Aren't things so much better now?")

that it's hard to have a fresh, genuine interchange. And it's hard to keep going once one of these lines has been spoken.

As part of an anti-racist organization, I have opportunities to talk about racism in casual social situations, and I am very aware of when I do and when I don't bring it up. When people ask, "What do you do?" I can choose to avoid the topic by saying I'm an editor and writer or I can choose to mention the UNtraining or the book I'm writing and invite a more risky conversation. So what makes me open up to taking the risk?

I open up when I feel there is some ground of relationship to begin with, some feeling of connection, which doesn't have to be around race at all. It could be with a family friend or someone in line at the grocery store. I'm not an "in your face" person, but I'm taking more risks by initiating conversations myself, particularly with other white people, even if it's not comfortable. White people, including me, need to be able to talk about race and racism in much more multidimensional ways. When we're not in denial about racism, we are so defensive, afraid of being wrong or wronged, that we don't know how to talk except in knee-jerk ways that deaden conversations. When I find myself in one of these, I tend to close down. Or get self-righteous or overly urgent in a way that doesn't help further communication.

I generally don't bring up issues of race with people of color unless they're a friend and that's something we talk about. Or I am in a workshop or class specifically for that purpose. I figure people of color have to deal with racism enough, so why should I ask them to think about it just because I want to? But I open up when a person of color initiates the topic. For example, the head of our group at a job I once had was an African American woman married to a white man. She once told a story about her daughter making "biracial" Barbie dolls by putting the head of her white Barbie on the body of her black Barbie and vice versa. She told this in a humorous way that let me know she was comfortable talking about race in her own life. I told her about the UNtraining work, and we ended up having a number of good conversations, including one about internalized racism.

I've noticed that sometimes, though, I'm so eager to talk that I go on and on and don't stop to listen or ask questions of the other person, or gauge where they're coming from. That is actually a kind of closing down too.

It's much easier to have conversations about the racism "out there" than to get personal about racism in myself or people I care about. Talking about personal experiences around racism is always edgy. I am afraid of being a target, but I also feel that, as white person who has some awareness, I need to be able to have conversations with other white people, just to loosen the grip of the taboo about talking about how we really feel about the subject. That's an opening up that comes from taking responsibility for being the kind of person I want to be.

Being afraid of making a mistake, saying something racist or ignorant, is a big thing that can close me up in talking with people of color. I'm learning that it's better to just relax and be myself and that if I make a "mistake," I can acknowledge it, rather than sink into a miserable heap of self-recrimination, which is sure to close down any further conversation.

On some level, talking about racism is never "safe," unless it's general or abstract. There is no way to guarantee safety on either side. We have to be willing to try it out, to test and be tested, to believe that the risk is worth it.

Eileen Kugler

I close down when the conversation immediately jumps to charges and attacks with no chance for dialogue. It doesn't bring anyone along; it doesn't change minds or behaviors.

I also close down when people enter a dialogue solely to change someone else's mind: If they only heard my side, they would believe as I do. You must enter a formal dialogue to change yourself.

I try to have real conversations in my life—to not let questionable comments by others go unnoticed. I work at making my initial statement truthful, but as non-threatening as possible, just to start the dialogue. At best, it opens up doors that would otherwise be closed and gets everyone thinking.

Barbara Imhoff

What opens me up is when POCs continue to talk with me regardless of any blunders I might make. And when they don't try to spare my feelings or not say something because they think I can't take it, or won't identify, or won't understand.

How do you think whites can be effective allies to people of color? Why?

TARA RONDA

I believe we must rid ourselves of these "color-blind" statements—we should NOT be teaching our children that color doesn't exist. Race is largely a social construct, but color and culture is not, and we need to teach our children that people are different. We should also be teaching them that our differences are not only okay, but also wonderful opportunities for all of us to learn something new every day. We need to stop trying to put our traditions and practices on other people and learn more about theirs. This is not about assimilation; it's about acceptance and celebration of those differences.

ROBIN DiANGELO

Bear witness to the pain of racism, have no criteria for how people of color express that pain, be humble and willing to not know, speak up, pay attention and use your position to challenge racism. Don't give up on our relationships with people of color, or only have relationships with people of color that keep us comfortable and affirm us.

EILEEN KUGLER

If we are to move beyond racism we need to be allies, or the country remains divided. As a white person who leads diversity dialogues, I find that sometimes I can open doors with people who look like me. I have come to see that I can play a role that a person of color cannot. I use the comfort level that comes from hearing a speaker who is "familiar" to white audiences deliver a challenging message. I believe they are then open to lessons that only a person of color could deliver (particularly personal experiences).

HOLLY FULTON

Whites must educate themselves about history and see how they feel about our history and ask themselves, "How would you feel if your ancestors went through this and you were treated like this in society? What would you want the privileged folks to do?" I feel fortunate to be part of the documentary film, *Traces of the Trade*, and being in the film and showing it to people and facilitating discussions is important ally work that I do and want to keep doing. The film gives me a kind of "platform" to do the work from and I hope to do many screenings in the San Francisco Bay Area with follow-up discussions or workshops. Whites need to talk to other whites and get them motivated to take action, talk, listen, read, and study. Often after screenings white people ask, "What can I do?" This is SUCH an important question from them!!!!

Bill Proudman

Whites are allies to POC when they don't look to POC for affirmation, when they confront racism without prodding. White are allies to POC when they can wade into potentially difficult conversations (ones where they risk being called a racist). Whites are allies to POC when they initiate more frequent conversations about the dynamics of race at play and they do it from a place of self-interest rather than to convince a POC that they get it.

Whites are allies to POC when they regularly initiate and engage with other whites about race without looking for POC for validation or confirmation.

Betsy Perry

I think the best thing I can do—I'm not sure about "whites" as a whole—is twofold: to listen, and to repeat. Listening is how I was changed. I try, when I hear a POC saying something that resonates with me, to link to it—not just to restate it, because when you do that, other white people listen to *you* rather than the POC. I try to say, "This person said something important, go read it." It took other people at least a year of linking to Martin Luther King's *Letter from a Birmingham Jail* for me to read it; I try to link to it regularly in hopes of encouraging other people to listen and change.

Finally, and this is painful for me, I need to confront. If I don't, I'm saying that it's the POC's job to be the bad guy, and I get to be the good guy. Nope.

Amy Fritsch

I think—and hope—that white folks who educate themselves about racism are taking steps to be allies.

I think that whites who speak up—with friends, colleagues, strangers, to newspaper editors, etc.—to point out racist language/"jokes," comments, attitudes and assumptions, and who also explain in what ways they are harmful, and how to reframe the comment or attitude in an accepting way are being allies.

I think that it is important for white people, who are often seen by other whites as less threatening, to frame the stories they know and the studies of which they are aware and the issues of racism in terms they know other white people can understand. This is particularly important when talking to white people who have experienced types of oppression and struggle to see the difference between their oppression and the pervasive oppression and degradation of institutionalized racism.

A white friend said something to me that became the most valuable moment in my understanding of racism in its institutional nature. She pointed out my family's lower-middle-working-class status, our lack of education, our geographic location, our short distance from rural farm folk, our lack of insurance when I was a child, and all the disadvantages I had. Then she said, "Now, imagine that all of that was exactly the same, but that your family was black. Would you have been in the same situation, or would you have been better or worse off?" I could see immediately that, of course we'd have been worse off. My father would have won far fewer bids, had fewer jobs, and we'd have had even less money. And that, as my friend gently and firmly pointed out, was why institutionalized racism meant that a person of color was at a greater disadvantage.

Too many people see concerns from a member of a group in question as "biased" or "self-interested." Often white folks will only listen to another white person. Thus, until people of color are given appropriate credence for speaking to their own experiences, there need to be white allies to speak the language of anti-racism to the whites who will listen, at least to another white person.

CRAIG MORFITT

I think whites can be effective allies by taking an active role in tackling racism and by standing up to bias and stereotyping. By sitting back and taking a passive stance, we condone the status quo. We have a responsibility to take on some of the work in dismantling the system of racism.

White people can become active in tackling racism without becoming organized activists. They can simply commit to tackling racism whenever they encounter it in their day-to-day lives. Whilst seemingly an easy task, it can require courage for people to challenge their friends and family members on their behavior. Failing to take action is tantamount to condoning the behavior.

Some ways in which whites can begin to tackle racism would include:

- Not telling racist jokes;
- Challenging the racist nature of jokes told by others;
- Challenging racist comments made in their presence—at the time the comments are made and in front of whatever audience heard those comments;
- Challenging racist stereotypes when they hear them;
- Challenging racist conduct when they see it;
- Engaging in conversations about race and racism;
- Developing personal relationships with persons from other racial and ethnic groups;
- Seeking to educate themselves further on race and racism.

When white people challenge racism that occurs in their presence, they send a clear message to the perpetrator that all white people don't think the same way. They also make it clear that racist behavior can and will be challenged. Openly challenging racist conduct in the presence of others ensures that more than just the perpetrator becomes aware of the fact that the conduct is deemed unacceptable. I think this is particularly important when the target of the racism is present, as the message is clearly sent that white people are prepared to stand up against such conduct. The TV show *What Would You Do?* often demonstrates the power of a single person speaking up and challenging inappropriate behavior—even when many others seemingly turn a blind eye to the situation. Doing the right thing isn't always the easiest choice but if we want to be effective allies we need to make the tough choice when it is the right choice.

Janet Carter

For me it starts with becoming aware of what whiteness means and how I carry the cultural identity and privilege of a white person, whether I like it or not. Being white means something, however culturally derived it is and no matter how much I want to be seen as an individual. Race will be an element in all my relationships with people of color, no matter how far in the background it may be.

I remember back in the sixties hearing a news report about Malcolm X and how the Black Muslims saw white people as the devil. I was shocked, offended, and scared—"those people" would hate me just because I'm white! They don't even know me! Looking back now, I realize that I was getting a tiny taste of how it felt to be seen as part of a group, not as an individual person. And that my youthful reaction of outrage was experienced a thousand-fold by people of color most of their lives.

My sense is that being an ally is not something I can declare myself to be. The people of color in my life are the judges of that. If they don't experience me as an ally, then all my good intentions are just a way to make me feel good. The question is, "How does it feel to be on the receiving end of my good intentions?" I have to be open to feedback on that.

It can't be all about me. I have to be able to get out of my own way to really listen and be present to other's reality. And I have to be willing to stick my neck out when I feel something racist is going on.

One thing I've learned is that I will never be able to truly understand what it is like to be a person of color, especially the relentlessness, pervasiveness and unpredictability of racism. I can only use my own empathy and experience to imagine what it is like. Some years ago our organization was the target (via email) of an attack by a white-supremacist group. I was handling our e-mail and, as the violent and nasty messages began coming in, I was shocked and terrified. We were about to hold a public event, and even though this group was based on the other side of the country, we didn't know what might happen. After assessing the situation, it seemed to be all words and no action, which turned out to be the case. But as I sat with my fear and outrage, I suddenly realized how sheltered and privileged I was as a white person—that people of color experience some level of this aggression or the threat of it ALL THE TIME. It took my breath away and rapidly snapped things into perspective.

Structurally, I can think of two things needed for white people to be effective allies. First of all, white people need to take responsibility for working with other white people around racism, to shift the conversation to how white supremacy structures our identities, our organizations and our ways of relating. We need to get that racism is about US and that the good news is we can do something about it. It's hard work, but we don't have to stay stuck with guilt, denial, bewilderment, frustration. We need to be able to talk about racism among our white families, our white friends and our white groups. And we need to learn how to do this directly and sincerely, and, ideally, with love rather than self-righteousness.

When I began writing my book, *Good Little White Girl*, about the invisible ways I learned to be racist growing up in a white-liberal family in Vermont, I was really nervous about how my brothers and sisters would take it, not to mention my aunts, uncles and cousins. Both my parents were gone, but I loved them and did not want to hurt their memories. I knew I couldn't proceed out of defensiveness, fear, or preachiness. I needed my family's support, their stories, their memories. I needed their love. I decided that the only way was to invite them into the process of looking at our upbringing together. How did we learn about race and racism? And they have responded beyond my wildest dreams. We have had conversations we never would have had. They have spontaneously helped me with research. They have shared their new-found awareness of racial-justice issues. We are in it together.

Second, when white people work with people of color, especially around racial-justice issues, let the people of color take the lead. They are the ones with first-hand experience. I am amazed at how strongly I am trained to be the one to "help," to "save," to prove what a good white person I am. So I practice not jumping in thinking I have all the answers. On the other hand, I try not to hold back my ideas and questions. I want to be a real partner, not a know-it-all "helper." I am there to learn as well as give. We are in it together.

Douglas Detling

When white folks speak up against poor or indeed racist treatment, they are effective allies of people of color. When people of all races speak up against injustice in the courts, they are effective allies of change. It is when nothing is said, when enough people do nothing, that racism is permitted to survive.

CHAPTER TEN

WHAT IT WILL TAKE

What do you think it will take for people
of color and whites to trust each other?

JIM LANGEMO

First, it will happen individual-by-individual as relationships are built through listening, validation, transparency and confidence.

Second, for it to happen more often on a cultural scale, I think we need to start with parents and with our school system. If we can tell more of our nation's story, if we can teach children when they are young how to listen, if we can help them retain their curiosity into their adulthood, we may be able to help. If we can help parents model these same behaviors, as well as help them be more active in their children's learning, everyone will be more enriched.

Third, if we can influence the workplace, the parents of children will see that trusting each other isn't just theoretical and it isn't just some pipe dream—it can really happen. What's more, those adults will see that when it does happen, people live more enriched lives, they are more productive, the businesses they work for are more successful. When they see that, they will want to ensure that their children can experience it too.

ROBIN DIANGELO

I think it will take a very long time, and we are not on the right track. People of color have good reason not to trust us. I think they will begin to trust us when we begin to get honest about our racism, to not give up or walk away when they get real about race and it gets hard for us to hear, and to be willing to bear witness to the righteous rage and pain they have as a result of our racism. When we walk our talk, move beyond intentions and actually demonstrate our commitment to end racism through action.

As for whites not trusting people of color, that is baseless and rests on a false understanding of what racism is and how it works.

SARA KRAKAUER

I think there need to be more spaces that are mixed-race. Once you know someone face to face, it's hard to be afraid. When we work together, we learn about each other and see each other's humanity. I wish that I had more friends of color, and honestly, I think it would take a lot of effort on my part to change this. I do think I need to do that work, though.

BARBARA IMHOFF

Everyone's willingness to stay in the room; a level playing field (better jobs for people of color, equal opportunities, etc.); an end to genocide everywhere; compassion; honest, respectful dialog; walking our talk (especially we whites). In general, we need to start with the truth, wherever that is for each of us, and even if it's not pretty.

JOHN ALEXANDER

A certain amount of distrust is probably unavoidable and possibly even desirable. Despite that, the distrust can be minimized if there is continuity in the discussion and some basic "ground truths" can be established. Those ground truths include the reality of the traumas that people have suffered that are denied societal privileges. But despite that ground truth there needs to be a respectful agreement that there is no hierarchy of suffering. In other words, whites also suffer because of both their privileges and their guilt. And further, when whites become aware of and committed to working against white privilege, they will experience additional suffering. All that suffering is real and deserves respect and sympathy. I have frequently been in discussions where whites felt that their suffering didn't count or that the suffering of racial and ethnic minority folks trumps theirs. Despite the fact that the suffering of racial and ethnic minority folks is great, arguably greater than that of privileged whites, it does undercut trust if whites feel that their suffering doesn't "count."

At the same time, whites must understand that they will be challenged and that they do not get a free pass just because they understand and even work against the privileges they've been granted. This is why a certain amount of distrust may even be a good thing. When people come together about such difficult and complex issues, it would be surprising if there weren't a fair amount of distrust.

BETH ELLIOTT

Honest conversation, apology when needed and everyone taking responsibility for their own stuff.

BARBARA BECKWITH

When white people, myself included, are willing to acknowledge the dynamics of everyday, structural and cultural racism and acknowledge it when an instance happens and is pointed out to us, trust is likely to grow.

I have found that women, Jewish people, and LGBTQ people sign up in disproportionate numbers for the anti-racism course I co-teach. I think it's because they've experienced discrimination, and are therefore more likely to believe the prejudice that other groups have experienced. I know that it's helped me to have gone through women's liberation. Clearly, racism is very different from sexism, but remembering our struggles helps me "see" more easily the dynamics of racism. Back in "women's lib" days, what I wanted from men was to accept, to believe, to feel in their hearts the effects on me of their words and actions. And I wanted them to stop sexual abuse. It was their problem, after all, not mine.

So when white people point to the election of Barack Obama as president of the United States as if proof that people of color should stop pointing out disparities, I remember when men would say that women have progressed so far in this 21st century that "they" (we) should stop pressing for more female Supreme Court justices, legislators, engineers, or wage parity. In the same way, for people of color, "progress" isn't enough when the goal is equality.

JANET CARTER

At a workshop one time, a woman of color asked our small discussion group, almost rhetorically, "Why are white people so mean?" The answer that popped out of me was, "We are clueless and afraid." I should have added that often we have no idea we are being mean, but are acting out of entitlement and privilege we don't even know is there. For me, trustworthiness starts with trusting myself, and that comes out of knowing myself both as a white person and as a human being. I think we white people need to educate ourselves about our whiteness before we can be trustworthy.

- White people can't be trusted until we understand that we are white and that that means something beyond checking a box on a form.

- We need to know ourselves as white, as part of a history of white supremacy, a collective history that we benefit from individually whether we want to or not. We need to know the true history, a history told from different points of view that make us think and feel the complexity of what we have all inherited.

- We need to really get that our everyday experience around race is different from our friends, neighbors, classmates, and coworkers of color.

- We need to understand that our good intentions can sometimes result in hurtful situations and that we can take responsibility for that in ways other than falling back on our intentions, feeling paralyzing guilt and/or expecting the other person to take care of us.

- We need to develop the capacity to be with the intensity of our own feelings, so we don't project them onto others, or have to shut down others' intensity.

- We also need to get that we are decent loving human beings who want to be loved and accepted for who we are—and that loving and accepting all the parts of ourselves is the place to start. Mistakes don't diminish our basic goodness as human beings.

Trust is based on authenticity. How much of my full self can I bring to my encounters? How much am I really willing to see and learn from and about others? How willing am I to be uncomfortable at the beginning of conversations in the hopes that we can bridge the distance our cultural conditioning has created? How open am I to hearing feedback about how my whiteness affects someone else?

I realize I am speaking personally here, because that is the arena I have some control over. But on the societal level, we need more ways to share both histories and personal stories, starting in grade school, so that the cultural field shifts to one where we can all identify with each other while at the same time delighting in and respecting our differences.

A sense of humor can go a long way on both sides.

BILL PROUDMAN

We each need to foster deeper partnerships where we can regularly be "messy" with each other. It will take making a long-term commitment with each other, rather than thinking that because we now have a mixed-race African American president that the conversation and challenges of race are somehow over.

Amy Fritsch

I think it will take a great deal more time, a great many more conversations that are difficult and have depth, a great deal more adjusting of the inequities of society, a great many more people seeing the inequities as they have stood and accepting them as real before trust can begin to take hold. I think that white folks will need to know more people of color—and have more people of color say that, yes, they experience and see racism—and develop a personal stake in the situation of those people of color for whom they have come to care. For people of color to be able to have more trust for white folks, whites will have to see and acknowledge societally-pervasive racism as real, work actively against that racism both personally and institutionally, check and modify their own racist ideas and actions and comments, and keep promises about working for change.

I cannot imagine a world with trust between whites and people of color that does not first balance many of the existing inequities so that the statistics of arrests, those imprisoned, politicians, people in power in business, high school graduates, college graduates, etc., are more proportionally balanced and representative of the actual population of white folks and people of color. As long as those inequities persist and are supported by false claims that people of color/poor folks/women/etc., just need to "work harder" and "deserve" better, I cannot imagine people of color being able to trust white folks who perpetuate and believe in—and often remain blind to—a system of such widespread inequity that oppresses them. What is there to trust in someone who denies your very reality and then blames you for your circumstances in that reality as though you had made what they say doesn't exist?

John Lenssen

A. I believe that for white people to earn the trust of people of color it will require honesty—the honesty about the ways that we whites benefit from racism, the honesty about the times that we do not speak up about racism, the honesty about our continuing racist bias that is so deeply unconscious and a lifelong struggle to unlearn, the honesty about the times that we whites can relax and escape the daily harsh and painful impacts of racism, the honesty about the times that we have hurt people of color. And also the honesty about the times that we do speak up about racism, and the honesty about the ways that we too have been hurt by racism, and the honesty about how we sometimes lose standing and status with other whites when we speak up about racism.

B. I believe that for white people to earn the trust of people of color it will require days and months and years of individual and collective action to follow and accompany the words of anti-racism, solidarity, alliance, and community. We whites must walk the talk.

C. I believe that for white people to earn the trust of people of color it will require an authentic interest and commitment to collaboration that is not based on the superiority of missionary attitudes.

D. I believe that we white people must embrace the fact that the struggle against racism and that forming alliances across difference is actually in the interests of white people.

What do you think it will take for the United States to heal from racism?

ROBIN DIANGELO

A serious radical revolution. Or just a very long time, because racism is a very clever thing—it adapts and mutates and becomes harder and harder to name while it accomplishes its work more and more effectively.

BETSY PARRY

"Heal?" I don't acknowledge the word. I think it's too simple. I think we can get better. Our goal should be getting better. Getting better is achievable. "Healing" is so broad I don't think it's even meaningful.

LAURA K

Time. Courage. Honesty with ourselves and with one another. Intermarriage. Symbolic reparations. Respected individuals who represent "the other," whoever and whatever "other" represents. Exposure and relationship. Paradigm shifts we cannot ignore. I hope it does not take more bloodshed, but I fear it will. Whites in South Africa did unspeakable things to keep the power out of the hands of majority blacks, and whites are becoming the minority here. I do wonder what kinds of nasty things will emerge as that reality moves closer and closer to home...

AMY FRITSCH

Time. I think that healing will only come after honest self-examination from white folks and time for the expression of that self-examination to be proved in action as well as intent. I suspect that much of that work from white folks will only follow yet more frightening, soul-baring sharing of experiences from people of color. I think that public, steadfast, and consistent acknowledgement from white Americans and the American government of the harms done to people of color in America, accompanied by sincere and earnest apologies and changes of policy, attitude, and results are the only things that can begin to chip away at the damage done to people of color by the pervasiveness of racism. I don't know if there is any recompense that can help. I think the time factor is necessary to healing because I think there will not be opportunities for healing until white America has proved that any good intentions that are communicated are followed up with actual change. Until that change (finally) happens, I would not expect any person of color to believe that "this time it really will," since there have been so many failures of promises in the past.

Amy C. Orecchia

Time. Lots of time. It's crazy to think about it, but we're really only a few generations removed from slavery. I've heard from multiple African American friends, colleagues, and clients that they feel they've experienced more overt racism since Obama was elected. It could be possible that whenever public progress is made, we experience a little backlash. I think it's going to be a long process. However, we absolutely cannot be passive in this process. One important approach is to advocate and contribute to early hands-on education/awareness of all racism (but especially institutional/systemic racism) for whites. We need more white people who "get it," because that breaks down a barrier and hopefully opens up dialogue.

Holly Fulton

Having a black president is certainly one little start; notice my word "little." Lessening of white-supremacist groups, though it almost seems like they are growing now. The demographic changes whereby white is the minority, and they predict that will happen within the next 30 years. More awareness of racism and classism. The two need to go hand in hand more than they are. Most of all—A LONG AMOUNT OF TIME.

——·——AUTHENTIC RELATIONSHIPS ——·——

What do you think it will take for white folks to unlearn racism?

SARA KRAKAUER

Is this possible? Racism seems like a circle that we are caught in. We need to make a change and in order for perceptions to shift, that change needs to be in place. But we can't make that change happen without the shift in perspective. I don't know how to stop the cycle. I do think that some change happens through every relationship that is built across racial lines.

AMY C. ORECCHIA

From my perspective, which is the experience I had growing up in predominantly white communities in the upper Midwest, one of the most important pieces that is missing is actual contact with diverse groups of people. It's a very interesting phenomenon to me, how we were always taught about history and that racism was wrong and everybody is equal and should be treated the same, but almost all of the kids in my class were white and almost everyone I saw on the street and at the grocery store was white...and I think white people who grow up like that are extremely uncomfortable when they do find themselves in diverse settings. We've also been taught not to talk about race and that it doesn't matter. So, we have no words to talk about the things we notice that we've never seen before. We don't realize that it would be more appropriate to ask about something we are unsure about instead of making incorrect assumptions. In my opinion, the biggest thing white people need to unlearn racism is desegregated communities.

BETSY PERRY

I don't think it can be done. I don't think racism is a binary: on/off. I think it's something you work on every day, and that you never entirely defeat.

TARA RONDA

I think that offering white people the opportunity to get to know people of color would make it easier. Certainly, it's harder to be prejudiced against someone you have befriended and genuinely like. We should put ourselves out there into the communities we fear so much (for example, cities where large cultural centers are often housed).We need to stop being afraid of being the only white person in the room and accept that's a role people of color often must take on. We need to put ourselves in other people's shoes and we must do all these things genuinely, not just as an empty token of change.

TOM MOORE

We will, unfortunately, unlearn racism sometime after we become the minority. A less cynical answer would be that we'll unlearn racism when we start caring about how the inferior education of some of us impedes all of us. We'll unlearn it when we realize that inner-city crime and drug trafficking is our problem too. We'll unlearn racism when we really get it that it's as important to "us" as it is to "them."

MAC SABOL

In order to unlearn racism, white folks have to have enough self-confidence and self-worth to boldly recognize that unlearning an "ism" requires that we let go of "us versus them" and embrace the reality that "we" are not better than "they," that the we/they comparison has no meaning. Actually, it goes farther than that—if we are honest with ourselves, we have to face the reality that "they" were better than "we" were all the time. Now, THAT is a place where REAL TRUST is needed in order for all of us to be successful.

Ignorance sure seems like bliss sometimes, doesn't it?

And yet, I also wonder how we will ever be able to sustain anything like unlearning racism when the world continues to reinforce other "isms" elsewhere in our lives and in our society. If the unlearning is to be successful and long-lasting, we cannot let the open area created through unlearning to be filled by other "we/they" isms. Christians versus Jews, men versus women, America's culture versus Iran's culture, fill-in-the-blank-for-us versus fill-in-the–blank-for-the-other. These are ALL opportunities for us to slide back into the behaviors that have brought us here in the first place.

A Presbyterian church where I worship in upstate New York opened its doors to an African American congregation that was seeking a place to worship. For a while, we co-existed: Our church's services were held in the early morning and the African American congregation worshipped in the early afternoon. We even held several joint worship sessions, which touched me deeply, sharing different traditions yet worshipping the same God through different avenues.

Then something began to slowly shift in the relationship. Our church's members began to complain about "the other congregation" and children messing up the church. The African American congregation began to complain about our church's congregation members not being respectful of their traditions and not even speaking to them. The recession that occurred about the same time led to more definitive differences: One church was on stable financial ground, while the startup began to falter. I was the Clerk of Session at the time and I could never seem to be able to get both sides to get to the "what is going on" place—the pain kept getting stronger and stronger. Eventually, the rift in the two groups came to a head and racism was cited as the "real" reason for the split and the divorce. The startup church left. It was a painful end for many of us.

Was it racism? I am not sure. I do know that having to set aside "we" and "they" so we could coexist was ultimately more than many could handle, and that was true for both congregations. Even today, many years later, it deeply hurts me to think that, for the sake of maintaining/restoring our two separate entities, we trashed an opportunity to become something so much more.

Amy Fritsch

I think that the process of unlearning racism and any prejudices involves knowing and caring about individuals in the stereotyped group. One of the primary ways in which I've seen negative attitudes about homosexuality shift over the past twenty years has been the ever-increasing number of folks who know and love someone who is gay and whom they know is gay. I do believe that the more people of color a white person knows and loves, the less able that person is to stick to the ludicrous position of, "Well, you're not like 'them'; you're different." I think that the route to more white folks caring about and being personally connected to people of color has to start through a greater number of people of color having access to better education, improved opportunities for jobs and career advancement, and thus being in "white" spaces more, so that white folks start to see and know people of color more and begin to see their stereotypes fit less and less.

Unfortunately, this theory also assumes that the white folks will accept and respect the people of color in their workspaces and churches and playgroups for their kids rather than merely grumbling and becoming more hateful as has been seen in the past. It also presumes that white folks will not merely use every interaction as further "proof" of their own racist stereotypes, especially if the people of color in their lives do not assimilate and "act white," thus altering their cultural identification, personality, or self-expression in order to appease the white folks.

I do think that, at least in highly diverse areas (such as Chicago, where I currently live), the ever-increasing inter-ethnic dating and marriage hopefully will also bring people of color into white families in a positive way and bring, by way of the treatment of their loved ones, white attention to the racism faced daily by people of color. This, again, presumes that the white family will love and welcome the person of color and know and accept that person fully, getting to know their lives and loves and struggles.

BILL PROUDMAN

I am not sure we will ever unlearn it. As aware as I think I am about the benefit of white-skin color privilege, I am still amazed at how quickly I lose consciousness of its pervasiveness in my life.

The first step for me is to be conscious of the everyday effects of racism, without any residual self-inflicted guilt or shame. I am responsible for noticing how racism impacts the depth and quality of my relationships while understanding it is not my fault that racism exists. I am responsible for noticing how I and others hear each other due to the impact of racism (regardless of whether I caused it or not).

Second, we whites have to step up and better initiate dialogues and efforts exploring the impact of race on communities/organizations, relationships and individuals. If I am solely dependent on POC to initiate these conversations, nothing will change long-term. I and other whites must continue to discover what it means to be white—both the positive and the negative. I need to better understand how it impacts and affects most everything I do. Asking myself what I love about being white is an interesting question that should not simply be relegated to white supremacists. I am what I am, and to not understand that more fully can lead to my collusion with wanting to minimize or negate the impact of skin color.

John Lenssen

For white people to unlearn racism it will require:

- Truly believing the experiences with racism from people of color;
- Studying, reading and questioning the history of oppression, the socio-political-economic foundations of capitalism/imperialism/colonialism, i.e., the structures that support and perpetuate racism;
- Examining our own biases and the ways that we perpetuate racism every day;
- Honest dialogue with other white people;
- Anti-racist alliance and action with people of color and other white people;
- Authentic relationships and community with people of color;
- Ultimately, the will to unlearn.

Janet Carter

At the end of his book, *White Like Me*, Tim Wise talks about racism as a "soul wound" in this country. This really struck a chord with me. White people won't really take on unlearning racism until they see how it is hurting them. Us. Me. This is a deep question. What happens when we see that the world we believe in is not that way?

Growing up in a white-liberal family, I saw injustice in the world. I watched the struggles of the civil rights movement on TV; I read *The Diary of Anne Frank*, and wrote an essay on how everyone should see *A Raisin in the Sun*. In college in the sixties, I heard Stokely Carmichael speak and watched as black pride spread. I boycotted lettuce and grapes in support of Cesar Chavez. I protested the war in Vietnam. But all that didn't touch a core of fear inside me, an intense vulnerable spot I barely knew was there. Until I came to the Bay Area, I had no close friends of color. Once I did, race was not a conversation we engaged in for a long time.

But, as a meditation practitioner, I could see my own mind. I began to notice a kind of low-level fog of thoughts, feelings, small reactions—a clenching in my stomach when a group of young black or Latino men approached on the street, envy of white people who seemed so at ease with their friends of color. I knew something was affecting me and I didn't like it.

At the time, my husband, a white man, was learning about white privilege in a psychology training program and through friendship and mentoring with a woman of color. Through our conversations, I began seeing a new level of how I had been conditioned, against my knowledge, to be in the oppressor role. I read Malcolm X's autobiography and cried because I had assumed that it was not a story that I could relate to—and I was so wrong. I heard stories, finally, from my brother-in-law about his experiences growing up in a mixed-race family, of police encounters, racist treatment by his grade-school teachers, the way he experiences racism still, every day, everywhere. The pain had become personal.

I began to see how white cultural norms shaped how I was raised. A lot of these have to do with control—controlling the body, controlling feelings, not questioning authority: Stand in line. Raise your hand. Don't all talk at once. Don't be too intense, too loud. Don't interrupt. Do what the teacher says. The police are here to protect you. Do what the doctor ordered. Listen to the experts (who mostly are white). Don't ask too many questions, especially the ones that can't be answered. We don't do that. Those people are....

So while I benefited from many aspects of privilege given to me as a white person, the price of belonging was to live behind a veil of ignorance, disconnected from parts of myself, unable to really stand up for my beliefs for fear of not belonging.

Something has to pierce that veil for white people to be motivated to really unlearn racism. It could be a personal encounter, a challenge, a cognitive dissonance that becomes imperative. I think of a moment in a "privilege" workshop at a diversity conference at my job. A black woman shared the story of how her adolescent son one day in class spontaneously stood up in response to an interchange with his white teacher. Her son was tall and, in that moment, looked threatening to the teacher, who sent him to the principal's office. He had done nothing but stand up. "So," she sighed, "we had to have the conversation."

"What conversation?" one of the white women asked. But the people of color in the room already knew—that one where you have to tell your child that they are going to be seen and judged not for who they are, but from the fear and racism of those in authority. The one where you have to make sure they keep their self-respect, but also do their best to be safe in those situations. "Oh, my

God!" the white woman said when she heard this was a common challenge for parents of color. "I can't believe this! That's terrible!"

We, as white people, have to believe it. We have to understand the history that got us here, the roles we've all inherited and are passing on. Until we believe it and know that we ourselves can't live with it, we won't begin to change.

AFTERWORD

LETTER TO MUN WAH

—·— WHAT IT TOOK ONE MAN —·—

Dear Mun Wah:

I hope that you and your family have had an enjoyable holiday period. I just wanted to update you on another step in my personal journey.

You may remember our previous communication concerning Mr. Clyde Best, the Bermudian who was one of the first black football (soccer) players in England. He suffered a lot of racism during his playing days from fans in the stands. I had written to him confessing the occasion when, as a child in England, I joined in racist chanting aimed at a black player from an opposing team at a football game. The letter expressed my remorse and offered an apology to him, as I do not know the identity of the player I verbally abused. Following receipt of the letter, Mr. Best telephoned me and we were supposed to meet but that meeting did not happen.

Anyway, on Christmas Eve I telephoned Mr. Best and asked if I could visit him to make the apology in person. He agreed and I drove to his home where we had a brief conversation and where I apologized and handed him a gift as a token of my apology. Mr. Best was extremely gracious. He said that we all make mistakes in our life and that the important thing is that we recognize them and learn from them. He told me not to dwell on the incident "as it would make me sick." I told him that I was aware of how much he had to struggle with racism as a player and he responded along the lines of, "Someone had to go through it—it just happened to be me, but it helped to make things much better for the black players of today." I was so impressed by his ability to suffer years of racial abuse and yet maintain such dignity and to demonstrate such benevolence. I was reminded of Nelson Mandela, a man for whom I hold much admiration and respect. Mr. Best has already indicated that he would like to use my letter in his autobiography, and he said he'd get back in touch later to arrange for a photo of us both to accompany the letter in his book.

I think that my personal meeting with Mr. Best has gone a long way to helping me to achieve some level of resolution for my racist actions all those years ago. Hopefully the inclusion in his book will help others in some way.

I owe a great deal of thanks to you for helping me in my journey of self-discovery and personal healing.

Many thanks and best wishes for 2010.

Your friend,
Craig